Unsuitable Company

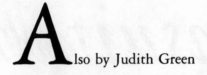

Also by Judith Green

SOMETIMES PARADISE

WINNERS

THE YOUNG MARRIEDS

Unsuitable Company

JUDITH GREEN

BANTAM BOOKS
NEW YORK · TORONTO · LONDON · SYDNEY · AUCKLAND

This novel is a work of fiction. Any references to real people, events, establishments, organizations, or locales are intended only to give the fiction a sense of reality and authenticity. All of the main characters, organizations, events, and incidents in this novel are creations of the author's imagination, and their resemblance, if any, to actual events or persons, living or dead, is entirely coincidental.

UNSUITABLE COMPANY

A Bantam Book / August 1991

*Lyrics from "What a Difference a Day Made" were
used with permission of Stanley Adams.*
*Lyrics on pages 126, 128, and 130 are from "I Remember You" by Johnny Mercer and
Victor Schertzinger and are used with permission. © by Paramount Music Corporation;
© renewed by Paramount Music Corporation.*

Library of Congress Cataloging-in-Publication Data

Green, Judith H.
    Unsuitable company / Judith Green.
      p.   cm.
    ISBN 0-553-07006-1
    I. Title.
    PS3557.R3727U5   1991
    813'.54—dc20   91-4422
                                                       CIP

Published simultaneously in the United States and Canada

*Bantam Books are published by Bantam Books, a division of Bantam Doubleday Dell
Publishing Group, Inc. Its trademark, consisting of the words "Bantam Books" and
the portrayal of a rooster, is Registered in U.S. Patent and Trademark Office and in
other countries. Marca Registrada. Bantam Books, 666 Fifth Avenue, New York,
New York 10103.*

PRINTED IN THE UNITED STATES OF AMERICA

BVG   0 9 8 7 6 5 4 3 2 1

For Ann and Al

Unsuitable Company

*F*rom the heavy glass doors of 823 Fifth Avenue, Art Rooney watched a brisk October wind swirling leaves high above Central Park. Then he watched the lines of limos immobilized in gridlock. Gone were the days of leisurely two-way traffic: Checker cabs lining up to take men to their offices in five, maybe ten minutes; women strolling arm in arm. Now people walked in a hurry, heads bent, no time to chat. Gone were the proper nannies pushing large Silver Cross carriages to the park to meet other nannies, each proud of *her* family, *her* baby. Gone was the sense of neighborhood.

Those were the days when Rooney's father had been 823's superintendent before him, when Art was just a little boy watching the seasons change from behind these same rich doors. Still, Rooney thought, nothing had changed as much as 823's tenants. Not all of them, of course; there were still some who weren't billionaires. But there weren't many fine, elegant people left—like the Archer Blairs, for example.

Rooney shrugged and checked his watch. He ought to go upstairs, turn on some lights. Clive van Arlyn and his big-bucks client were coming. They'd better be on time; the MacDonald dame was bringing another prospect right after van Arlyn, someone flying in special from London. Rooney laughed out loud. Imagine people waiting in line to spend eleven million dollars, even for a Fifth Avenue penthouse. It had to be the most expensive apartment in New York.

"I'm goin' on ahead," Rooney said to Mike, the doorman.

"Don't worry, Art. I'll send van Arlyn up," Mike answered. In his impeccable gray uniform that exactly matched the gray of the awning, he looked like the commandant of West Point.

Mike was part of the Irish mafia that Rooney's father had installed long ago. Although the unions were making it almost impossible for most apartment houses to keep their Caucasian staff, so far the top luxury buildings had managed.

Tall and wide-shouldered, Rooney seemed a lot younger than his fifty years. It was the black hair and the broken veins in the chubby cheeks, which looked like wind flush instead of too much whiskey. It was being clean-shaven and suited up, too. Unless he was making repairs, Rooney was in jacket and tie, as his father had taught him. "When you're representin' people, you got to look like 'em to get respect." Not that Rooney's father would ever have appeared in anything as inappropriate as today's prevalent sweatsuits, no matter who was wearing them.

Waiting for the bronze elevator doors to open, Art Rooney took a slip of paper from his jacket pocket. Holding it at arm's length, he tried to decipher his own scrawl.

"Mrs. George Wheaton, Omaha," he mumbled. That's

who that full-of-himself bastard van Arlyn was bringing.
Rooney took out another slip. Again he muttered the
name: "Mrs. John Kaplan from London." Doesn't anyone come
from New York any more? he wondered, entering the elevator.

"Wait till you see the view. All of Fifth Avenue. Your own Central Park. Eleven million dollars is a very fair price."

As he spoke, Clive van Arlyn was trying to convince himself that this astonishing figure was indeed reasonable. He had learned to lie gracefully while adapting to the new ironies of New York life, such as the fact that he had sold a similar apartment ten years earlier for two hundred and fifty thousand dollars. In those days, however, no real estate broker in all of Manhattan would have considered showing the Wheatons an apartment at 823 Fifth Avenue.

"Actually, I'm surprised it's not more. They're asking nine million for the one in Mrs. Onassis's building."

Van Arlyn's lean build accentuated his sharp features, and though only forty-three, his thinning gray hair and time-warp manners made him seem generations removed from Erica Wheaton. His archaic, upper-class New York accent was almost all that was left of the vanished society of proper clubs,

Hudson River mansions, and strong Christian morals in which Clive van Arlyn and his wife, Mary, had their roots. The new Clive van Arlyn, like most of present-day New York, had given in to money, for when the blood thins and the great house is long since gone, a roof over one's head often depends on the wiles and charms inside oneself.

That was why van Arlyn had left the trust department of Manufacturers Hanover in his late twenties. He'd watched too often what happened when apartments inherited by people who didn't want to live in them were given to brokers to sell. Armed with little more than a fact sheet, they made more in commissions in a month than a bank vice-president earned in a year.

After becoming a top society broker, it was a natural hustle for van Arlyn to propose a few choice clients for membership in one of his prestigious city clubs, the Racquet, Brook, or Knickerbocker. Several had even made it to Long Island's swank Piping Rock, where van Arlyn soon had them teeing off with the likes of Ogden Phipps and Alfred Vanderbilt. Not only did his connections help van Arlyn to sell apartments, it helped him to buy into this new computer issue or to know when that tobacco company was about to merge. Easy for those who never went back to shirt sleeves to call him a traitor. He preferred to think of himself as a survivor. As for Mary van Arlyn, the business world interested her as little as did Manhattan. Being childless, she was happiest breeding her Cavalier King Charles spaniels at their gatehouse cottage on the grounds of the old Gould estate in Sands Point.

"And Ten-Forty Fifth Avenue is so far up," van Arlyn continued, walking excitedly in front of Erica Wheaton, almost backward, in order to face her with his argument. "Not to mention the museum blocking the view. The layout there doesn't have a patch on Eight Twenty-three."

Erica knew 823, even some of its recent tenants: people like herself who were not only taking the town but sweeping the world. But she didn't know this particular apartment and couldn't imagine what made it so spectacular.

"Dear sweet Jesus, Clive. Eleven million might sound awfully fair to you, but to a gal from Nebraska you're closing in on our state budget," she said, shaking her great mane of hair and laughing her rough, sandy laugh. Erica was hip enough not to let van Arlyn know that she thought herself lucky to be in on this bonanza. After all, bonanzas worked in a lot of ways. If the apartment was right, she wouldn't let George Wheaton think twice about the big eleven. Anyway, eleven's lucky, it's a football team!

During the time Clive van Arlyn had been showing apartments to Erica Wheaton, he had grown fond of this big blonde, which was more than he could say for most of his clients. He liked that she didn't try to hide who she was—or, more important, wasn't. He admired her straightforwardness and healthy spunk. And he liked how she looked: solid, sexy, natural. Her coloring was mostly from the outdoors, and her clear blue eyes gleamed. But best of all was her laugh, big and bold and irresistible. Though George Wheaton's money was highly visible, Erica—unlike most wives—didn't feel she had to wear it.

The biggest difference, van Arlyn decided, between Erica Wheaton and most of his new clients was that she was in love as well as in business. Sure, she liked the money, but she would kill for her husband without it. That's why van Arlyn, who'd seen a lot of rich women, cared for *her* as well as for his six percent.

Erica Wheaton was pure Midwest and proud of it. She was purple mountains and fertile plains. Born Erica Phelps, upriver from Omaha in Bellevue, her father was a meat packer and her mother a part-time filing clerk at the Strategic Air Command, headquartered a mile from their house. Erica's people, as early as Lewis and Clark, had been lured by Nebraska's beauty and the riches of the mighty Missouri River.

After honors in high school, Erica stormed Nebraska U. Being head cheerleader was big-time, and marrying the captain of the football team was the jackpot. But Erica's star quarterback never made it big off the playing field. At twenty-six—too old, they said, to win—Erica Phelps became Miss Omaha and then was crowned Miss Nebraska. You've got to be determined to escape via the beauty queen route. There are a lot of tough Kiwanis, Elks, and carnival roads to travel before that last parade down the runway.

When the year's tour was over, so was her marriage. That's when Erica went to work and became what was then called a stewardess.

If van Arlyn hustled, so did Erica—before meeting George Wheaton, of course. Her days as a "stew" had yielded her a lot more than miniature liquor bottles. Sure, she was looking. Sure, she seized the opportunities.

As a flirtatious flight attendant she met fellow Nebraskan Johnny Carson on the red-eye from LA. When Carson had joked about their wheat fields not being as sweet as they're cracked up to be, Erica let loose that sexy laugh. Luckily for Erica, next to Johnny Carson was George Wheaton, an Omaha businessman in his late forties who had just divorced his wife of twenty-five years because she had remained all the things he'd married her for.

Now at thirty-three, married almost three years, with her daughter Georgette nearly two, Erica Wheaton and her husband George were beginning to figure in a world peopled by the new Four Hundred. Light-years away from Ward McAllister's Four Hundred, today's list was culled from the

Forbes and *Fortune* pyramids up which George Wheaton had climbed steadily. Not even the rise of the colossi in the frenzied finance of the 1890s could have matched the mogul mania of Manhattan in the 1980s.

Although Erica liked power, she liked to feel she had earned it. Power came from going and doing, being part of things, not just a party *to* them. She'd helped with Wheaton Industries, advising George to put cineplexes into his malls and to get rid of the fast-food franchises. During the few years they'd been married, the companies where George Wheaton used her ideas had turned good profits. She never wanted her name chiseled on a museum wall or engraved on thick cream-colored charity invitations unless she had helped to make it happen.

Even at the ranch, it was Erica who'd insisted on bringing in the best heifers and bulls to breed. A prize bull might cost millions, but she spent when it counted, and she knew how to spread it around so it did.

"How many people do you really think might want—and can afford—this apartment?" Erica asked, as they walked over the lobby's Persian rugs. Until today, she thought she'd seen everything, from Jock Whitney's grand double townhouse to an Arab billionaire's triplex with a private elevator and indoor pool, where she was told guests lounged on semisubmerged benches watching erotic films at skinny-dipping soirées.

"Incredible as it sounds, twenty-five or thirty. That's the urgency. That's why you had to fly in."

Erica smiled at the twenty-five or thirty, mostly because the figure included her.

Although the Wheatons still lived in Omaha, near the big house George had given his ex-wife, Wheaton Industries had spread its tentacles from the poured-concrete malls of suburbia to the steel-and-glass behemoths of Wall Street. Now George needed headquarters in the hub.

As they waited for the elevator, Erica caught van Arlyn staring at her cleavage, his brows knit as tightly as her angora. It wasn't just the great divide that anchored van Arlyn's attention, it was everything: the bold plaid of the suit in criss-crossing turquoise, black, and green; the wide nailhead belt pulled an extra too-tight inch; the jam of Chanel chains. One or two chains, maybe, but five? He understood it attracted attention, but in his world it was the wrong kind. Van Arlyn sighed aloud. Why couldn't Erica's naturalness above the neck carry on down?

She obviously liked to be noticed. But Clive knew there was a better way. Much better.

"Clive, do I see from your look of horror that I'm due for another session in which you tell me how to dress so as not to offend some stuffy co-op board? Won't this work wonders?" she teased, whipping off her jacket for a better view.

"It'll work wonders, all right. *After* they vote you in!" Though Clive van Arlyn had sidestepped many of his family's traditions, how to dress was not one of them. He was still the Brooks Brothers boy he'd always been. Everything was just a little older and, needless to say, more threadbare.

Erica was a van Arlyn rarity in that she was not intimidated by what he called his "wolf in class couture wardrobe": the hacking-back herringbone jacket with leather patch elbows and the button-down shirt whose cuffs were held together by old crystal links so cloudy one could hardly make out the hunting scene inside.

But she'd gotten this far because her brain reacted when it really mattered. Like the first time she had made love to George Wheaton. She understood what George wanted her to do with her mouth, and she knew also that the woman he was leaving never had.

Erica still made the same kind of love. She knew that when she got excited, it made George all the more so. Erica's flight plan had taught her that when she really dug someone, he knew it. She could be twisting and turning and pumping the exact same way, but if there was no passion the signals were different. She remembered the first guy who got the message. He was out of control, crazed. She was embarrassed at first, then flattered. She'd never made a guy react like that. Rising to the challenge made Erica like sex all the more. And if Erica had liked sex before, she loved it with George.

She'd think about it before she went down to his office, deciding what she would be today: a shy, pubescent virgin, a dominatrix wearing spike-heeled boots, or the brazen hussy who'd arrived flashing her hot eyes and body with only her Miss Nebraska ribbon under her sable.

She'd think about it all the way, getting more and more excited as George told his secretary, "No calls." He'd lead her into the exercise room with all the expensive avocado oils, otherwise unused, and make wild love on the tanning bed. It reminded her of the time in Las Vegas in the presidential suite at Caesar's Palace, when she'd been poor and had first spread the free fancy bottled creams over her body. Her computerized conventioneer missed his meeting, but she never missed a beat.

With George she spread the expensive balms over herself as if it were a ritual, until her body glistened like gold. She'd parade to the bicycle, all the time watching George watching her, even while he was tearing off his clothes. She knew just what she was doing as she pedaled naked, her breasts jumping up and down, the oil between her legs wetting the hard leather

UNSUITABLE COMPANY ———————————— 11

seat while she twisted with passion until George pulled her off
and entered her.

And when she left her husband's office, she did so with
the seeming casualness with which she'd arrived, stopping to
chat with George's secretary as if she'd just delivered a child's
report card.

At home, their king-sized bed could be transformed into
a black satin den or a nun's retreat of purest white. Who cared
what the servants thought? George had never considered
himself a stud or even a weekend warrior, but with Erica he
became someone who didn't let what he couldn't do interfere
with what he could. . . .

"Don't worry, Clive," Erica said, turning to a frowning
van Arlyn. "I'll be your perfect person. Of course, if they don't
think so, I'll rip it all off and show them they've *really* made
a mistake."

"Pul-eese," he said, making Erica's favorite van Arlyn
face by rolling his eyes high and letting them rest mischie-
vously in the corners. It expressed just what you suspected he
was thinking. However, he'd learned to say outright, without
the slightest hesitation, things like "Look at that sunlight
pouring through," when a new concrete tower would soon
block the view, or to marvel at "the peace and quiet" when the
children who lived on the floor above were in school.

Clive van Arlyn had eloped with Mary Tompkins in the
late sixties. A passive and pretty girl three years his senior, she
had always adored Clive. He was smart and clever and fearless
in fighting her two older brothers, who were jocks and jerks,
with his own greatest weapon, his wit. The van Arlyns were on
lists for dinners, yachts, and everybody's island, often because
Mary van Arlyn preferred staying in the country and Clive was
such a desirable extra man.

Mary van Arlyn never knew, however, about the lurid

event just before their elopement that had precipitated the marriage. Van Arlyn and three other friends, all male, had been on Fire Island for the weekend. There had been a party. Everyone had to come dressed as a bride. The wedding cake was laced with LSD. The icing was sprinkled with coke. The sex turned to torture. The following morning, one of the "brides" lay in the middle of the dining room table, with a blue garter around his neck. Nobody remembered anything. That's what they all swore, and it was a vow that had to endure. But nobody really did remember. Too many drugs and too much liquor had blotted the party out for everyone. Immediately thereafter, van Arlyn's particular friend and companion had vanished, leaving van Arlyn terrified and in need of respectability.

"The super's waiting upstairs," the elevator man said, after greeting van Arlyn and nodding to Erica. After the first employee strike in the building, 823's elevator had gone automatic, but the building still boasted a daytime button pusher. Now his white-gloved finger pressed PH.

Stepping from the elevator, Erica and van Arlyn entered what was certainly one of the city's most glorious duplex penthouses. The highly polished marble gallery, mirroring a waterfall of light from the majestic crystal chandelier, made Erica feel as though she'd wandered into a Busby Berkeley extravaganza. And the way the long rectangular rooms flowed one into the other, enfilade, was like a great European château.

"How's it going, Rooney?" van Arlyn asked, after introducing Erica Wheaton.

"Able to take nourishment," he answered, annoyed at being bothered. He'd answered this same question yesterday in front of another of van Arlyn's clients, who he also knew, from the first glance, hadn't a prayer of getting voted in. Rooney liked to believe he was of the old school like his father, giving less of a damn for the new big tippers than for the old purse-proud swells. His father, hired when the building went up just before the First War, had told him of times when money also poured, but, unlike now, it didn't reign.

"They think they own you for a ten," he'd say—and today Rooney could say exactly the same thing, except the ten was now a fifty. It wasn't only in this building where money screamed and orders were barked, where high heels clicked on marble and the last look given was to the mirror instead of to the person being addressed.

Rooney hardly glanced at Erica Wheaton. That first flash of wild hair and turquoise sweater was enough not to warrant a second look. He wondered why van Arlyn bothered. Not that there weren't worse in the building, but they had gotten in before the board started keeping their kind out. That's what all the supers in co-ops talked about. Their snobbery was little different from that of their tenants. "Nothing is like it was." "It won't ever be the same." "Treat 'em like pigs, they won't know the difference."

Van Arlyn was incensed at Rooney's indifference to Erica. Stubborn bastard! He should know as well as anyone that in today's mad-money world, with priceless virtues peddled daily, the Wheatons had a good shot at making it.

"You wanted views," van Arlyn said, waving his arm from the glassed-in terrace that ran the length of the living room and leaned over Fifth Avenue like an exotic spaceship.

"May I have the pleasure of presenting you, my darling Erica, with not only a slice of heaven, but with two and a half miles of Central Park for your own front lawn."

For once, van Arlyn hadn't exaggerated. Beneath the border of distant high-rises, a breath away from Tiffany's and Bergdorf's, lay the autumn splendor of Central Park, with bursts of gold and orange spreading across acres of green. Directly below, just beyond the pavement, was the Central Park Zoo, where Erica could actually see seals sunning and polar bears swimming. And every now and then, when some tiny hand would lose its grip, one of the helium-filled dots would soar into the breeze, past the lake with its rowboats, the Sheep Meadow with its kites, the playgrounds, even beyond the new-monied wings of the old Metropolitan Museum of Art.

"It's a miracle!" Erica said, overwhelmed.

"Wait till winter. Between the snow and the skating rink, you'll think you're in Wonderland."

Fortunately neither Erica nor van Arlyn heard Rooney mutter, "Or out in the cold." Rooney'd bet the world a free round that Erica Wheaton had about as much chance at 823 as the proverbial snowball in hell.

The entire penthouse was unique, having been specially built for one of the thirty Carnegie millionaires created by "Uncle Andrew" after he sold Carnegie Steel to J. P. Morgan. Morgan's resulting giant, United States Steel, was capitalized then at $1.5 billion, a figure to stagger all but an astronomer. At this moment, at least three of 823's tenants were worth that or more.

Since the first Carnegie, the apartment had changed hands only within the family, and fortunately they had all had the good taste to leave the good taste. The Carnegie crests remained in the high corner moldings; the green and blue colors of their racing silks still glistened in the marble mantels and patterned marble floors. And today, with air rights in New York being bitterly fought for, ceilings an extravagant fourteen feet high were truly diamonds in the sky. The apartment harked back to an age when one went to the races to see one's own horses run, when manners mattered, and when friends cared about one another as much as they cared for themselves.

The downstairs of the duplex was definitely in the grand manner. The living room ceiling with its hand-carved octagons had been copied from one of the great houses in England, while the parquet floor looked as if each piece had been laid by an artist. In the old days, this room would have been called the salon. "Living room" was hardly appropriate for a space van Arlyn knew had been furnished with signed Louis pieces, where seat cushions on ornately carved bergères were plumped halfway up their backs, where museum-quality Aubussons covered the floor instead of the walls, and where even the oversized bronze doorknobs were cast with crests. But then people did not "live" in this room. They received.

"When the Carnegies were here," van Arlyn said, as they entered the gold-and-white Venetian dining room with its frescoes of the Grand Canal, "liveried footmen served." He watched as Erica's eyes glistened.

The only obvious renovation was the kitchen, modernized two years ago at a cost of a million dollars. As they walked through, van Arlyn pointed out the banquet-sized charcoal grill, the walk-in freezer, and the see-through wine refrigerator that was like a small room.

Climbing the wide stairway to the second floor, van Arlyn stopped midway. "This is what's known as a picture staircase," he said, gesturing toward the landing. "The big money man's portrait always hangs on this wall to allow ample space to admire his genius. The descendants descend as far as space allows."

Erica shook her head. "My great-granddaddy was hanged for real. How about that for a picture?" She laughed as van Arlyn again rolled his eyes.

The dressing room especially intrigued Erica. Behind the

beveled-mirror doors an oval rack stretched the length of four closets. At the flick of a switch the rack revolved, bringing each hanger within immediate sight and reach. Fascinating, too, were the metal identifiers inserted into the shelves, and the amount of space designated for hats and gloves.

"Look at this," she said, amazed as the drawers pulled out with ball-bearing efficiency. But then they came from a time when things were made sturdily, people cared, and "built-in obsolescence" was not yet a phrase. It was a day when costs were still in proper proportion even if you were as rich as the Carnegies.

The five bedrooms were all big and bright, but Erica's favorite was the painted nursery. On one wall a life-sized Snow White danced with the Seven Dwarfs, while on another wall Snoopy and Lucy played football. How appropriate for a Big Red fan!

Erica also loved the mother-of-pearl buttons tucked in strategic positions in the wall of every room which van Arlyn told her were once used to call servants.

Rooney shrugged his shoulders so van Arlyn could see his "what would she know?" gesture of disgust as he walked away.

After a final rapturous sweep, Erica was on wings. "Clive," she cried, "I don't like it, I adore it! It's Christmas. A thousand Christmases. I can't wait to tell George! I can't wait for him to feel the magic!"

Since Rooney hadn't even had the customary courtesy to follow them around, van Arlyn dismissed him when they were ready to leave with the same disdain Rooney had shown Erica. "Why don't you stay, Rooney, and lock up. And make sure the lights are out."

"Nice meetin' you, Mrs. Wheaton," Rooney said, sure he'd never see her again.

"Thank you. See you soon. Very soon, I hope."

Waiting for the elevator, Erica Wheaton turned to Clive. "I could be crazy, but maybe eleven is low. Say they had an auction, what do you think would take it?"

Van Arlyn didn't answer. He couldn't. What Erica didn't seem to understand was that it wasn't a question of money.

"It's tough to know who's bidding. They'll stretch for this one. Not that the highest necessarily matters." He wanted to warn her. Too high to the vulgar could be, God forbid, vulgar! Knowing her chances were slim, van Arlyn was suddenly sorry Erica wanted it so much.

The elevator man was taking a break, so van Arlyn poked L as they got in and started down. Suddenly, they heard sounds, muddled and low, far away. As the elevator descended, the sounds became clearer, more distinct. It was a man and a woman, shouting. Van Arlyn and Erica stared at each other.

Without warning, the elevator doors opened at 6 and the voices exploded in both volume and hysteria. Van Arlyn and Erica stood frozen.

"Fucking whore! Cocksucking whore!"

"Not yours! Not yours anymore! You won't have any balls between those legs when I'm through with you, you fucking turd. And that's now. Now! Now!"

A good-looking young girl, her open robe showing she had nothing on underneath, hurled whatever she was drinking, including the glass, at a graying man in a jogging suit. His back was turned to the astounded observers in the elevator. Not only was he oblivious to the open door, but to the fact that his hand was leaning on both the UP and DOWN buttons. Without releasing them, he reached for her body with his other hand and caught the hem of her robe. Off balance, she slipped and fell to the floor of the elevator hall. Her legs apart, the robe like a doormat between them, she scrambled to raise herself as the soft velour, still clutched in the man's hand, left her body completely.

"My God!" Bettina Blair suddenly moaned, staring at the open elevator.

Turning to see what had caused the new outcry, the gray-haired man's mouth began to tremble. "Fucking Christ almighty!" he mumbled. His arms fell limply to his sides. And as the elevator door closed on this fascinating vignette, van Arlyn smiled to himself. Erica Wheaton would now get her apartment.

2

*L*ong before the elevator doors at 823 Fifth had closed, the boardroom doors of Triomphe, Ltd., in the heart of London's fashionable Mayfair, had opened. Throughout the night, Triomphe's founder and chairman, the brilliant and successful John Kaplan, had been mentally preparing for today's meeting, a meeting that might prove to be the most important of his life. He wasn't certain if he'd even slept. He remembered saying "Damn it!" and "Hurry up!" more than once to the luminous hands he'd had Asprey's paint on the antique carriage clock by his bed.

He was glad Zara was in New York. Not that J.K. didn't adore his wife, nor did he doubt for an instant that their life was satisfying in every way. But this deal needed his complete attention. He must remember to call Zara's father and cancel the shoot. He laughed to himself. All the English seemed to think about was shooting and fucking. He wondered why both targets were called birds. He must ask Zara's father. He'd think it a lark.

Actually, a tarty little bird was exactly what J.K. would want later. Not someone who knew how to love, but someone who knew how to please. The easy release. To feed his ego. Massage his balls. But discreetly. He was not like those idiots who paraded their manhood in "private" clubs whose "hostesses" couldn't wait to tell the press they'd serviced the likes of Fergie's father. Of course, were anyone to suggest that Kaplan's first love was the deal and that dealing gave him the greatest sexual pleasure, he'd have thought him mad.

At six-foot-three and well over two hundred pounds, even with his dark hair receding until he was almost bald on top, John Kaplan seemed a good deal younger than forty-five. It was the dashing way he moved, his pheasant strut, the seductive eye and ready smile. Even his eyes, with their catlike amber streaks running through gray irises, were young and darting.

Yet if one looked closely, the lines read differently. The forehead creases formed easily and, to judge by the depth of their ridges, had done so for years.

Although his Huntsman suits were tailored with conservative straight-cut jackets, narrow lapels, and cuffed trousers, the extra-wide pinstripes, like those he wore now, and the horse-blanket plaids he wore on weekends, gave him the dazzle of a riverboat gambler. And why not? On today's green felt, John Kaplan was emerging as one of the world's top players.

His appeal was electric and sexual to both men and women; people felt complimented when he stopped to talk. He exuded a compelling force. Everyone, it seemed, including those he'd whipped to a pulp, wanted more of John Kaplan. Each believed he might be the one to tame him.

People who knew him well called him Jack. Not because

it was the familiar for John but for blackjack, at which he excelled. He could count cards in as many as four decks and was an unheard-of "ahead" in London's gambling clubs. He'd started the name himself to appear more cavalier, more devil-may-care than devil.

J.K. could trace Triomphe's exact beginning to the day, eighteen years earlier, when he'd observed a sudden flourishing of Oriental restaurants throughout London. England's old-time fish and chips no longer seemed to satisfy the newly hot fast-food taste. Only in his mid-twenties, Kaplan managed to convince—"con" being the operative syllable—a willing-to-wager bookmaker on the odds that Chinese takeout would sweep the country. Almost two decades later, all across England, people still poured money into Triomphe's coffers every mealtime.

From there it was a natural progression to freezing the dinners, to buying supermarkets to put them in, shopping centers for the supermarkets, to more real estate. More of everything. From the start, Triomphe's profits set records. Had the bookmaker left in his original loan of fifty thousand pounds instead of taking his promised seventy-five at the end of the year, his investment in Triomphe would now be worth millions.

As John Kaplan entered the gleaming, teak-paneled boardroom with its custom-weave, arch-motif carpeting, he was delighted that the full complement of directors had come on such short notice. It was a tribute to his imposing financial stature. He couldn't wait for the meeting to start, to stun them out of their conglomerate minds with the company he was proposing to take over.

The spacious boardroom occupied half the second floor of Triomphe's elegant townhouse, once the hideaway for the Prince of Wales during his "harmless" flirtation with "that vulgar American divorcée." In fact, two Vuitton trunks found in the basement with Mrs. Simpson's w.w.s. emblazoned in yellow were now used as coffee tables in the Kaplans' country home.

The white Georgian building had been loaned to the Prince by his knowing friend, the Duke of Westminster. Ironically, three hundred years earlier, when the Westminsters, then *and* now London's largest landowners, first acquired the district of Mayfair, it had been called "a worthless area of vice."

Kaplan relished intrigue. He enjoyed picturing the future king being dropped at the corner, pulling the brim of his hat low, the lapels of his fur-collared coat high. He imagined him sneaking through the conveniently servantless servants' quarters and hearing him call, "Wallis! Wallis!" as he took the circular stairs two at a time.

Mrs. Simpson's bedroom was now J.K.'s private office, a fact he particularly savored. On the sunny side of the second floor, it overlooked a garden where Virginia creeper climbed whitewashed brick walls. At the garden's end, an old stone fountain spouted steadily from an appropriate statue of Eros.

Before John Kaplan purchased the house, it had had a succession of owners but no renovations. Instead of corporate planners, J.K. hired a design team specializing in domestic decoration. Except for the boardroom, Kaplan wanted, and got, antiques in polished fruitwoods, landscape paintings, and inviting fabrics.

The reception rooms, with their fresh flowers and overstuffed sofas and chairs, resembled parlors, and the offices looked like libraries. During the overhaul some of the bathrooms became bathless to utilize space, although Kaplan insisted on keeping the double tub in the master bathroom, installed at Mrs. Simpson's request. For J.K., it was a conversation piece, an off-balance opener, proof of how informal and down-to-earth a chap he could be, discussing the Duchess's sexual expertise.

What made J.K. especially proud was the mark *he'd* made in England, the monies he'd brought into Britain. Except for its former owner's abdication, John Kaplan had certainly done more for the Crown than Edward VIII.

After the success of his original takeout chain, Kaplan was able to borrow and expand easily. And when Triomphe went public eight years ago, it was so hot an offering that it yielded Kaplan profits to the jolly tune of forty million pounds. Now, with Triomphe becoming global, the stock was hotter than ever.

J.K.'s genius was not only in spotting trends and maximizing undervalued situations but in predicting worldwide trouble spots. Long before the Marcos ouster, Kaplan had sold Triomphe's huge Philippine embroidery companies; before any devaluation in Mexico, he'd vetoed bidding on two Coca-Cola bottling plants outside Guadalajara.

Chewing on his unlit twenty-eight-dollar Davidoff cigar, John Kaplan compulsively checked the points of pencils, the thermoses of coffee and water. He'd already rechecked his carousel of slides making sure of their order. Again, he aligned the long yellow pads on the table where the directors would soon be sitting. Crafted by England's most fashionable furniture maker, Viscount Linley, son of Princess Margaret and nephew of the Queen, the table was a replica of the one at 10 Downing Street, ingeniously curved so that, without ever leaning forward, everyone was visible.

As Kaplan thought about the details of this new deal he wasn't at all worried about its complexity. He'd learned long ago that people paid attention if you made them believe they were able to grasp intricate concepts. Actually, it had been more tedious for J.K. to uncomplicate today's facts than it had been to structure the whole thing. Not that the board had to understand every word. One of the main reasons their votes stayed solid was that, besides their fees, Kaplan provided substantial year-end bonuses and generous travel allotments to take their families to "investigate" new Triomphe activities. J.K. was aware that nobody loves luxurious freebies better than the rich, because only they know how much they are worth. He was also aware that those working for you can be more dangerous than those who oppose you.

Little in Kaplan's life, whether it was a finely sharpened pencil or a marriage, was unplanned. He lived by a meticulous and deliberate design, a design woven into the fabric of his being as painstakingly by his mother as by himself.

Displayed in identical frames on opposite walls were the words that said it all:

> Victory at all costs, victory in
> spite of all terror, victory how-
> ever long and hard the road
> may be, for without victory
> there is no survival.

These words were spoken by J.K.'s hero, Winston Churchill, before the House of Commons on May 13, 1940. That was also the day, month, and year on which John Kaplan's mother took her last look at her beloved Arc de Triomphe, before her perilous escape from Paris and the Gestapo when his father, a leader in the Resistance as well as a Jew, failed to return after completing another perilous mission.

"He was very brave, your father, and very handsome, like you," J.K. remembered his mother saying over and over as she pressed his little hand in hers. "He designed big, beautiful cars for people to have good times. That was before the factory he bombed changed to tanks."

She didn't add, tanks that were meant to crush the likes of your father under France's new Nazi wheels.

"After a few days when your father still didn't come home, and when those days became a week, I knew the worst had happened. But I also knew they had heard the explosion he caused over all of Paris and the Nazis would never make another Peugeot tank!"

Her voice was as ardent as "La Marseillaise" on D-Day. It was a fighting voice. Marie-Louise Kaplan was John Kaplan's greatest legacy.

"But my angel, don't ever believe that life is over. I believed my life was over when your father died, but suddenly came the most wonderful part of my world. You."

John Kaplan could still feel his mother's fingers as she cupped his head in her hands. He was too young to understand that she was remembering her fear when she'd discovered she was pregnant.

After weeks of travel, hiding and changing her identity, Marie-Louise had finally reached Normandy and a small camouflaged boat. In this boat, built to hold seven but with twelve aboard, Marie-Louise spent four death-stalked days before they sighted the English coast. Thanks to one of the passengers, a priest, she then found refuge in the rectory of a tiny Covent Garden church, not far from where Henry Higgins gave new life to a cockney flower girl.

In a country unable to support its own, where dogs were put down for food and children were sent to work instead of school, Marie-Louise was lucky to have lavatories to scrub. Yet as often happens, the greatest hope springs from the greatest despair. And so it did on the afternoon she entered Her Majesty's Halcyon Clinic.

The first labor pains had started early that morning, soon after the siren's warning had sent all London underground. When at last the all-clear sounded, Marie-Louise could barely crawl to one of the ambulances used to haul dead and broken bodies that would lead her to David Ramsey.

Although Ramsey had started the war at the front, a Nazi attack on a clearly marked Red Cross unit had sent this young physician back to London with a punctured lung. With his life a constant swirl of death and destruction, he was thrilled to deliver a healthy eight-pound boy. Raised on a small dairy farm in Dorset, Ramsey had always looked more like a farmer than a surgeon. However, with his life consumed by medicine a pallor had replaced his country bloom. Therefore, when Marie-Louise entered his world, he gladly offered her a room in his tiny flat. Since his lack of leisure had made it difficult to develop a permanent relationship with anyone, the arrival of Marie-Louise became the miracle he needed. When the blitz increased, London seemed no place for the infant he was beginning to consider his son and for the woman who, almost without him noticing, was dropping into his thoughts and into his dreams. Marie-Louise needed little convincing to go to his family in Dorset. When David could manage to visit, Marie-Louise would revitalize his entire being. She felt in-debted to the Ramseys, while they in turn felt blessed that so loving a woman was brightening their son's life. During the day she would take baby John and work in the nearby orphanage, and in the evening, with the family, she would crochet wool squares for soldiers' blankets while they all huddled around the voice of the BBC as Hitler, thank God, invaded Russia rather than crossing the Channel.

When the war ended, Marie-Louise and David Ramsey were married. Never, however, would her husband know that her seemingly unrestrained climaxes contained no passion, that sensuality for her had been extinguished in Paris. Her ambition now was for her son.

As it happened, she and Ramsey were perfectly suited. The time he spent with his wrap-around nurses, whose admiration he fed with his enormous sexual appetite, allowed Marie-Louise more time with her son.

That she didn't desire more children also suited the increasingly busy doctor. Because of the thousands of shattered limbs and faces he'd operated on during the war, Ramsey now specialized in reconstructive surgery, which gradually turned into a lucrative cosmetic surgery practice.

Though the Ramseys were hardly *Burke's Peerage*, they were not excluded from society as they might once have been. After wars, service records often become insignias of acceptance. Were it not for the consistent stream of "amusing parvenus" the wars created, England's deadly upper-class drawing rooms would have stayed that way. Therefore a chap like Ramsey, who'd not only sewn Sandhurst blue bloods back together but was capable of sculpting their mums back into debs, was more than welcome.

Though she was aware that much anti-Semitism still existed, Marie-Louise refused to change her son's name or have Ramsey adopt him. She believed the prejudice he would encounter was a part of his legacy and that the insecurity it generated would guard against his becoming lazy or self-satisfied.

When he was old enough to understand the barbs at school and had already been called "Jewboy," Marie-Louise gave her son his own choice. But with his father's strength and bravery already instilled in him, for John there was no option. Even at the tender age of eight, he had already adopted his "I'll show them" mind-set.

No, there would be no registration at Eton or Harrow for John Kaplan, but neither would there be buggering by upper-class prefects who forced the new boys to warm their beds with their virgin bodies, making the sheets toasty for when they slipped in beside them. There would be successes, but never because Kaplan ran races where one stopped for hurdles or helped a bloke who stumbled.

The school in which he was enrolled was just outside Dorset. Having her son at home during his formative years and her husband's active ones suited John's mother just fine. Her constant proddings were instrumental in his becoming valedictorian as well as in his easy entrance to Oxford.

When he graduated with honors, Marie-Louise Ramsey encouraged him to attend Yale Law School—"America, my darling, is where it is all happening!"

Since John's mother had always known where the meaningful games were won, she had filled his head with a lust for winning that she knew would far outlast any playing field, cramming his mind with philosophy, politics, economics. Though her special friends were La Bruyère and La Rochefoucauld, when she'd tell her son about his father, she quoted the words of Churchill:

> Not in vain may be the pride of
> those who survived and the ep-
> itaph of those who fell.

Marie-Louise Courbeille Kaplan Ramsey died in a car crash on her way to surprise her son at Heathrow Airport. He had just finished his first year as a young attorney with the prestigious American law firm of Sullivan & Cromwell. At the funeral, his grief and frustration were almost uncontrollable. Smashing his right fist against his left palm, he knew nobody could ever again tell John Kaplan that life was fair. Chiseled on her headstone, beneath her name and dates, were the prophetic words NOT IN VAIN.

3

*T*he Courbeille fire coursed through John Kaplan now as he greeted each member of Triomphe's influential board. With conglomerate warfare raging, such top board members as global tycoons, crack politicians, and expert bankers—as well as ex-presidents of everything—were scarce. Even Gerald Ford, whom J.K. had wanted, especially in light of today's meeting, was already on five.

Little wonder that headhunters, once hired only to scalp top management, were now in constant search of directors with big bucks and hot contacts. Since a board's primary function was to help its company achieve its goals, the more powerful the directors, the more empowered their leader.

With a sharp eye on 1992, when 350 million Europeans would create an omnipotent economic whole, J.K. had restructured what had once been an almost exclusively British domain. Out of twelve Triomphe members, excluding himself, only four Brits remained, though all were well placed, either in Parliament or in the press.

There was also a leading Irish distiller, two French business tycoons, one Swiss and one German banker, and, from Japan, the shogun of Tokyo real estate. Though a million dollars an acre might sound absurd in Beverly Hills, in downtown Tokyo land went for a hundred times that much.

The last two members were American. Archer Blair had been J.K.'s roommate at Yale as well as his first introduction to New York's monied aristocracy. Tall and spare, Blair's craggy looks mirrored bedrock New England, as did his hidden sexual desires. Although Blair was J.K.'s oldest friend, the fact that the Blair name was still revered on Wall Street was why J.K. included him.

Jack Minton, the other American, was known as "New York's hottest risk arbitrageur" and had already made more money honestly than insiders ever thought of stealing, though J.K. never quite understood the talent associated with arbitrage. He saw arbs as ferrets: ratters unearthing already known facts about companies from brokers hungry for commissions, buyers needing backing for takeovers, and lawyers and bankers forever on the muscle. After sifting the guts from the gossip, they would buy the stock of the supposed takeover for their firm and pray the buy-out happened. If it did, their firm got richer, and at Christmas a million dollars could easily end up in their stocking. More basic was J.K.'s loathing of Minton's lack of class.

Yet no matter how diverse their origins, their one uncommon denominator was their belief in the words on the plaque J.K. presented to each new member. LIFE'S A BORE WHEN THE SCENERY DOESN'T CHANGE. IT NEVER DOES UNLESS YOU RUN WITH THE LEAD DOG. As far as track records went, J.K. was far ahead of the pack.

* * *

When the directors finally sat down, all eyes focused on J.K. The air was alive with expectation.

"A very good morning, gentlemen," J.K. said, smiling. "Again, let me thank you for coming on such short notice. With the facts now complete, there's no question but that we must act at once."

J.K. never sat during a presentation. He didn't pace, either. He stood tall among his peers. As he rested his cigar on the only ashtray in the room, in front of *his* chair, J.K. squinted, much as an artist might study the horizon for the right perspective.

"We've all been aware that for some time the buy-out of America has been savage. Last year alone, over a hundred and fifty billion dollars was knifed away, sixty-eight percent more than the year before.

"In a small way, Triomphe has participated in this American shopping spree. Yet our cart is virtually empty, compared to what it will hold." As J.K. pressed a button, the lights dimmed and a screen lowered. One by one, universally recognized logos stretched across the screen: Firestone, Pond's, Doubleday, Saks, Carnation, Tiffany, Clorox, Tropicana.

"This is but a part of the American dream gone sour. Even establishment names such as Brooks Brothers and J. Press"—he smiled at his pal Archer—"have crossed the Atlantic." At Law School, Press had been his and Archer's sartorial haunt.

"Yet most Americans are unaware these stars have been shot from their flag. The fact that Yankee call letters such as RCA are now German, and that Mack truck, hallmark of the U.S. highway, is a weak sister to Renault, would doubtless stun every man and woman on Main Street."

J.K.'s surging voice was broken only by the click of a new

slide showing American skyscrapers awakening to a new rising sun.

"Well, Aki," J.K. said. "What about the pillage of this skyline? Two billions' worth to date and much of it yours. Japan's not even as big as California, and you've already managed thirty-four billionaires. In all fifty U.S. states there are only sixty-eight. What genius said, 'America's the land of opportunity if you're Japanese'?"

"I think I did." Aki Yoshoto laughed. No one joined in.

"Not that Britain's doing badly," J.K. continued. "So far, believe it or not, we've devoured the largest slice of America's pie. And if all goes according to today's plan, another big wedge should be coming our way within months."

Kaplan paused, not so much to get his breath as to make sure the board got his message. All at once another slide flashed before them. "As everyone knows, only one finish line counts, the one at the bottom. Look at the foreign ownership in America, over a trillion and a half dollars, last year it grew a staggering twenty-five percent. That bottom line is soaring off the chart. With today's rate of exchange, America is irresistible. And don't forget, it's a country where one needn't worry about Communists or guerrillas overthrowing the government. In America our only enemy is another investor."

Sweat began to break on J.K.'s brow. His mouth was dry, but his adrenaline was surging; he was too excited to stop for water. "I now want you to look at a company whose name is a byword but whose vast riches are secret. A company so layered with misconceptions about the future it soon won't have one. A company so poised for a killing—pardon me, turnaround—the Street will be thunderstruck. A fruit tree so overripe, it's begging for a good Triomphe shake."

Although J.K. wouldn't admit that the words "hostile" and "raider" would have anything to do with "a good

Triomphe shake," they would be as much on target as J.K. himself.

"Gentlemen," Kaplan continued. "The situation I'm about to show you, in good American lingo, will blow your minds!"

His breath tight, Kaplan finally sipped some water, as a buzz of excitement whirred through the room. Hearing the stir, he looked at his watch, worn on the inside of his wrist so he could check it unobserved. Not quite yet, he thought. Let them salivate a bit more. Not that J.K. ever forced enthusiasms or opinions. As he put it, "I merely adjust them."

Looking at the time made him think about Zara: what he'd have to tell her later. After all, his deals, and this one in particular, had a lot to do with that apartment she was going to see.

Archer Blair was also thinking about Zara. He couldn't believe he'd come to London while she'd gone to New York. He purposely hadn't called her, wanting it to be a surprise. Obviously, she must have done the same, because she'd never phoned either. Though Blair never thought he'd be glad to know Minton, let alone be indebted to him, today he was both. Minton's offer of a ride home in his company's plane at least meant he'd be back in New York for a late dinner. Blair wondered if Zara would laugh or cry when she got his message at the Carlyle. Now Blair checked *his* watch. He wished like hell Jack would get on with it. Who gave a damn how much bigger Triomphe got? Christ, the only reason he was even here was Zara!

As J.K. felt the tension mount, he was especially pleased to see that Archer—who served more as a friend—seemed particularly on edge. Unwrapping the cellophane from a fresh cigar, J.K. rolled the rich Havana between his thumb and forefinger. Just about right, he thought, his eyes narrowing anew. His board was just about where he wanted them: on the edge of their chairs, ready for him to grab by the seat of their pants.

His voice throbbing with excitement, J.K. began. "Not millions, not even hundreds of millions, but *billions* of dollars can drop into our laps from this prize."

All at once WHEATON INDUSTRIES, a name as famous and American as Mickey Mouse, blazed across the screen.

J.K. smiled, acknowledging their shock. "You'll be more startled in a moment." Eyes didn't blink and minds didn't stray as J.K. laid out his facts.

"For years, George Wheaton has ruled this public company as if it were his private fiefdom. That's great, when things are going well. But stockholders get restless when shares drop and dividends are threatened. Men like George Wheaton insist that morals have changed, that people don't want to work anymore. Morals haven't changed. Times have. And people like George Wheaton haven't!" J.K.'s words fell like thunder as he smashed one fist into the other.

"The dwindling giant you see on the screen is the perfect example of a man's blindness to today, to a company that could be bankrupt tomorrow. But our deal will not only allow us to control Wheaton, it will enable us to do it with Wheaton's own money!"

It was true that George Wheaton was still running Wheaton with lessons he'd learned at the University of Chicago. As a disciple of the brilliant economist Nikolai Kondratieff, Wheaton still believed in his theory of long wave cycles: that no matter what happens short term, every fifty years or so certain economic cycles are inevitable, and these cycles, or waves, govern inflation and deflation.

Though Wheaton was sure deflation was here, J.K. believed the opposite. "I predict the future will be the precise reverse of Wheaton's timing. Maybe not forever, but long enough for Triomphe not to have to worry about the rest."

J.K.'s voice grew stronger as each slide illustrated how George Wheaton's selling many of Wheaton's companies and converting them into cash, stock, bonds, and mortgages was responsible for Wheaton's crisis.

"George Wheaton is betting that these paper assets will prove more valuable than the hard-core assets he's sold, that a pervasive deflation will let him buy back what he's sold at much lower prices; he also assumes he'll make a windfall from the accumulating interest and dividends.

"What's worked in the past for Wheaton hasn't a chance of working now. The only shot his company has to grow its way out of danger is mine."

All that was heard were some deep inhalations. Then Otto Scharfstein broke the tension that filled the room.

"I don't want too many deals not using other people's money," Scharfstein said, half laughing.

"Me either," said Gunther, the Swiss franc.

"Gentlemen, when you see the monies this deal will generate, I hope you'll have enough ventures for the cash that will flow through your banks. Or better yet"—J.K. winked —"back into Wheaton, the company we are *saving* from ruination. Remember, Triomphe never wants to appear the corporate raider; only the corporate builder. That Wheaton has the potential to be one of the biggest buy-out bonanzas of all time is something we may notice later. After all, how can we resist such benefits for our shareholders?"

"Wheaton has some properties in Canada I could do very well with," Aki said, his voice charged.

"I'll bet," J.K. answered. "Everything Wheaton's got left

is good except its credibility." Again, J.K. pounded his fist. "And even if George Wheaton is foolhardy enough to want to compete with our bid, the banks won't lend him sufficient money. Bank generosity doesn't go as deep as Triomphe's pockets." Scharfstein and Gunther nodded agreement.

"Furthermore, Wheaton's classy Wall Street firms with their old-boy networking won't know what's up their family arses until the bomb on which they're sitting, called complacency, explodes. No offense, Archer, old chum," J.K. said good-naturedly.

At the sound of his name, Blair forced a laugh. Ever since chapel at Groton, Blair could look as if he were listening when his mind was straying—the way it had been now, over Zara.

"The idea of buying this giant without putting one cent at risk—buying Wheaton from Wheaton with Wheaton's money—is, as my children might say, awesome. Every cent can be raised from leveraging Wheaton's existing assets. But the reason for haste is that there won't be enough existing assets to leverage if we give George Wheaton time to keep selling."

As J.K. paused, he realized there wasn't a cough in the carload.

Quickly, easily, J.K. showed how he'd take the remaining company apart, maximize every option, minimize any loss. He showed the divisions he'd sell, the management he'd prune, the bones he'd leave to bury. Without a doubt, it was a company whose time to be raided had come.

"Yesterday, Wheaton Industries closed at thirty-two dollars a share, staggeringly less than its true value. Its five hundred million in cash and paper alone comes to half that. But the Street doesn't know it; I know through a source I cannot divulge. Also, Wheaton's remaining assets, those operations still functioning, are worth two billion more. Why, you might ask, doesn't today's market reflect Wheaton's worth even without that half billion in cash and paper? Because George Wheaton has unnerved his investors. Even after twenty years of building solid value, Wheaton's recent unpredictability has made the market fearful. And a frightened market not only sells but sells off. Who cares if Wheaton still pays dividends? In the takeover world, success has to do only with cash flow and assets.

"What Wheaton's obstinacy has brought about," J.K. proclaimed, again banging one fist into the other for emphasis, "is a great opportunity for Triomphe. We can offer twice the current market price for Wheaton, sell off the remaining entities for at least that, and still be left with Wheaton's stash of half a billion!"

If, as Rockefeller had said, "most business is stealing without resorting to violence," John Kaplan was a master thief.

4

*T*he meeting over, the board gone, an exhilarated John Kaplan dialed his private number at the Carlyle. Never had there been so fast a vote or such eagerness for a deal. He'd have called Zara sooner, but the directors had stayed for a celebratory lunch, all except Minton and Blair. J.K. wondered what in hell kind of dinner Archer had in New York that was so important.

Zara Kaplan almost tripped getting to the phone. She hadn't even read her messages or put down her purse. She'd called Archer from JFK even though she knew it was too early for him to be at his office. But she couldn't call him at home, and she knew the receptionist would tell him as soon as he got in.

"Hello?" Zara's voice was high and excited, a smile sweetening her lips as she looked out the picture window at all of downtown Manhattan: the rivers, the bridges, even Wall Street, from where Archer would be calling.

"Darling? Hello. You sound out of breath."

"What?"

"You sound out of breath. Did I take you from something?"

"No, no. It's all right. It's fine. John?"

"Yes, of course. Are you sure you're all right? You sound odd."

"No, no. I'm fine." As the smile faded, Zara motioned to the bellman. "Put it here. There. Anywhere."

"What? Zara?"

"Nothing, darling. Just my valise."

Although J.K. felt slightly deflated, he understood that, with the bellman there, Zara must have just arrived. She had probably been expecting that real estate girl to phone and was thrown off. "Sorry, darling. I didn't realize you'd just arrived. Time difference and all. Anyway, the meeting was a smash. Went off like a top."

Zara pouted into the receiver. "I'm happy for you," she said, not really aware of what her husband was talking about. She remembered his mentioning some meeting or other. But then he was always mentioning some meeting or other.

"And don't worry, I kept my promise about Archer. I never said a word to him about your looking at an apartment in his building. The number eight twenty-three never passed my lips."

Zara Kaplan's heart fell. The corners of her eyes filled with tears as she realized where Archer must be. "What did Archer say?" she asked. She wanted to make sure of her bearings—or, rather, Archer's.

"Say about what?"

"About the apartment."

Now J.K. understood. She'd *mis*understood. "He never said anything, darling, because I didn't mention a thing. Anyway, that wasn't really uppermost in my mind till after our meeting. You know I wouldn't say if I promised. But we both can now, if you like the apartment, because Wheaton's as good as done. I'd have called with the news sooner, only it was still a bit early for you and they've just this moment gone."

"How nice they all stayed," Zara said, finding it almost impossible to feign happiness, though she knew she must. Actually, she *was* happy for him and would have sounded thrilled were she not so disappointed about Archer.

Naturally, it never occurred to J.K. to mention that Archer hadn't stayed for lunch or that he'd hitched a ride back on Jack Minton's plane.

"Anyway, darling, it's a glorious day for us both. I just wish you were here with me to celebrate. But if you like the apartment, that will be celebration enough. Call the instant you've seen it. Promise me, my angel, my exciting little girl."

John Kaplan recalled the first time he'd ever set eyes on Lady Zara Thorne. It was at her father's shoot, one brisk October morning in Cornwall, almost fifteen years ago.

"This is my daughter, Zara," J.K. thought he'd heard Lord Ballard say, but he was obviously mistaken. It couldn't be this tall, whip-thin girl extending a heavily braceleted hand, looking untamed and uncouth, not to mention unwashed. Her long aubergine hair was obviously dyed and her matching plum-painted mouth with an indecently large lower lip was outlined in black. Her eyes, slanting ever so slightly to pagoda-arched brows, were as green as the freshest of God's greens. They were the most beautiful eyes he'd ever seen. If she were his daughter, he'd tear off those rags, give her a thrashing she'd never forget, and scrub the daylights back into her ladyship. Since she was not, the very thought excited him.

"How do you do, Mr. Kaplan," Zara Thorne said. The voice John Kaplan heard bore little resemblance to the studded denim jacket, the ludicrously high-heeled boots, or the three earrings dangling from one lobe. "I'm surprised you're here," she went on, her heritage coming through after all. "My father is virulently anti-Semitic."

Although Kaplan's ethnic origins hadn't caused any stir in years, or at least any he'd heard, his rise to the bait was instinctive.

"I'm well aware of that," John Kaplan said matter-of-factly. Actually, he was thunderstruck, but he was not going to give her the answer she expected.

Even though he was aware it was a challenge, he was surprised at her using the term "anti-Semitic." He was more intrigued, however, by the way "virulently"—a difficult word for a socialite to master—rolled off her tongue in the same deep voice, certainly a startling contrast to her Holly Golightly appearance. Unable to take his eyes from hers, he watched as she smiled into an exhalation of smoke.

An air of well-being filled the room. He and Lady Zara stood beside the pine-scented fire in the library of the Ballards' house. Far from a stately mansion, this fine Tudor home of gray fieldstone quarried on the property was built in 1535 as a hunting lodge for Anne Boleyn, only a year before her husband, Henry the Eighth, had her beheaded. It had been owned by Ballards as long as any Ballard could remember.

Of the twenty or so guests at the shoot, Kaplan knew only two others. The group ranged from apple-cheeked twenty to preserved ruddy, while the dress, for both sexes, varied little from tweeds and suedes, broken only by colorful vests and ties.

Although J.K. was a fine shot, a shoot for him was

always more business than sport. The Ballard shoot was no exception. Ballard, who had no idea how to get money unless someone died, had heard that Kaplan might be interested in a small chain of greengrocers he'd just inherited and had therefore invited him to Cornwall. What more attractive milieu to transact anything as unattractive as business, especially since Ballard had no office?

Although it was still early, two brass-buttoned butlers passed ponies of brandy that people either downed in a single gulp or used to lace their tea or coffee. J.K. watched transfixed as Zara Thorne threw back her Rémy Martin before the silver salver had even passed.

"One must brace oneself for these harsh fall winds," she said as she walked away, using her tongue to lick a last drop from that devastating lower lip.

His eyes followed her around the book-lined room, past the gleaming wood tables laden with family photographs, Victorian baby rattles, and porcelain bowls filled to overflowing with cabbage roses. The greens, grays, and blues of the landscape outside dominated the chintz that covered everything inside. Through the leaded glass windows, calendar-perfect sheep grazed on the brow of a hill and a small river followed the contour of the land until it disappeared in a grove of beeches.

When Zara returned, she held a fresh unlit cigarette for J.K. to light. He was stupidly pleased she'd returned and eagerly fetched a match.

"Tell me," he asked, noting the gold wedding band on her long slim finger, whose plum polish matched the succulent gloss on her mouth, "which one is your husband?"

Zara's eyes remained fixed on J.K.'s. "He's just served the brandy." It was an attempt to apologize for joking about her father's anti-Semitism. She was sorry she'd said it, but whoever

Mr. Kaplan was or wasn't, he had looked at her as if she were the one who didn't belong.

"At least he knows his place." His eyes smiled into hers.

"Anything to be near me," she said, laughing through another exhale of smoke as J.K. felt the entire room and all the people in it, except for Zara, melt into a blur.

"Zara, are you all right?" a slender, faceless man asked.

"Perfectly, my dearest," she answered, taking a sip from his glass. "Sweetheart, meet John Kaplan. A great friend of Daddy's moral inconsistency." It was ever so slight, but she knew Kaplan would catch her wink.

So this was Zara's husband. Immediately, his precise manners, his deference, even his diction became an irritant. And that idiotic loden cape over those nasty, tight jeans made him appear like some Carnaby clown. No wonder Zara dressed like a gypsy.

Philip and Zara were not quite twenty-one when they married. Now, five years later, Philip could still pass for a minor. With his jeans excessively narrow and his body even thinner than Zara's, he looked like a strung-out teenager growing into himself. A strange contrast to Kaplan, who, large and looming, seemed almost twice Philip's age, although he was only six years his senior.

"Is your wife with you, Mr. Kaplan?" Zara asked, threading her arm through her husband's. She was as devoted to Philip as he was to her. Although Zara, a designer of paste jewelry, and Philip, a successful scenic designer, believed they'd grown up by creating their own lives, the parental cord had never been completely cut. Her jewelry and his sets were merely the beads and paints of precocious youngsters.

"John. Call me John, please."

"John-please, is your wife here? Pretty please, John-please, is your wife here?" Zara said as Philip roared with laughter.

John Kaplan, although unable to divert his attention from Zara's animal eyes, wondered what absurd game she was playing with that taunting, childish phrase. Was it for him or for Philip? Whatever, it was oddly effective. It had the power of making Philip think his wife was hilarious while making Kaplan clench his fists to stop himself from punching Philip right through his cretinous roar. What had someone said about chinless wonders? That's where they hold all their brains.

Curiously, each felt superior to the other. John Kaplan, by his proven worth, and Zara and Philip by an inherent worth they didn't have to prove. Kaplan would have liked to have had both.

"My wife is in London. She loathes anything to do with killings," Kaplan said, still riveted by Zara's eyes.

"As long as I don't eat what I shoot, I don't mind killing," Zara said, running her dark nails through Philip's blond, wavy hair. "Aha. I think I see Daddy getting out his whistle. That means we're about to start."

Zara and Philip's sister were the lone women guns out of twelve. Four drives were scheduled before lunch and three after. Lord Ballard and John Kaplan walked together toward the tall grass, a hundred yards from the house. "No excitement like wild game. Better than birds hatched on some rearing field by a gamekeeper," Kaplan said, his practiced, offhand delivery leaving no doubt to anyone except, of course, Kaplan that he could tell the difference.

Ballard looked at Kaplan curiously. "Quite so. Quite so. You know, there's a fallacy about pheasants. People think they love the woods. Wrong. Dead wrong. It's the border they like. Like there," he said, pointing. "I cut that opening through those woods myself. Called giving the pheasant the edge.

Wouldn't you say, Kaplan?" His chortle turning into a cough, Ballard's face turned an apoplectic red. Pulling a flask from his pocket, he took a hearty swig.

As they approached the first drive, John Kaplan's loader set down his supply of cartridges and Kaplan's other gun. Although there was a six-year wait for a matched set of Purdys, Kaplan had ordered his years before he'd ever taken a shot. He'd then taken lessons at Purdy's and practiced thousands of hours until people called him a natural. He'd done the same with golf. There was no such thing for him as an "amusing" round with the boys until he had broken ninety with the pro.

While Kaplan worked one gun, his loader replaced the cartridges in the gun just fired, then held it in readiness. Although the proficiency of this relay appealed to J.K., the retrieving of the birds by Ballard's dogs was pure poetry. But to J.K. it paled in comparison to the way Lady Zara held her gun and dropped her bird.

As a wrangler is born to a saddle, Zara seemed born to a gun. Even in those preposterous boots, it was extraordinary how she would sight her prey, swing the long barrel just far enough in front of its path, and pull. Watching her manor-born ease and undeniable class, J.K. knew he had to know Lady Zara better. During lunch, he invited her and Philip to have dinner at Annabel's with him and his wife the following week.

John Kaplan had married Fiona Lytton two years after his mother's death. David Ramsey had made a last valiant effort to be his stepson's best man. His lungs, weak since the war, almost gave way completely, and Ramsey died only weeks later at his home in Dorset.

J.K. had met Fiona at Hyde Park corner listening to a Sunday morning political rabble-rouser. Selfless and instantly devoted to him, it didn't take long for J.K. to believe he was in love. A brilliant political scholar at Cambridge, Fiona had worked tirelessly for Harold Wilson's Labour Party, but once married to John Kaplan and his ambition, she worked even harder to get Wilson out and Edward Heath's Conservative Party in.

Except for John himself, who couldn't match socks or put links into cuffs, their seven-year marriage remained childless. A life without children became instead a life with J.K.'s ambitions, and without knowing it, Fiona became less and less able to crawl out from under her husband's future. Had John Kaplan not fallen into the shelter of habit, or had he assayed his marriage as a deal, he could easily have spun Fiona off for an efficient majordomo.

The week following the shoot seemed like an eternity for J.K. During his most complex meetings, Lady Zara kept popping into his thoughts. The exaggerated mouth and crazy hair, the animal eyes and animal nails: he kept seeing them all, all over him.

At long last, the night for Annabel's arrived. Obscured in the basement of an unpretentious townhouse in Berkeley Square, Annabel's was without doubt the most glamorous nightclub in all of London, probably in all the world. Its members included everyone who figured prominently any-where, from society's backbone to the new global glitz. Its waiting list was longer, by miles, than the list of the thousands who were members.

What fascinated J.K. most about nightclubs was that in all London, as in most great cities, there was only one club that mattered. If a new one opened, either the old or the new one would close. It was as if it was too tedious for society to be confused.

Small by disco standards, Annabel's was a masterpiece in brass and sexy lighting. As the Kaplans and the Thornes went to their table, they passed Princess Grace and Prince Rainier hosting a small dinner, as well as Bianca and Mick Jagger in a cozy corner. The table that J.K. found most interesting was the table where the real Annabel sat, not because she was the ex-wife of the club's founder, but because she was the present wife of the dazzling James Goldsmith, one of the world's biggest takeover players. Goldsmith had coined the term, "the new blue," the chip worth a billion. Although J.K. didn't, as yet, know Goldsmith well, he'd make it a point later on to say hello to "Jimmy" and a bigger point of making sure that Lady Zara was with him when he did.

No sooner were they seated than J.K. asked Zara to dance. He couldn't wait to hold her, press her to him, get closer to her scent. "Someone like you," he whispered, holding her painfully tight as they danced above the ribbons of lights embedded into the floor, "should never share housework and orgasms." Zara had told him earlier that their maid hadn't come and therefore they almost hadn't either. "Or don't you have orgasms?"

"Verbal truths create complications," Zara replied, rubbing against him.

Fiona Kaplan knew how much her husband hated to dance and smiled to think how hard J.K. was working to get Lord Ballard to deliver those greengrocers. Little did she know an agreement had been reached at the shoot.

Since there is never an orderly progression to love, when the compelling possibility of Zara Thorne struck the upwardly mobile John Kaplan, it became an obsessive force.

The first time they made love, there had been something crazy and exhausting and devouring about taking Lady Zara like a whore, and even more so when it occurred to him that she wanted him to. He'd known it was going to be like that since the moment at Annabel's when she let him press himself into her, then let her hand fall down onto his trousers.

They met in Zara's loft. Philip was at the theater. Zara thought it great fun to show John Kaplan the skylighted fourth-floor walk-up with its peeling paint and unmade bed, the makeshift tables of wooden planks covered with rhinestones, feathers, bracelets, belts, and pins.

As much as Kaplan saw himself the conqueror of Zara, it was Zara, as it is always the woman, who permitted it, who allowed him to rescue her from boredom. She begged him to tie her hands with the rhinestone belts, to use the feathers. She did the same to him. He loved her long body, the way her toes touched his. Her head moved every which way as their lips found every part of each other's bodies. One hand grabbed her tied wrists and pinned them over her head while his free hand went everywhere, opened everything, putting his fingers first into his mouth, then into hers.

Breaking free, Zara gripped the headboard and pulled herself high while pushing his head down. The violent rhythm of his tongue made her heave as if the bed were motorized. Her contractions were almost more than she could bear. More than Kaplan could bear. He had to enter her. He lifted his head hopelessly, apologetically. At the same moment that his flesh exploded, her face contorted as she wailed and thrust her body with such force that Kaplan arched in unison.

Each time they made love the fervor mounted. Kaplan, always excited by the decadence and flamboyant hedonism of the aristocracy, never seemed to tire. For the elite, it wasn't really challenging tradition. It was merely carrying it on.

The Saturday following Annabel's, J.K. drove Zara to a small country inn. Nestled in the gentle hills of Kent, Kaplan chose it because it was only a stone's throw from Chartwell, Churchill's asylum from his "black dog" days of depression, from the burdens of life in office, and his rejuvenation when he was booted out.

The silk of Zara's blouse was so sheer that her nipples as well as the tiny goose bumps around them were delineated as if she were naked. When Lady Zara wasn't leading John Kaplan's hand there, she was putting it under her loosened skirt to the crotchless knickers.

Suddenly Kaplan swerved his forest-green Jaguar off the highway and pulled into the cobblestone driveway of a deserted village church. Grabbing the blanket covering the spare, he threw it on the damp grass, then ripped at her shirt and skirt while she tugged at his pants. In less time than it had taken to jerk the Jag to a stop, he was on her and in her with such fury that he came immediately. Too immediately. Unashamed, Zara spread her legs wide and, while he watched, showed him exactly what she liked.

Before registering at the inn, John Kaplan drove Zara to Chartwell. Although she hadn't been there since childhood, she hadn't forgotten the exquisite views of pastures, lakes, and tile-roofed cottages Churchill so often painted.

Holding Zara tightly, the wind binding them even tighter, Kaplan told her how another Churchillian prophecy was proving its power. "'Change is the master key. The mind must be strengthened, not merely by rest but by using other parts.'"

"I agree, my darling. He'd have been proud of how beautifully you're using them," Zara said, nuzzling his cashmere sweater.

Although it was the furthest thing from John Kaplan's mind, on the way to the Fox and Hound they followed a FOR SALE sign down a long dirt road to an old stone farmhouse. High on its own hill, it shared the same splendid countryside with Chartwell. In as much time as it took to drive to the estate agent's office, have her ride back with them, and open the old wooden doors, they decided it was theirs. Not a man of impulse, yet a man of many purchases, John Kaplan was possibly happiest with this.

Soon the lovemaking loft in London was exchanged for suites at Claridge's, and the small country inn gave way to country houses belonging to Zara's friends, as they waited for theirs to be finished. Not that this stopped them from picnicking on the lawn, lighting fires in the oversized fireplace, and loving under the dark oak beams. Obsessed and consumed by each other, they were rarely apart.

Although Zara Thorne would have described herself as happily married when she and John Kaplan first met, her marriage, like much of her life, had been maintained by a dream rather than by reality.

For John Kaplan, Zara was more than a physical obsession. Not that he could admit it, but sex had only been a bridge to their marriage, to the titled Zara and to the seats at the dinner tables of the entrenched establishment. That was John Kaplan's real obsession. Of course it mattered what happened to Fiona. That her future could be told in a single sentence was desperately unfair, but then, as J.K. knew, so was life.

5

*I*t had been fourteen years and two children since John Kaplan had convinced Lady Zara that her game of house with Philip had been played out. Even now, as Zara paced the living room floor of their Carlyle duplex, having just hung up from speaking with her husband and with tears of frustration about Archer being in London blurring her vision, she didn't have the slightest regret about her marriage. Nor had she ever. She felt as much love for her husband as ever and believed that any outside life she had only made her less demanding of his time.

Zara adored being Mrs. John Kaplan. She loved his larger-than-life defiance of everything she had been bred to believe in, his proving that one could grow rich again in England by working. She preened as others wondered how he made the millions they were sure he'd lose, going after companies they'd rejected as fully priced.

She especially liked the free flow of new money after being raised in the gluepots of conservatism. The quality of her toys, such as the cornflower-blue Rolls Corniche waiting downstairs, had vastly improved.

Not that Zara ever lost her appetite for the unique. At one white-tie dinner, a huge white tie had been all she wore, but it was the clever way she'd had her dressmaker drape the bolt of satin about her body that made it elegant. At a ball at Blenheim, she'd arrived with a parrot screeching "Fuck thou" and "God bless" by squeezing its left or right foot to make sure it didn't confuse to whom it said which. And when the mood struck, she'd paint patches of violet, turquoise, or green in her hair to match her gown, jewels, or eyes. Her language could be the Queen's in front of the Queen, but that of the parrot when she wanted to shock. She was excited by the excitement she gave, her passion coming from the passion she inspired rather than the passion she felt.

No, Zara was hardly the usual English deb, corrupted early and bored ever after. She was fey and fancy, wearing her husband's successes like the lady she was born to be, opening doors J.K. could never have pried apart.

As Zara went to her dressing room, seeing herself in the mirror made her even more unhappy. Everything had jet lag. The new streaks in her "electrocuted coils" were dull and vapid, while the "waterproof" mascara had run down her face. Her lipstick, more exaggerated and film-star-of-the-forties than ever, had smeared over the outline of her lips.

Sinking onto the king-sized bed, even Zara's new toys and games didn't stop the tears from falling between those palm-frond lashes. It reminded her of when she was little. She was on just such a big bed in her parents' room in Cornwall, staring at the faded roses on the wall, crying those same lonely tears. She'd been riding her bicycle with her friend Beth. A storm had come up suddenly. There was terrible thunder and lightning. The dark roads were thick with mud. They were shivering and had to walk their bikes along the flooded gutters. All at once, blazing headlights stopped in front of them. Beth's mother and father got out of their car. They had been looking for the girls since the storm began.

When they got to Zara's house, Zara's parents were putting buckets under the leaks in the ceiling and towel-drying the furniture. "We didn't know she wasn't upstairs," Zara's mother said distractedly, trying to catch the drops of rainwater. "Thank you ever so much. That's what happens when Nanny's off."

She glanced in her daughter's direction, but neither of her parents ever scolded Zara as Beth's had scolded Beth, as Zara wanted them to do. Instead, they told her to take a hot bath and get into bed. She did. Into their bed. Tired as she was, she waited and waited for them to come up.

"Well, what have we got here?" her father finally said.

"It looks like a hungry and tired little girl," her mother answered, giving Zara a kiss. "Run along to your room. Nellie is coming with supper." Too bad, Zara thought, her tears didn't make a noise so her mother could hear them drop.

Zara's parents never recognized Zara's needs. And since childhood memories are selected to justify adult ways, Zara never remembered her father saying, "I'd have fretted to death had I realized Zara wasn't in her room!" The same way she left out her mother's "I love you."

Actually, everything had been fine until Paul went away to school and Miss Darby left. After Amy Darby, there were six more nannies, but none so loving. Zara's parents, doting on each other, were like pretend parents. Soon Zara started her own world of pretend. Sometimes she'd be a scruffy on the telly. Other times, a model in *Harpers & Queen*. Sometimes the Queen herself. It was lonely living among people who pretend.

If she wasn't noticed the way she was, she had to be somebody else.

As big grown-up tears kept falling on Zara's Pratesi sheets, the Carlyle operator was about to give up ringing the Kaplans' apartment. Although Zara heard the phone, she couldn't answer until she stopped crying. She knew it was only Ray, the Carlyle doorman.

"Miss MacDonald is here to see you. Says she has an appointment. She wants to know, should she come up?"

"No. No, thank you, Ray. Tell her I'll be down in just a minute. Ask her to wait in my car, please."

Dragging herself from the bed, Zara pulled off her travel jeans and triple-ply cashmere sweater. As she opened the top drawer of her dressing table, at least a hundred lipsticks were arranged like little soldiers, and brushes of the finest sable, from skinny to fat, lay in Lucite trays.

The next drawer held everything for her eyes, including dozens of sets of prescriptionless contacts, their color depending on her outfit, which depended on her mood. The bottom drawer was filled with foundations and rouge, depending on how tanned and "healthy" she wanted to look.

Pulling top after top off the lipsticks, Zara chose a vivid geranium, the plum color having long since gone the way of the black outline. Slamming the drawer, she left every lipstick open, as always. She was that way with everything she used: not lazy, just impatient.

After reapplying her eyes, rubbing on more than enough "health," and teasing her hair into what looked like an ungovernable vine, Zara picked a black Armani suit with a thigh-length skirt and a silk crepe blouse. After a final look, she felt a lot better. Grabbing her alligator Kelly handbag, she put on her jewelry, typical thirties and forties and typical Zara, while waiting for the elevator.

Zara Kaplan was Doris MacDonald's favorite client. Doris admired the madness of her makeup, the newest designer clothes, the stratospherically priced skin bags from Hermès, and the great jewelry, like the Cartier panther pin she wore on her shoulder that had once belonged to the Duchess of Windsor. Zara had told Doris how John had given it to her after a night at Annabel's, after they'd just met, when only he knew he was going to marry her. She'd even showed Doris the card she always carried: *To replace the paste and tell you I'm stuck on you.*

Most of all, Doris liked Zara's extravagance, her never caring what anything cost. Forget about apartments. Even in a store, when she was buying for others as well as herself, price was one thing Zara Kaplan never shopped.

"Hello, Doris, my love," Zara said, bending low, in order to angle her long body into the Rolls.

Doris MacDonald's blond *Town and Country* looks and safe tailoring were quite a contrast alongside Zara.

"Doris, I swear, if I didn't like the idea of owning a Rolls, I'd trade it for something comfortable. But one gets so much better treatment in it."

Doris liked Zara's saying "honest" things that other people wouldn't have the courage to say. Doris didn't realize, however, that it was Zara's position that made what was unacceptable in others acceptable in her.

"Eight twenty-three Fifth. Right, madam?" the driver asked.

"Where?" Suddenly Zara forgot everything except Verna, whom she suddenly remembered she'd called from the plane, telling her to be at the Carlyle at twelve. But now without Archer it wouldn't work. Zara's stomach tightened.

Doris MacDonald felt hers sink. "*Where?* Only to the find of the century. The reason you flew in!"

You should know the real reason, Zara thought. "Do you mind, Doris? Just a second?" She took the phone from the armrest between them. "I must make a call. Then I'm yours." She didn't add, unfortunately.

As Zara dialed, Doris began to panic. Was Zara putting her on? Wasn't this *the* special trip? Wasn't the head of the 823 board their special friend? Wasn't this the best deal ever? For Doris MacDonald, it was. Her commission alone would move her permanently from her walk-up in Tribeca to easy street and she wouldn't even have to pay off a super, as she'd done over and over, for his tip on a divorce, a death, or even a pregnancy that would make an apartment too small. Curiously, when her firm had given her Kaplan's name months ago, they all thought he was just another climber who wanted to be where he wasn't wanted.

Since no agent wants to waste time or embarrass clients, it's tricky omitting apartments that clients have heard about. But every broker knows full well the unspoken rules for rejection in certain buildings: Jews, blacks, homosexuals, Orientals, celebrities, divorcées. Singles because "they stay out all hours and have strangers overnight." United Nations delegates because "they constantly change, entertain undesirables, and tie up the elevator." And anyone who would have the press hanging around.

"Hello. Is this the service?" Zara asked, without mentioning Verna by name.

"Yes, it is. Miss Gundstrum is out."

"Did she leave a number? Any place where she can be reached?"

"No. She didn't. All we know is she's in town."

"I know that," Zara said irritably.

"She'll be calling for messages. Do you want to leave one?"

"Tell her today is canceled. That today at twelve must be postponed. Make sure you say 'postponed.' And ask her to call Mrs. Kaplan at the Carlyle." Zara knew that Verna had a *Vogue* booking later. That's why they didn't make it later. Night shots at the Statue of Liberty. Damn! The three of them would be fantastic. Archer was always talking about it. Zara was drenched with desire just thinking of it, even though she hadn't seen Verna since they'd first met months ago. But thinking about her had only heightened the anticipation.

They'd sat next to each other on the Concorde. Ridiculously beautiful, Verna was returning from London after a shoot for *Bazaar*. Her bombshell body, never feeling the cold, was covered by the skimpiest, purposely overfitted teal-blue sheath. Her short white-blond hair was swept back, and her strong, firm features were like a man's except for her nose, which she had bobbed when *Vogue*'s top fashion photographer told her it cast too many shadows. Her cheekbones stopped just underneath her straight-set blue eyes, and when she remembered, she kept her wide mouth slightly open, because at a party Norman Mailer had told her the gap between her front teeth was sexy. Her only makeup was a sea-foam blue eyeliner; she wore no jewelry at all. She looked as if she should be sitting in a Saint-Tropez café in August, but not for long, just long enough for the best invitation to the biggest yacht. In their three hours together, Zara and Verna had consumed as many bottles of champagne.

"Vonderful," Verna had said after several glasses. "Dom must be just so." Her voice was mock know-it-all as she took a bit more than a genteel sip.

"Just so what?"

"So chilled. Fifty degrees." Verna slurred her words.

"Filthy?" Zara asked.

"I had zees boyfriend. He vas always talking temperature and how grapes must be from a vonderful Chardonnay harvest. Zey never vere, but never did he send it back. He couldn't vait zat long drink."

Verna touched a lot when she talked, and they giggled a lot into each other's necks. After a particularly familiar hug, Verna told her she found her very attractive. She also told her that she was married to the wealthiest man in Stuttgart. "A maker of parts. Too bad zey didn't do better vith his." This time they laughed so hard they had to hold on to their glasses. Zara was amazed to hear herself confide that she was on her way to meet her American lover.

"Ve three should have a party," Verna said, squeezing Zara's hand while staring into her eyes. By the time Zara and Verna landed in New York, they were good enough friends to have decided they definitely would get together, all three of them.

When Zara told Archer, he wanted it that minute. So did Zara, but when she called Verna, she had already left. She was rarely in New York. That was what was so frustrating about today. Today was the first time that Zara had tried Verna's number and actually found her there. She'd just returned from posing for the swimsuit issue of *Sports Illustrated*. She even had a chance for the cover. "More important," Verna said, "my Chardonnays are ripe for harvest and my bikini lines show you vere zey start." Her laugh triggered everything, even more intimacy than Zara remembered.

"And please," Zara said again to the service, "emphasize the word 'postpone.'" As she replaced the phone, Zara could just picture Verna's voluptuous body naked. Inhaling deeply on her slim gold-tipped cigarette, she rolled down the shaded window, blowing the smoke away from Doris MacDonald, who was thrilled that Zara was finally done with her call.

"Well, I guess life could be worse than going to look at an eleven-million-dollar apartment my husband's dying for me to like," Zara Kaplan said, laughing.

Even in Zara's world of helicopters and private jets, that was a hefty number.

As if she'd been a withering plant doused with Miracle-Gro, Doris MacDonald blossomed. When they pulled in front of 823, Art Rooney himself was there to help Lady Zara from the beautiful automobile.

"Hello there, Mr. Rooney," Doris MacDonald said, introducing Lady Zara while giving him a high sign of raised, happy brows. After greeting Lady Zara, Rooney winked back. Not that he liked the name Kaplan, but somehow this one seemed different. She not only looked but spoke like the kind of tenant Rooney thought 823 should have. Not like that other woman, the one in the sweater.

Nobody knew better than Doris MacDonald that in today's seller's market, money was easy. What was tough was connections. But with Zara's being a cousin, who cared how distant, of Prince Charles, and with Archer Blair being her husband's best friend, their combination of clout was as seriously big as the eleven million.

Before Doris's time, in the early seventies, when Manhattan moved to suburbia, apartments went begging. Co-op boards couldn't afford to be choosy, and barriers fell. But with merger mania besieging New York, co-ops were going, going, gone out of sight.

Now, last year's five-million-dollar Renoir was going for ten, and diamonds taken from vaults were sold for enough Swiss francs or German marks to buy hundred-foot yachts and country estates. Flowers for a much publicized wedding had passed the million-dollar mark, and in one fashionable Fifth Avenue bedroom a silk wall trimming, supposedly belonging to Marie Antoinette, was sold for the bargain price of a quarter of a million dollars.

Big and oafish, Rooney fairly danced alongside Zara and Doris to ring for the elevator. Zara never looked left or right. She knew where she was going. Long before her affair with Archer, she and J.K. had been here visiting.

"Mr. and Mrs. Kaplan are good friends of the Blairs," Doris MacDonald offered, noticing Rooney's curiosity that Zara knew the way.

"I must have been off duty," Rooney said, all charm. "Fine people, the Blairs," he added. "Don't come no—any better."

"He's my husband's oldest friend in America. They went to Yale together," Zara said, tapping the toe of her tight suede boot as they rode in the elevator.

"Remember, I mentioned this apartment belonged to the Carnegies," Doris MacDonald said, as the elevator doors opened and they stepped into the imposing marble gallery.

"Yes," Zara answered. "Something about their racing colors in the marble. Ah, yes, I see. How clever. Green and blue everywhere. I've never seen that before. And look, their crests in all those moldings. What fun. And that ceiling's divine. So English."

"The salon's a perfect room for any kind of entertaining," Doris MacDonald said. "Compared to what we've seen."

"And how," Zara said enthusiastically, whipping through the library and dining room. "It's nice to find high ceilings, too. John and I feel like Gulliver in most New York flats. 'Designed for Japanese,' John says."

"Better believe it," Rooney said vigorously. He was

liking her more all the time. And she didn't dawdle or ooh and aah over everything. She knew what was what. She was used to it.

"They modernized the kitchen, even put in a char—"

"John will love that. But my God, I must say whoever painted the dining room never saw a Guardi or a Canaletto. Well, that can be painted over." She laughed. "Let's see the upstairs. My word, what have we here?" Zara stopped at the landing. "A place for John's portrait! How perfect!"

Rooney's smile grew bigger all the time. If there was one thing he knew it was class, and this was it. Happily, Rooney raced ahead to turn on the lights.

"This is the master," Doris said, lifting her arm in a sweeping gesture.

"Just lovely. Lovely. Great dressing room. And for once John can't complain about closets. Doris, it's grand."

Doris MacDonald could have kissed Rooney in sheer bliss.

When they got to the other bedrooms, Zara just peeked to see if they were a good size and bright until she reached the nursery with the painted walls. "Who on earth created tacky town? Not the Carnegies, for sure."

Although Rooney and Doris liked Snow White and her group, they nodded convincingly, stumbling over each other in their eagerness to agree with Zara.

"Wait till you see the view from the terrace," Doris MacDonald said, quickly closing the door.

On their way, Zara noticed the call buttons embedded in the wall. "My God, Doris. Grandmother revisited."

Rooney sure hoped this one would move in tomorrow so he could be sure he'd seen the last of that other kind.

"Well, what do you think?" Doris MacDonald asked, as they surveyed the view. "Did I exaggerate?"

"Not enough. I'll take it. I love it. We can't show it to John, though, until day after tomorrow."

"You want to go through it again? Anything you want to know?"

"Like what?"

"I don't know," Doris answered, and she really didn't.

Rooney knew Zara wouldn't want to ask any nitpicking questions. Her kind couldn't be bothered. They hire people who bother for them.

"I do have one question," Zara said. "How about lunch? To celebrate. After all, Doris, it's not every day I buy and you sell an eleven-million-dollar apartment."

"Right on!" Doris MacDonald said, unable to refrain from hugging her.

Rooney sure wished he could. "Congratulations," he said, as he pumped Zara Kaplan's hand. "Welcome aboard!"

6

*R*ooney wouldn't have been so thrilled had he seen the elevator door close on Bettina Blair earlier that morning and watched Clive van Arlyn inhale the sweet smell of victory. In fact, once in the lobby, van Arlyn, in a clutch of rapture, had grabbed Erica Wheaton's arm and almost shoved her out the door, motioning her not to speak until they were far enough away. Not that she could have. The shock, the nakedness, the degradation of what she'd seen had left her limp. That girl was so pretty. And so young.

"No need to get in the car," van Arlyn said, unaware that he was pushing her down the street. "You know how drivers listen. How they talk."

No, quite honestly, she didn't.

Van Arlyn's mind was also on the girl. After all, he'd known Bettina Blair forever. He couldn't believe what he'd seen. But this was business. Big business. And he certainly couldn't worry about her pain.

"Erica, my sixth sense tells me, it's going to work out perfectly," he said, as they started across the street. "Do you have any idea who that girl is? Bettina Blair," he whispered. "Archer Blair's daughter. I can't believe it. Little Bettina. I knew her before she was born. Erica, you'll never know what a break this is."

"I haven't a clue as to what you're talking about, Clive, but there must be a good reason you're so excited about that sordid scene."

"Listen, Miss Nebraska. I'm looking way beyond that sight we saw. And take my word, it would have shocked the bejesus out of me even if Bettina hadn't been Archer Blair's daughter. But, Christ almighty, she is! And Blair is head of Eight Twenty-three's board. It's not my fault this fell into our laps. I just have to figure the best way to use it." As van Arlyn spoke, he measured every word. Every sentence became a pronouncement.

Erica had been through this before with van Arlyn. He became excessively impatient if she didn't immediately read his mind.

"Look, Clive, no matter what you think about west of the Mississippi, we can be pretty good at chewing up and spitting out the Big Apple."

"Bravo! Bravo!" Clive applauded with a slightly nervous laugh.

"Furthermore, Clive, I'd be ashamed to be confused with that pathetic girl and your mighty establishment. So do me a favor and don't ever mistake me for those Flopsies and Mopsies whose plastic surgeons can't keep up with their baby names. And one last thing, Clive, before I throw up. In Nebraska, when we're having as good a time as Bettina Blair was having with that jogger, we shut the goddam door!"

Van Arlyn recoiled. Erica's words had triggered something. He remembered the shock in the jogger's face. Would it have been there if van Arlyn were a total stranger? Something, too, about those dark eyes and mouth. They were familiar. Twisting his ring furiously, Clive van Arlyn was suddenly frightened.

"I know that fellow," van Arlyn said, more to himself than to her. "But from where?" It was not like him to forget. Maybe he couldn't place him because he was so out of context, like the time he saw his doorman out of uniform on the street.

"Clive, I just don't get your gloating over that girl."

Suddenly, Erica's bare-assed honesty, which van Arlyn usually admired, gave him a swift pain in the gut. Why couldn't she, just for a minute, be one of his ghastly arriviste clients, the kind with no inferiors? At least they'd know they'd hit pig heaven. But no, now that his ship was coming in, he had to get one so fucking square he could rig her.

"Erica, my pet, it's not about her. It's for you. There's still a lot of takeover money out there wanting that penthouse, that instant ancestry. From the date they conquer Wall Street, they want to date from William the Conqueror. And what better platform?" Clive's voice was strident and his words came fast. "They may not be highly cultivated, but they're highly cashed and they buy class like crazy."

"Who cares?" Erica asked.

"Lucky for me, they do. And for anybody else on their ride. Like the auction houses. No sooner does the van from Sotheby's pull up than those pieces become heirlooms that have been dust catchers at Granny's for years."

Erica was aware of overachievers turned overconsumers. The ones George Wheaton called "greed-driven bastards," who'd mortgaged the apartment for the house, the house for the paintings, and the paintings for the new wife. In fact, just as George had predicted, in what *The New York Times* called "a blur of waving hands and shouts," the crash not only demolished 22 percent of Wall Street but those mortgaged jillionaires as well. But, as he also said, "When the dust settles, a lot of big-time rich will be a lot richer."

"I swear to Christ, Erica, if fig leaves were crests, they'd go back to Adam and Eve."

Erica's gravelly laugh rang through van Arlyn like a Las Vegas payoff. Finally, he too began to laugh. High and giddy.

Erica was relieved to have both of them return to some kind of norm. Their concentration on that girl had put them in a sort of stupor. Not until now did Erica even realize they'd left the car behind.

"Clive, where's the car?" Her voice was tentative.

"We can walk." Clive's voice was firm. "We'll call the driver from there."

"From where?"

"From this swell shop in your new neighborhood."

"What kind of shop?"

"You'll see. It's just a hop, skip, and a jump." Now that Clive truly believed Erica and George Wheaton could get the apartment, it was time for her to get the proper clothes.

The saleswomen at Martha's openly ogled van Arlyn and the dazzling Erica. A Park Avenue fixture for over forty years, Martha's attracted the elite in patrons as well as couture: Adolfo, Scaasi, Saint Laurent, Fabrice, and Lacroix were just a few of the top designers who came personally to present their lines to Martha's Rolodex of socialites and parvenus, old-timers and newcomers, out-of-towners and locals and those looking to look like the cover of something. But then, wasn't fashion's function to give one the look of who one wanted to be?

Even Martha herself was a fixture. Well into her eighties, she still waited on favored clients, although the recipients of

Martha's bills were her most guarded secrets. It was not unusual for unsuspecting wives to watch as their husbands' mistresses tried on gowns identical to theirs.

Though van Arlyn didn't make a practice of taking women to dress shops, he had a good eye and had selected clothes for special friends, especially big business friends like Erica. And after what happened at 823, van Arlyn wanted to get this package wrapped as soon as possible.

"What's so urgent about going now?" Erica asked.

"Trust me, Erica," van Arlyn said.

"The last time a man said that, he emptied my flight bag in a motel," Erica said, squeezing Clive's arm. She loved van Arlyn's thinking she was a lot of brass for his tastes, because his tastes were not her worry. "Anyway, Clive, we get these same names in Omaha. We even get them in person, pinning and prancing and flattering. What does Martha's have that our Omaha trunk shows don't?"

"Me! What you can put together in Omaha isn't exactly the put-together look you're going to need for Eight Twenty-three."

While sitting on the showroom's striped cushioned chairs waiting to be helped, van Arlyn pointed out the soft lighting, thinning mirrors, and pale pink walls. "Washes the 'old' right out of the girl."

"What happens when the girl gets home?"

"She goes on a diet and calls surgery." Van Arlyn was only half joking.

Martha, always with the eagle eye, waved to van Arlyn. Suited in the latest Chanel and with every flaxen hair in place, Martha was still a sturdy little dynamo, working as hard as ever to make a sale.

As Erica watched the tireless saleswomen show gown after gown, unzipping the most fragile from plastic bags, she wondered what they really thought when they tried to convince a woman to pay more for a gown than they paid for a year's rent.

"You know, Erica," van Arlyn said, "you have to show these board members you're not doing what they've been guilty of, lowering the quality of the building."

Erica knew nothing about buildings and boards and the requirements Clive suddenly started to spout: mandatory letters attesting to finances, sobriety, schools, clubs, "and what a jolly good fellow you are. And it's a must, you know, that these letters have the proper names—"

"Stop! In the name of my sanity."

"Erica, take it as a fucking game, but know you'll be the one screwed if you don't play. And you only have to be judged once to be a champ forever."

"Clive, the last time I went before a group of judges, I wore the tightest swimsuit you ever saw, and any credentials I needed were in plain sight."

"Somehow, I believe Eight Twenty-three requires more than those dimensions."

"Why not just tell them I'm a winner, Clive? You're my friend."

"Precisely, my dear. And friends never tell the whole truth. That's for the enemy to do."

A strange chill ran through Clive as he said that. It was again something to do with that jogger. But what?

"Erica, you know what I'm saying. The simple rich feel victimized. Their inconspicuousness has been invaded by vulgarians flaunting it all."

"Like me?" Erica asked.

"Pul-eese, Erica. The rich I'm discussing aren't familiar with graduates from the school of hard knocks. All they learned is, 'Put not your trust in money, but your money in trust.' Their only business is making sure their world survives. They're all part of that invisible club, each other. They always greeted Jock Whitney when he walked into the Brook. The bartender even gave him a chit to sign, when Whitney wasn't a member."

Erica knew about the Brook from Clive. It was where he said he "retreated" when he couldn't stand the fake world. Or maybe it's where he went to find it. She never could remember.

"What I'm saying, Erica, is he never had to join. He probably never knew he wasn't a member. It didn't matter, because he was. And nobody wanted to make waves. If you're what they want or expect to see, you're one of them. Look, Erica, you're the one always telling me how you love business. How George loves you loving it. Look at this as another deal. Don't tell them what's wrong with the company until you've got the job."

"And you the commission."

An over-rouged, old-time saleslady, wreathed in black with hair dyed to match, greeted Erica and van Arlyn with a kindly smile.

"Are you looking for something for evening? Daytime? Travel?" As she spoke, she shifted her weight as someone does who's constantly on her feet.

"Nothing like that over there," van Arlyn said arrogantly, pointing as a fortyish woman with the help of a salesperson pushed excess flesh into a feathered strapless dress, only to have it pop out again. "Something more tailored than trimmed. For daytime," he added.

When she left to look, Erica turned to Clive. "I didn't know you wore dresses."

"What's that supposed to mean?"

"She was asking me."

"I'm sorry."

"No, you're not."

"I'm not. You're right."

"But you were wrong."

Hating confrontation, van Arlyn got up and walked about the salon, looking at the bags and jewelry, at the continuous video of Valentino's resort collection. Seeing himself in the mirror, he nervously arranged the foulard in his breast pocket. The red of the paisley matched exactly the slim thread in his glen plaid suit, as well as the jacket's red lining. It was a van Arlyn trademark to have his few better jackets lined in a color of the weave. He wished that obvious good-lookers, such as Erica, understood it only took that small amount of flair.

On the other hand, Erica Wheaton wished van Arlyn understood she hadn't come to Martha's today because she wanted to dress for Clive van Arlyn and the 823 board. If George Wheaton wanted nondescript suits and stacked heels he'd have married a librarian.

When the saleswoman returned with her arms loaded, van Arlyn ambled back.

"Anything you like?" she asked, diplomatically turning to them both.

"I'm not sure what he wants," Erica answered testily.

"Let's look in the back." Van Arlyn was impatient with the poor choices.

As in all dress shops, the back was not only stocked with current merchandise but new arrivals not even tagged. Every now and then, pet clients and friends like van Arlyn were let loose there.

With a practiced eye, van Arlyn pushed through the racks of two-, three-, four-, even ten-thousand-dollar machine-made dresses. Flicking his wrist, he discarded anything with sequins, beads, padded shoulders, a low bodice. Every now and then he put something aside. When he'd finish a rack, Erica would go through it again, putting her choices in a different spot.

"Eight Twenty-three specials, coming up!" Clive announced, as he presented his selections to Erica.

"Clive, these give 'safe' a whole new meaning. These are things a lawyer would put on a madam to sway a jury."

"Erica, please look at it as a challenge. Once you put them on, you'll give them new meaning."

Finally, it was settled: a honey tweed suit with a white blouse that tied in a bow. Not a total loss, Erica felt. Only the blouse would live the rest of its life on a hanger.

After the dressmaker pinned the skirt shorter, Erica pointed to the dresses she'd be back to try. The saleswoman's eyes brightened at the beads and sequins, low necks, and happy colors. "If someone as beautiful as you doesn't wear them, Mrs. Wheaton, nobody should," she said, genuinely but softly.

"Ready, my pet?" van Arlyn called.

"Ready?"

"I've planned a celebratory lunch at Le Cirque."

7

*I*t was exactly 1 P.M. Le Cirque was swarming. They were all there: the inviting smiles and the ready laughs, the ones whose world-weary eyes gazed at life with the sightless stare of a sphinx and the ones whose eyes popped from over-carved lids. In zip code 10021's window on the world, one could count six accents at five tables and hear ordinary conversation about what colors to paint the stripes on their private jets.

Here, master chefs and pastry kings had been brought from all over Europe at bank-robber wages, while guests merely toyed with their arugula and grilled sole. Maybe in today's high-risk arena, the embrace of wealth and power strangled the taste buds. The crash? Oh, yes. When was it, exactly? Isn't it funny both crashes were in October?

For those whose party was over, *tant pis!* Though they hadn't really left. The same sorts still sat at their tables.

Sirio, Le Cirque's owner, had a gentleman's smile and a bouncer's eye. Like every top restaurateur, he saw in a flash where they all should sit. His judgment was so severe that many a new-hundred millionaire was still working his way to the swell of status at the front of the room.

From busboy to waiter to captain of the exclusive Colony, to financial disaster when first on his own, Sirio was one of New York's great success stories. Smart and tenacious, he allowed no detail to escape him, even telephoning old customers who hadn't been by, despite all the new ones hanging from the rafters. After all, the new needed the old to be assured that this was *the* place.

A courtesy drink, a sampling of pasta, even the delivery of favorite dishes to one's hospital room—all was done to make the special feel more special. Yes, he'd made all the right moves, but perhaps the smartest was the one he didn't make: moving in on his customers.

Immaculately groomed, charming as ever, he bowed to kiss the air above Erica's hand, giving a doubly warm welcome to van Arlyn. For van Arlyn was not only the old world, but old world bringing in new money.

"Your friend is already here, Mr. van Arlyn," Sirio said.

As if just remembering, van Arlyn checked his watch. "Erica, I've invited this great chum, Brice Oldfield, to join us." Van Arlyn always slipped in pompous words like "chum" when he knew he'd been wrong. He hadn't mentioned he'd called him from Martha's. "Great decorator. Brilliant color sense. Could be perfect for the new digs."

Oldfield was someone who, van Arlyn believed, admired him in a more-than-a-business way. But it was tricky. Though such encounters hadn't been van Arlyn's thing for years, he didn't want to discourage Oldfield, either for business or possible pleasure. However, were anything to emerge, what better lure than 823 Fifth Avenue?

"Fine," Erica said, weaving through the crush, trying to

avoid being bumped even by those already seated, who kept shifting direction in order to wave their cushion-set stones, huge as cushions, at their friends.

"My God!" van Arlyn stammered, as he stared at the second banquette, where Mrs. Archer Blair and her nineteen-year-old daughter, Bettina, were chatting.

Cornelia Blair, every inch the quintessential private person, looked as women still look who age gracefully. Her short, tight gray hair, waved close to her head, appeared tamped down by an invisible net. Her only attempt at cosmetics was two slaps of rouge perking up the watery blue eyes and two little lines of lipstick, amazingly straight, considering she always applied them without a mirror. Her face, however, looked far more indulgent than she was. The laugh lines that had formed over the years into a pattern of kindness and approachability were deceptive.

Although her clothes were quality, they were from another era. Even with money no object, the look they achieved was the one she and her friends had always had, the one their mothers had bought at Hattie Carnegie and Elizabeth Arden. For evening, the dresses still had little jackets, and for daytime, the same. Since Cornelia Blair wasn't tall but was growing plump, her nipped-in coats and long hems were less flattering than ever. This woman wouldn't have the foggiest notion of how to wear a shoulder-strap bag, so attached was she to the handle on her arm. And, when "the girls" gathered at home for bridge, in their boxes at the races, or at the club for a dance, they thought they looked fine.

Bettina Blair presented quite a contrast next to this escapee from a time capsule. Her sable-brown hair had the just-shaken-dry-from-the-shower look, because that's just what it was. Today's makeup, beneath today's necessarily dark glasses, was extra thick, but the thin, arched brows were still visibly provocative. The nostrils of her short nose flared like those of a Thoroughbred, while her sullen mouth glistened with colorless gloss. The short drab olive dress ("I'm into earth tones") was basically an oversize shirt, cinched even shorter by a three-hundred-dollar brown lizard belt. Though piece by piece she was a disheveled mess, all together she had class. A dozen ads in *Paris Match* or *Hola* looked exactly like Bettina Blair.

Had Cornelia Blair witnessed this morning's spectacle, she probably would not only have denied it involved her daughter but denied it had even taken place. It was part of the continuing psychodrama of her life that didn't allow anything to sully the Norman Rockwell painting in which she lived.

As a little girl, Bettina remembered her mother listening to her father on the phone with other women while tears welled in her mother's eyes. Even then, her mother pretended nothing had happened, just as Bettina's bid-for-attention tantrums were brushed off as "strong-willed Blair blood."

The final détente between mother and daughter happened during a weekend from Hotchkiss when Bettina had come home with a boyfriend. She was only fifteen. The Blairs knew the young man's people. He was very polite and attractive. He got up when Mrs. Blair walked into the room. He dressed nicely and said all the right things. How on earth was Cornelia Blair to know about dilated pupils or the smell of marijuana? Bettina had wanted her to. Just as she wanted her to notice that her friend *hadn't* slept in her brother's room. But when Bettina became pregnant, Cornelia Blair became the dutiful mother. She took her to the doctor and, after it was taken care of, it was as if it never had happened.

From that day on, it was sadly obvious to Bettina that she could never liberate her mother's mind, any more than Cornelia Blair would allow society's new parasites to unravel her own view of the world. Emancipation for Cornelia Blair would never go beyond shedding her white gloves in summer.

As Cornelia sat next to her daughter, their conversation remained on a no-seams-opened, no-gaps-closed level. She didn't want to see the swollen eyes beneath the dark glasses, or the bruises under the heavy pancake, or wonder why an ugly piece of crystal dangled from Bettina's neck on a brown leather string instead of her nice pearls.

As usual, Cornelia Blair's conversation was simple and direct, as one who has but one mind, her own. She spoke of charities and clubs and used words such as "interloper" and "social staple." Her phrases sounded like homilies from needlepoint pillows. Not that it mattered. All Bettina heard was a replay of this morning's argument with her lover.

"See the woman over there in the checkered suit drinking the martini, next to the one in beige, pushing her breadstick through the butter?"

No, Bettina couldn't see her. "Yes."

"Well, that checkered suit wants to chair the dinner for the Hospital for Special Surgery." Names were often lost for people Cornelia Blair didn't feel were suitable. "You tell me how she could possibly deal with beverages, knowing bottles only from the inside? Naturally, if she isn't made chairwoman she'll think it's because she's being persecuted, as they all do. . . . Manners certainly make the lady," Cornelia said, seemingly out of nowhere.

However, Cornelia Blair was very pleased to be having lunch with Bettina. She felt motherly as well as dutiful. In fact, when people asked her about Bettina, she would answer, "We've been very lucky. She's never caused us a moment's trouble." Then her cold eyes would crinkle warmly.

As van Arlyn and Erica followed the captain, it was impossible for van Arlyn to avoid Cornelia Blair's table.

"Hello, Cornelia. Hello, Bettina," van Arlyn said, as casually as possible. "I'd like you to meet Mrs. Wheaton. We've been doing—what else?—the apartment bit." Clive purposely omitted "Blair" from his introduction to Erica so she wouldn't react.

"Hello, Clive, dear," Cornelia Blair said. "So nice to meet you, Mrs. Wheaton. I must say we never thought of Clive's turning to anything so honorable as trade, but I hear he's quite good." Although the word "honorable" made Clive feel a bit queasy, it wasn't sufficient to alter his good mood.

"I find hardship quite ennobling." Van Arlyn laughed, his eyes avoiding Bettina's.

Cornelia Blair looked with affection at Clive. His family had known hers back in the old brownstone days. Mary van Arlyn was a longtime friend, and, though they didn't see much of each other now, their lives had many threads that meshed.

If Erica hadn't seen a sudden streak of fear cross the teenager's face, she never would have identified her as the crazed girl of earlier that morning.

When Bettina Blair took Erica Wheaton's hand, she squeezed it twice with that fugitive pressure children use.

With the same complicity, Erica squeezed back.

"A pleasure to meet you, Mrs. Wheaton," Bettina said, trying to regain some composure, her frenzied brain bursting with thoughts of Gary. In fact, it was all she could do to stop from screaming "Shut up!" at Clive as she listened to his drivel about "Aunt Gertrude Vanderbilt" and "What has it all come to when Ralph Lauren is selling shirts in what was once Auntie's home?"

Typical hypocrite Clive, Bettina thought, trying to jolly up her mother and impress Mrs. Wheaton, whom tomorrow he'd most likely call "that horribly vulgar woman."

"Well, good luck with your search," Cornelia Blair said dismissively, already back to her food.

Staring into her plate, Bettina prayed Clive would keep his mouth shut about the morning. Not that the elevator door opening was the worst part, although God knows what would have happened if it hadn't.

This had been Gary Dellos's fourth trip to New York since Bettina first met him last June, though his arrival this morning was completely unexpected. He'd just come from Athens and was still in the jogging suit in which he traveled. Luckily, Bettina's father was in London and her mother in the country. Even the servants were off.

Bettina was so excited when he called from the airport, she had champagne and orange juice waiting. She even surprised him with some cocaine knowing he couldn't bring it through customs. Almost immediately, Dellos emptied it onto the coffee table and with his American Express card separated it into thin lines before rolling a crisp dollar bill into a straw. For Dellos, it was still nighttime. Bettina put the stereo way up and the blinds down. She asked him to dance. They stopped for a few more lines. He ordered her to dance naked for him. "I am the pasha. You are the new girl in my harem. You must do everything I say." His black eyes glistened. After dancing wildly, Bettina began writhing on the floor, as she'd seen harem dancers do in the movies. The coke told her she was better than the movies.

Dellos loved sitting back and making this rich American debutante his slave. As he pulled her hands away from herself, he told her that when he clapped once he wanted her to untie his pants and put coke on his cock. Two claps meant she should lick it off. At once!

Between coke and booze and very little sleep, Dellos couldn't manage to get it up. Even using his fingers as a splint didn't work. Suddenly, he went berserk. Besides getting the dough, getting it off with her had been the only decent part of this deal.

Shoving her away, he took a huge swig of brandy.

"What's the matter?" Bettina was fuzzy, confused. Feeling cold, she reached for her robe. Lying next to Dellos, she kissed his hair, his ears, his eyes.

Pulling her arms from his neck, he started to get up. That's when her nails accidentally clawed his crotch. Wheeling around he caught her under the eye with the back of his hand. It was more from pent-up aggression and coke than from pain.

Unaware for a second what had happened, but seeing his crazed eyes, Bettina was panic-stricken. "I'm sorry. I'm sorry," she screamed over and over as he clutched himself.

"I love you. I love you," she called desperately, stumbling after him toward the door as he pulled up the pants of his jogging suit.

"Love? Love? You can't even fuck!" Before he opened the door his saliva hit her on the other cheek. It was then she kicked him there hard as she could. This time it was no accident.

Before George Wheaton had hired Gary Dellos to spy on Archer Blair's daughter, Dellos had coincidentally met Bettina at what the English call a "drinks party." It was during Ascot, and the hospitality tents were jammed with men in morning suits and women in gay print dresses and flowered hats. Although everyone was betting a good deal, no one seemed too sure about who was winning.

Bettina was with an English girlfriend. Gary Dellos was standing beside them, talking animated Greek to Maria Niarchos, whose gelding was in the next race. Bettina's friend knew Maria and made the introductions. To look at Gary

Dellos, one would think he had been born in Ascot attire, the way it suited him and hugged his body. While his gray hair set off the suntan, the flash of perfect teeth enlivened his deep, ink-black eyes.

Dellos surveyed Bettina as he did all women—the body, then the face. He liked class. Used to social mountaineering, he liked conquering it. He knew Bettina was class by the way she spoke and because she was a houseguest of the Northamptons. And although her outfit was mostly ragamuffin, she had the knack of pulling things together that made even the thrift-shop boa and button boots look smart.

Dellos liked American girls, too. He liked it that the classier they were, the less they picked up on the titles the English always dropped. He could tell this one was attracted to him from the way she tried not to look at him. And he knew the way to attract the attention of someone used to getting her way was to discourage it. Therefore, he left before she did, hoping they'd "meet again sometime."

"Sometime" was three days later. Dellos called. No, she wasn't busy that night, although she was. To say Bettina found Dellos seductive was an understatement. To say he was proficient in bed was the same. Though the number of Bettina's young lovers hadn't been limited, their experience had.

What also intrigued Bettina was the aura of mystery surrounding Dellos's business, the idea that he had no office, just his cellular phone and beeper. And, although his temper seemed to grow shorter the longer she knew him, nothing had ever been like this morning. Had Clive van Arlyn stayed at their table another second, Bettina was sure she'd have thrown something at him just to get him to go away.

As van Arlyn threaded his way through the Le Cirque crowd, he made his usual calculated pit stops, introducing Erica to everyone, until she left him and rushed ahead.

"Excuse me," Erica said, tapping Notre Dame's Father Hesburgh on the shoulder. "I'm from Omaha. I was a cheerleader for the Big Red." Her voice was fast and throaty and thrilled. "My husband and I never miss Homecoming. Notre Dame was something last week. You really creamed us. Not that I'm cheering you on, but congratulations." When van Arlyn caught up, he almost laughed out loud. The one person Erica knew, in a group that included the brothers Trump and Tisch, was a priest.

Brice Oldfield, who had been talking to the women at the next table, jumped up as Clive and Erica approached. Boyishly blond and still on the sunny side of forty, Oldfield was fast becoming society's pet interior designer. It had been almost twenty years since Billy Baldwin had hired this talented young man fresh from the Boston Institute of Fine Arts.

Oldfield was a quick study. It didn't take him long, after working with class, to dress like it and marry into it. In fact, had any of Oldfield's clients, including his wife, learned that his "venerable" family tree was rooted in the potato famine rather than George III, and that the name Oldfield had more to do with saloons than the Boston Tea Party, his swags and swatches might never have been as much in demand.

However, it was just this background that made Oldfield so acute. He understood what the new rich craved. While his appreciative laugh gave them confidence, his deliberate indiscretions made them feel special. And he never forgot Billy Baldwin's warning: "Anyone who thinks his client isn't everything should try doing without him!"

Van Arlyn had worked previously with Oldfield, helping him get the clients to whom he'd sold apartments—a mutually lucrative move, although Oldfield had always wondered if kickbacks were van Arlyn's real motive.

As Clive van Arlyn introduced Erica Wheaton to Brice, Brice introduced them to Lady Zara Kaplan and Doris MacDonald, whom, of course, Clive knew. Erica was fascinated by Zara's bizarre glamour, while Zara immediately dismissed Erica as one of those tarted-up new rich, the type her husband positively loathed.

Clive van Arlyn kept staring at Zara Kaplan. He knew the name. But who was she? His eyes narrowing, he waited for the click of recognition. The accent did it. Zara Kaplan. Of course. The society half of the half Jew who's making it big, or as they say in London, "monstrously!"

Van Arlyn had first heard about the Kaplans from Oldfield's wife, Paige. She'd gotten Zara's name when, along with two other girls who didn't need to work, Paige had started a fabric firm transplanting English gardens onto American sofas. She'd heard that Lady Zara was looking for a sumptuous New York flat and called to ask if when she found one she would use her fabrics.

Actually, van Arlyn had even suggested the name Chintzy for Paige's firm after telling her the story of the well-born Virginia woman who'd moved to Britain and bought a well-known English fabric house. Instead of continuing the tradition of importing the costly chintz from India, as England had done since the eighteenth century, she began making it much less expensively at home. After a great initial success she began farming it out to friends as a cottage industry, enabling the fabric to be marketed at a trifle of the cost. "You'll be carrying on a great southern tradition," van Arlyn told Paige.

Suddenly, van Arlyn spun on Brice. "That's Zara Kaplan? Of the 'looking for a sumptuous flat' Kaplans? With Doris MacDonald? What have you done to me?" Brice had promised van Arlyn he'd introduce "the divine Lady Z" to Clive as a client when she was next in town, in order for Clive to show her "something smashing." However, Oldfield had no idea that she'd be here now and was as shocked as Clive to see her with Doris MacDonald. Oldfield just wished Erica weren't around so he could tell Clive what a chicken's asshole he was, and how his mean-spirited mouth looked like one.

"Her trip, Clive, was a surprise. She only just arrived. I have no idea how she even knows Doris." Oldfield didn't know a thing about the apartment, either. Not that Zara would have told him, even if they'd had more of a chance to talk.

"I see," van Arlyn said unhappily. He knew Oldfield had no reason to lie.

"'Believe the best of everyone, and it will save you a lot of trouble.' Wasn't that yours, Clive?"

"Lighten the load, fellas," Erica said. Enough had already intruded on her day. "Anyway, *whoever* Zara is, I dig the look. Clive, you must admit her scenery leaves mine in the corral."

Oldfield wasn't sure as he watched Erica remove her jacket.

"Hers, dear girl, is a sandwich board screaming PAY ATTENTION," van Arlyn said. "You've got more *real* guts in an eyelash."

"Well, Clive, let me ask you. How would you dress that lady to go before the board?"

What van Arlyn couldn't say was that he wouldn't have to change a thing. "Nobody will ever have to try, Erica, because nobody but you is getting Eight Twenty-three."

The conviction in van Arlyn's voice startled Oldfield. It made him look at Erica again. Although he thought she was great and might well be the backbone of America, she was hardly 823 material. Not if they wanted the Carnegie look.

Suddenly, a flurry of waiters pulled out a table for Cornelia Blair to leave. As Cornelia and Bettina walked toward the door, Cornelia turned conspiratorially to her daughter. "Did you see the one next to us? Don't look yet. . . . Now, look at the ring. Did you notice how it kept banging the plate? You know, I read an article"—Cornelia Blair always "read an article" to reinforce her points—"about women who wear jewelry during the day for everyone to see. That the blacks and Hispanics looking for drug money will not only rob them but cut off their fingers."

"All ten?" Bettina asked, never believing the gospel her mother piled on.

Cornelia didn't hear. "Bettina. Don't gawk. Her kind interprets it as admiration."

Smiling to a few friends, even Cornelia Blair was not sufficiently skilled to avoid the checkered suit.

"Cornelia, I've been trying to catch your eye. I'm—"

"Yes. I know," Cornelia Blair said, still walking. Although one may not be able to help one's feelings, one can certainly help what one does about them, she thought.

Bettina wondered if she should say good-bye to Mrs. Wheaton. Not to ensure that she wouldn't betray her, just to be nice. But she didn't feel like dealing with Clive. If Clive did try something, for any reason, she'd make sure her father got him. She'd heard him complain about how Clive was hurting the clubs by sponsoring his new "best friends" as members. Clive's own membership renewals might just not arrive. In some places, it still worked like that for the Blairs of the world.

The waiters, the captains, Sirio, everyone made a big fuss over Mrs. Blair as she left. They genuinely liked her, and with good reason. She liked them and she showed it, not only with tips but by knowing their children's and wives' names, even the towns in Italy where they were born. Cornelia Blair enjoyed being sociable with people with whom she didn't have to socialize. They didn't want that extra inch any more than she did.

8

*U*ntil this morning, Socrates Garapoulos Dellos had always thanked destiny that he had been born poor. It had driven him to where he was today. Even as a kid, he'd hated working for his father, hauling in those rotten fishing nets, working all day with nothing to show for it.

Dellos liked hanging around the docks, though, sniffing the showy yachts, the big cigars, the fancy women. He had been only sixteen, but a beautiful sixteen, when one of those fancy women pinned him with her eyes. She looked to be about thirty, blond and brassy with long wavy hair that blew with the sea breeze. She ran a glistening tongue along her upper lip while curling a well-manicured finger in his direction. Dellos thought she was gorgeous. He was dazzled by her knuckle-sized diamond and the dozens of colored stones flashing from her wrists as she leaned against the shiny wood rail of the *OopsaDaisy*, out of Fort Lauderdale, Florida.

Dellos never said a word to Daisy Montana as he ran up

the gangplank and followed the curves of her body down the stairs into the master stateroom and onto a bed whose four posts were carved with daisies.

"Undress me," she whispered as she lay on the soft daisy-patterned spread. Her whole body smelled fresh, of flowers and rich things. "Don't be scared. I'll help." She laughed, undoing her bra while guiding his dirty hands to the zipper of her white pants. As Daisy began to grow excited, she tore at his black bikini. In seconds the tiny piece of elastic dangled from his foot, while his fishnet shirt became a collar around his neck. "Pull those off," she said thickly, pointing to her pants, which she had only managed to push to her knees. Gary Dellos was startled to see that she had no hair on her. None at all. Her mound of Venus was smooth and soft.

"I shave because my husband likes very young things," she said. "Do you? Or are you bored with them and want me?" Each word was said to the exaggerated rhythm of her body as it worked against his balls and cock. Putting her hands on his hips, she rocked him to her tempo. "Go with me, baby. Do it for Daisy. That's it. Faster, now. A little more. You got it, baby! That's it! Go! Go, you fucking Greek bastard! Go! Fuck me!"

There was no counting the young townies, harbor men, and sailors that Daisy Montana had had. If she had spent more time on land, they'd have been gardeners, delivery boys, and door-to-door salesmen. They were her recompense for selling out.

Gary Dellos had never been so hard or so big. Even with his girls—young girls, virgins—he'd never been this big. He had to be dreaming. His hands went around the base of his cock to make sure.

"Get that filthy hand away, you stupid kid. Oh, God. Oh, my God! My God!" she screamed.

Whatever Gary Dellos did, whatever it was she did, when it happened, it was primitive and untamed. Never had Gary Dellos felt so exhausted and so exhilarated. After catching his breath, he turned to hold Daisy, but she had jumped off the bed. Baffled, Dellos shook his head as if he'd just come out of the water, sweat dripping from his brow and hair.

"Hey, kid," she called, standing stark naked in the bathroom door. "Watch that smelly sweat." Her loose hair was already tied back. Water was running in the tub.

"Sorry," Dellos said, pulling down his shirt. It was the first word he'd spoken.

Going to him, she ruffled his hair. "Not bad, right? For you *or* me, right?"

Dellos nodded, smiling, but her smile was already gone.

"Here. Get yourself a haircut," she said, handing him a hundred-dollar bill. "Now *ciao*. Scram. Whatever. He'll be back soon." Daisy pointed to a picture of a white-haired man standing with a horse and jockey and herself.

Dellos got it all. The old man, her, himself. Mostly he understood what money could buy. Him for her, and her for the old geezer. He looked at Daisy. "Tomorrow?"

"Try me."

As she had known it would, the *OopsaDaisy* left the marina early that same evening so that their next port would be waking up at about the same time as Daisy. But it didn't matter. A lot more ships would be coming in for Gary Dellos.

Dellos's performances were foolproof. He would shut his eyes and imagine money to get it up. Old farts and bored perverts paid just to see him with their mistresses, girlfriends, even their wives. Once some drooling beer baron invited his whole crew to watch Dellos with his coked-up wife.

* * *

Gary Dellos was not quite nineteen when he met the urbane, well-connected Clive van Arlyn in Monte Carlo. By then he was a steward on the *Sophia,* the 220-foot-long yacht belonging to Dimitrios Andreadis, the richest of all the Greeks.

It was late July, and the *Sophia* was anchored off Monte Carlo alongside Aristotle Onassis's *Christina.* Between these floating sea palaces, a dazzling array of flotsam and jet set were continuous guests with a power and style to intoxicate the most jaded: the widow Kennedy and her sister, Princess Radziwell; David Niven with his young son, Jamie; Truman Capote; Giancarlo Menotti; Maria Callas; the Aga Khan, whom everyone called "K"; Noel Coward with a young blond boy; plus assorted royalty, social swells, and mandatory beautiful bodies accustomed to their place in the sun.

Andreadis had invited Onassis and his guests aboard for lunch.

Van Arlyn immediately spotted Dellos's smoldering Mediterranean looks, accentuated all the more by the starched whiteness of his tight uniform. What also intrigued van Arlyn was Dellos's attentiveness. Each time he drained the last of his champagne, Dellos would be there to refill the glass. Though van Arlyn never considered himself a bisexual, he did admit that he tried to live life to the fullest.

"Dear boy," van Arlyn said, in the British accent he packed along with his ascots and passport whenever he traveled, "do you speak English?"

"Yes, sir. Another drink, sir?"

Van Arlyn smiled. "You must never say 'another.' Some people don't wish to be reminded." That was van Arlyn's first lesson.

"Yes, sir. Thank you. Would you like a drink?" the boy asked, his teeth gleaming like mother-of-pearl.

"Tell me, how long have you worked on the *Sophia?*" Van Arlyn looked up from his deck chair by the pool, on the bottom of which was a huge mosaic. It was the queen of hearts with the face of Andreadis's wife, Sophia.

"Only this summer, but I am raised by the sea. My father he has two fishing boats in Athens." This man should know, Dellos thought laughingly, that his experience had been mostly confined to dockside staterooms.

Unable to break away from those romantic black eyes, van Arlyn believed this boy to be as beautiful as any woman with whom he'd ever been, and certainly more than any man. He wanted to take him in his arms that very night.

And so it started. Dellos knew exactly what van Arlyn was about. If a homosexual side trip was part of the dues he owed this dazzling world, Dellos could manage. Van Arlyn was so smitten that after one particular night at the Hôtel de Paris, van Arlyn took his young protégé to Cartier's to order a crest ring like his own.

Before van Arlyn's two-week stay was over, the liaison had paid off for Dellos. Clive van Arlyn invited him to the United States. To New York City. Broadway. The Empire State. The big time. . . .

Van Arlyn was the first at the gate after Gary Dellos cleared customs at JFK. Dellos held out his hand to show him the ring he'd taken care to wear. Van Arlyn was exuberant as he tossed Dellos's bag into the back of his red MG convertible.

"We're off to the beach," he said, as they headed east from Kennedy Airport. "It's the weekend. The city's empty."

"Then when do we go there?" Gary Dellos wanted to get closer to those skyscrapers, not farther away.

"Monday. First thing Monday."

As they sped down the parkway, with fortune on the horizon and opportunity at the wheel, how could Gary Dellos possibly have dreamed that in less than forty-eight hours he'd be on his way back to Greece?

"No cars are allowed," van Arlyn said as they stood at the railing of the ferry on their way to Fire Island. When van Arlyn put his arm around his shoulder, Dellos felt sick. His discomfort grew when he met the other "couple" and heard about the party they were invited to where they must all dress as brides. It took more, a helluva lot more, than a few drinks and a few snorts for Dellos to join in.

The following morning, still half drugged, he was the one to find the body. His vomit was splattered everywhere by the time the others came to stare.

"Oh, my God!" one of them gasped.

"Jesus, Mary, and Joseph and all the saints above!" another exclaimed, crossing himself over and over.

"But who? Why?" van Arlyn asked.

Then they all turned to Dellos.

Dellos had fled, believing they would blame him, the stranger, the foreigner, for the death. As it turned out, after the police were called and the autopsy performed, the cause of death was ruled as an overdose, a ruling Gary Dellos never heard.

Before this morning, when the elevator door had opened on him and Bettina, Gary Dellos's shadowy past had never caught up with him. For all those years he had never had to look back.

Gary Dellos had always prided himself on making the right moves. He knew exactly what he wanted to be: a mercenary for social swells. Servicing big shots around the globe made Dellos's adrenaline surge. He thrived on the hypocrisy of the elite, doing their dirty work to ensure their clean-cut reputations while their payoffs ensured his playboy style of life. After all, Gary Dellos was no two-bit promoter. He was a producer.

He was a pro at staging porno pictures for millionaires who wanted to frame the wives they wanted to dump; at running cocaine from Colombia and Laos; at magnetizing roulette wheels for Arab sheiks. Dellos had even disposed of a mistress of John Paul Getty's without so much as glancing over his shoulder. Except for van Arlyn, there'd never been a loose end.

Suddenly, whatever luck he'd had was gone and all he could do was stand there and watch it evaporate. It was as if some priceless vase were falling from its perch and he was powerless to catch it. The ingenious life-style he'd crafted for years was about to smash at his feet.

He had to think. Did van Arlyn show any trace of recognition? Anything at all? As far as Dellos could remember, nothing. Probably his gray hair saved him. A quirky smile twisted his lips. He'd always thought the gray was due to van Arlyn and his friends on Fire Island.

Dellos would have known van Arlyn anywhere, still twisting that goddam ring. All at once, Dellos trembled as he remembered throwing the one van Arlyn had given him into the sea, praying it would sink along with the memory of that terrifying morning.

As a frantic Bettina Blair left Le Cirque with her mother, a wild-eyed Gary Dellos was pacing up and down in his suite at the Commodore. Perspiration dripped from his body, and a knifing dryness in his throat made him gulp for air just thinking about that fucking, spoiled Bettina.

The worst part was that he had to make up with her. Not that she wouldn't kiss his cock from here to the moon. That was the trouble. Just thinking of her doing it made the idea of hauling fish with his father seem like heaven. Dellos knew he had to look at it as what it was: a job. Besides, the kind of cash George Wheaton was throwing at him was unreal. And guys like Wheaton didn't fool around. Not that Dellos did. And not that Dellos didn't think he was worth every dime.

Banging his head in frustration, Gary Dellos yelled at himself in the mirror. "Listen to me, you goddam idiot! So some rich bitch is in love with you. So you have to stick it out and stick it in a little longer. Don't blow a fucking fuse to blow the fucking deal. Just keep your goddam eyes fixed on that Bank of England deposit slip. Get that through your thick head, Dellos, you'll get it all! All!"

Again, he started to pace. He had to think how to get back on track. How to get back into this hot bitch's pants. After all, he had accepted Wheaton's contract. He'd done great so far. It should still seem like a lead-pipe cinch to be paid a bundle to fuck some loaded chick, just to find some dirt on a company her father was close to. Who would have guessed the bitch would fall in love? Love! He'd be lucky if he could get it up in a week.

9

"*G*reat lunch, Doris. Perfect day. Just perfect. I can't believe how right you were about Eight Twenty-three," Zara Kaplan said, as the doorman held open the door of the Rolls that waited directly in front of Le Cirque.

"Now do you see the reason for the rush? Even at that insane price?"

Zara nodded. "And you were right about its being so me. And John, too."

"It's everybody, Zara. Everybody's dream. But you're the one who will make it happen!" Doris MacDonald was on such a high, she had no cool left to keep. She didn't know how she got through lunch without dancing on the tables or dropping a seven-league boot on Mr. Piss-elegant-van-Arlyn, who said he only "sold the best to the best."

"Again, Doris, thanks," said Zara, climbing into the Rolls. "Let's stay in touch."

"Mind if I hitch a ride to the Carlyle?" Doris asked, not

wanting to lose even a moment's touch. "Our office is down the block."

"Of course. Get in," Zara said uncertainly. Until Doris said the Carlyle, Zara hadn't realized that's where she was going, though of course she couldn't wait to call John. It was unusual to have nothing to do in the middle of the day. Not that Zara's usual day was what anyone else would think usual except for those who also inhabited her world. For hers was a world where the titled and self-crowned fluttered around the most mercurial of flames, in a continuing search that made them basically homeless.

What it involved, whether it was in London or New York, the slopes of Gstaad, or the shrines of Nepal, was an event agenda. Continuous activity, be it a jet flight, a meeting, or a manicure, was essential. In fact, a manicure during a meeting in midair would be perfection. The more spheres of action in which one participated, the more inter-national territories to which one laid claim, the better.

Requisite, too, was a steady flow of people. Being alone was to be avoided at all costs. Thinking was perhaps the single activity Zara and her peers forbade themselves, since it provided a mirror into which they couldn't gaze.

Women like Zara, caught by the centrifugal force of their own whirling lives, became slaves to their schedules. No matter how shameless their luxury or how strong their power, they became servants to their agendas, bound to an event-filled day whose main function was to avoid being a typical one.

On such a day, Zara awoke early with J.K. Morning lovemaking hadn't been initiated by either one in years. In fact, Zara's first action, no matter how bad her hangover, was to jump out of bed, go to her dressing room, take off her gown, her wedding band, even her contact lenses from the night before, and weigh in. If her weight, always set at a mere

118 pounds for her five-foot-nine frame, tipped the scale even slightly, Zara would eliminate the protein slice of toast from her breakfast of herbal tea and a half of whatever fruit was in season. From her breakfast served in bed, she would chat with J.K., who would peer intermittently from his bathroom to catch the drift that the running water diluted.

Their talk was the sort of impersonal chat one would have with one's secretary. Lunch where? Dinner? Benefit function or private do? Sprinkled between would be talk about servants and children. In that order. After all, the former were impossible to replace and the latter one never got rid of!

While J.K. mostly listened, he could easily dress and organize his own day. With one last pat to his hair, he would give Zara's cheek a hurried peck, his thoughts already gone. "Good-bye, my angel."

"'Bye, my darling," Zara answered. "Call you later."

No matter who mentioned calling, and one of them always did, neither of them ever called unless it was an emergency about dinner or measles or, like today, a Fifth Avenue flat. But saying they would was their thread, tying together what they couldn't admit were disparate lives.

Zara liked J.K. breakfasting alone with his newspapers. It gave her time for a telephone canvass of the previous night, even though she'd forgotten most of what she'd heard by 9 A.M. when Noel, her exercise instructor, would start her peppy music. True, Zara knew enough about stomach crunches and buttock squeezes to lead most classes, but her lack of concentration needed a Simon Legree to oversee whatever agony kept the cellulite down and the pulse up.

When skinny Noel left and Eva, the hefty masseuse, arrived, Zara switched the phone back on. Patiently, Eva would shift the thick monogrammed towels from one part of Zara's body to another to accommodate her calls and her lack of modesty.

She would get on and off the massage table three or four times during the hour, perhaps to retrieve the number of a handsome Spanish jewelry designer, scribbled on a cocktail napkin the night before, before that fool maid, Maria, threw it away. Like all maids, Maria did everything Zara didn't want before she got around to doing what Zara wanted.

Often, Zara, hot-tempered, would yell into the receiver when, after buzzing the butler, all she could hear was Julio Iglesias blaring on the kitchen radio. "Tell Maria to shut Julio up and bring me my special. *Rapido.* And, Vincent, in case you don't know what *rapido* means, ask stupido Maria." Zara was convinced the only reason Vincent said, "She is a fine worker, madam," was because he was screwing her out of her Spanish fandango!

Zara's special was an extra-spicy, extra-vodka Bloody Mary, which worked miracles in mobilizing her frayed forces for the day ahead.

Nilu, Zara's Persian secretary—one never said "Iranian" after Khomeini—arrived midway through Eva's hour. Wandering in and out, she would go over Zara's notes from the night before. A master decoder of Zara's late-night hieroglyphics, she took it as a personal defeat if she had to ask about even the wobbliest of written words.

Nilu was a pro, too, at deciphering which plans to "definitely cancel," before Zara's Bloody Mary took effect. Otherwise, lunch at Harry's Bar, fittings at Thea Porter or Victor Edelstein, and charity meetings would only have to be reinstated. Zara left most afternoons "free" in order to fill them with a special "friend" or go to a gaming club and throw too many chips on the roulette table.

What took Zara the most time was to draw on her face.

Night or day, it was perfection that not even the makeup masters who'd taught her could capture as well. In truth, there were two Zaras, with the face and without: one bold, unique, and unconventional; the other still wanting to be punished for what the bold, naughty Zara did.

Zara's last stop each day was the hair house. There, in a private room, she would sip her special stash of Montrachet while Angelo painted or plaited her tresses and Daphne lacquered her nails to match her dress.

Where Zara mostly strayed from today's flock was that she didn't try to compete. She *was* the competition. In a world where ugly stepsisters were going to the ball instead of Cinderella, Zara had the class they tried to buy, the fashion they tried to copy. She had everything yet nothing to do with what was fashionable. Though her look might be excessive, it would have been so even if the world she lived in wasn't.

"What happens now with Eight Twenty-three?" Zara asked Doris, as the blue Rolls circled around Park Avenue and up Madison.

"Dreary mechanics: letters of reference, bank statements."

Zara smiled. "The board?"

"Soon as possible. Soon as I get the other stuff set with the home office. But not to worry." Not even for one single second, she thought gratefully. After hugging Zara good-bye, Doris MacDonald was as happy skipping down the street as Clive van Arlyn had been earlier.

The Carlyle's owner, Peter Sharpe, gave a warm welcome to Lady Zara as he handed her the messages she had been too rushed to pick up that morning. What Zara liked about the Carlyle was that it was more like a club than a hotel. Ever since its doors opened in 1930, guests had returned with a feeling of coming home. The staff, mostly regulars, took special pride in remembering the preferences of "their" people. The maître d' knew their favorite tables, the telephone operators their names, and the night maids remembered to turn down both sides of certain beds. Even Bobby Short played their favorite tunes when the old-timers came in.

Though she felt like rushing upstairs instead of going through the pleasantries, awareness of her position as Lady Zara and the importance of maintaining that position slowed her down. It was this same innate sense of values that made it possible for her to balance all the various parts of her life.

After the necessary cordialities, Zara proceeded smartly past the flow of guests, through the antiques-filled lobby, and into the elevator. Had she bothered this morning to look at her messages, she would have read, as she did now, *A.B. called from London to say he will be in New York in time for a late dinner.*

With renewed fervor, she called John as soon as she entered her apartment.

"I've never heard you so enthusiastic," J.K. said happily to his wife.

"I've never been so keen on anything before—except, of course, you, my darling," Zara answered. "I long for you to see it. I know you'll love it just as much."

"I do already," he said. Lately, his wife's spirits had seemed a bit damp and her behavior a bit distant. He was delighted to hear her so eager. The new apartment would be the perfect tonic to restore her normal liveliness. What a brilliant day, he thought. Wheaton this morning and now Zara. "When should we tell Archer?"

Just hearing her husband say the name of her lover excited Zara. It was the danger as well as the expectation that aroused her. "Soon."

"Actually, Zara, you're lucky he was here with me. You

could have run into him in the lobby. Now don't go running back until we tell him. You're bound to bump heads. That's the way things always happen."

"No. No, darling. I won't. I promise."

"Actually, Archer should be in New York tonight."

"Tonight?"

"He left before lunch. With Jack Minton. He loathes Jack and loves staying here, so it must be an important dinner."

"Is that what he said?"

"I think so. Anyway, my angel, what are you up to?"

"Nothing."

"Well, it won't hurt you. I plan to arrive tomorrow night, sometime after I'm through with Omaha. I leave at the crack of dawn. Can't wait. Not for Omaha, my sweet. For you. For Eight Twenty-three."

"I can't wait either," Zara said, loving the naughtiness of it. "And darling, congratulations on Wheaton. I'm so proud. You know, we've shot a double. Wheaton and Eight Twenty-three!"

When Zara hung up, her heart was beating too fast for a nap. But she knew she must try. She'd be sorry later. Maybe a bath would help.

As she lay back in the warm soothing water, the smell of night-blooming jasmine bath oil permeating the room, she already felt more relaxed. Closing her eyes, she allowed herself her most favorite luxury—thinking about the time, early last spring, when her affair with Archer began.

There had been a Triomphe meeting. Archer was staying the night in London and leaving early the next morning to join Cornelia in Paris. While John and Zara were dressing for the ballet, John received a call from Rupert Murdoch, some supposed brouhaha about Murdoch calling Teddy Kennedy "fat boy" in his *Boston Globe* and Kennedy trying to push a bill through Congress that would force Murdoch to sell either his newspapers or TV stations. J.K. couldn't possibly turn down "a pal in need," especially one *he* needed. Archer Blair just had to be a good sport and take Zara to the ballet, while J.K. met with Murdoch.

"Curious chap, Murdoch," J.K. had said, as they sipped champagne before going their separate ways. "At Oxford, he was known for keeping a bust of Lenin in his room. Now the interest on his four-billion-dollar debt alone could feed most of Russia. I must say, though, Rupert and I do exemplify the old saw of Oxford being the 'breeding ground of the ruling class.'"

Idly moving a large soap-filled sponge over her arms and breasts, down her flat stomach, and back and forth between her long legs, Zara smiled as she remembered how quickly Archer had agreed to be the "good sport."

As far as Zara was concerned, it hadn't really mattered who went with her to the ballet. She adored the ballet. It stimulated her sexually. All those beautiful men in tights! That night, she'd thought them particularly well endowed. Perhaps it was her mood, or the champagne. She knew she looked her best. And although she'd never considered Archer attractive, she remembered his flirtatiousness: silly things like brushing up against her or putting his tongue in her ear when they danced. She'd always thought it was more a reaction against his wife than a pass at her.

But this time she'd found his sharp, intense features arresting, and when he held her around the waist so his fingers fondled her breast, she didn't pull away. She even found the lemon scent of his after-shave arousing.

Archer had always thought of Zara as not only beautiful but hot-blooded. He fantasized that she was as wild as her clothes, as lascivious as her mouth. For him, the fire in her eyes held an unrevealed secret. Yet often, just when he thought he knew her, she slipped out of focus, like that night at the ballet, when he felt her hand underneath the paisley shawl she'd placed on his lap.

"Shall we go?" Zara whispered, her lips sliding down his cheek. "I mean, if you're able."

As if someone else were living in his body, Archer Blair felt himself stumbling over knees until he made it to the aisle.

Zara's selection of a mate was never predatory. The spirit divined and the body followed. Her moral climate depended on her need for excitement. Perhaps one reason she never feared betrayal was because betrayal, too, was part of the thrill she craved.

The modest birdwatcher she'd met in Windsor was so terrified at making love to *the* John Kaplan's wife in *the* John Kaplan's bed, it heightened her passion. But when his fear subsided, so did her interest. With the youthful naval buddy of Prince Charles whom Zara met in Scotland when Charles invited the Kaplans grouse shooting, instead of feeling old, Zara became the young, hot teenager she'd never been with Philip. Her desire to please, combined with his insatiable desire, made her mouth do new things, while she shrewdly kept her body restrained until the last possible moment.

Then there was Michael, an artist who showed at the Waddington Gallery. She and J.K. bought a painting of a boy on a beach who looked like their son. John thought Michael great fun and asked him to dinner. The idea that J.K. had arranged the liaison and the three of them could be civilized together was excruciatingly erotic. The others who followed, like those who went before, never lasted long and never mattered later. For Zara, Archer Blair was unique. He was her

American counterpart. He was tradition and convention, guarded and circumspect. And for her he was defying it all.

For Archer Blair, women weren't unusual. But it was always plural, never just the dangerous one woman. Though relationships might last weeks or months, they were mostly professionals. He liked to pay. It soothed his conscience and didn't threaten his world. It also wasn't unusual for Archer Blair to sleep with his wife. It was all part of their enactment of the perfect painting.

As much as Archer Blair believed himself safe from the tawdry age of overload, he thought himself safe from such lapses in breeding as having one's base instincts surface or losing control of one's emotions. Somewhere, however, along the genetic trail, Archer Blair missed a turn after meeting up with Zara. At age forty-five, ever since that first startling night after the ballet when they'd gone wild in his room in her house, he was defying the law of sexual gravity.

Stepping out of the tub, Zara slipped into a short, monogrammed terry robe and snuggled between her favorite Pratesi sheets, the ones with the tiny blue flowers and blue scalloped trim. What a pity about Verna, Zara thought, hoping she was just a pleasure deferred. And not for long, either.

Flipping the television remote control until she came to an old black-and-white film, Zara was just in time to catch Barbara Stanwyck scream into nothingness as she heard her killer climb the stairs in *Sorry, Wrong Number*. In about as long as it took the killer to reach Stanwyck's room, Zara was asleep. Zara had forgotten that the killer happened to be her husband.

When she awoke, it was already dark. She wouldn't have roused had it not been for the phone.

"Zara?"

"If that's who you want me to be," she said sleepily.

"Always. I can tell I've waked you. Stay in bed." He laughed. "You got my message."

"Yes. Thank heavens. What a foul-up."

"I couldn't believe it."

"Where are you now?"

"Still at the airport. Just cleared customs. That moron Minton bought some brandy or something to save a buck. But I won't be long."

"What time is it?" Zara asked, stretching her arms.

"Almost eight. What's that noise?"

"Oh, the telly. I must've left it on. I can't believe I slept so hard."

"Don't go back. Order something sexy like oysters, olives, and you. Actually, darling, never mind the oysters and olives. Oops, got to go. Minton probably bribed the customs more than he saved."

It was well after nine when Archer Blair finally got to the Carlyle. Zara hadn't bothered with makeup. What for? She had, however, ordered oysters and olives and had already drunk a couple of pick-me-up glasses of Dom downstairs in the living room when the bell rang.

Archer was still in his banker's gray, but he had managed a change of shirt on the plane. He liked looking crisp for Zara. She was always so fresh and appetizing. Even now, just her smell drove him wild. As he took her in his arms, she stood on tiptoe to meet his lips.

"Hello, Zara, my darling, my love," he whispered into her hair.

"Hello, sweetheart. I'm so happy you're here. What a foul-up," she repeated, almost fouling up again by mentioning 823.

"Is that a touch of Dom I taste on those lips?"

"Look what else is here."

Archer Blair laughed at the platters of oysters and olives. How he loved her extravagance, so different from his own New England thrift.

As Zara poured more champagne, she told him about missing Verna.

"I could kill J.K.," Archer said.

Zara never felt even slightly that way about Cornelia. She would never want anyone full time. That's why life was so perfect. "How *was* the meeting?"

"Boring. I think for your husband, however, tomorrow's the world. If that's enough. He's inexorable. But who wants to talk about him?"

Taking off his jacket and jerking his tie through the collar, he led her upstairs.

"Good thing half of these sheets are still fresh," he said.

In a second his clothes were on the floor and he was beside her, in bed. Zara wrapped one leg around him as he moved his hands over her body, kissing her everywhere.

Taking her hand, he put it around his limp cock. Slowly at first, then faster, she moved her hand up and down, up and down. Archer put his hand on top of hers, making her go even faster.

Zara slipped her mouth down from his lips to his chest, biting his nipples, first one, then the other. She moved to his thighs and buried her head between his legs. But little if anything was happening. Suddenly she felt like more champagne. She certainly didn't feel like working on Archer anymore.

As she started to move away, he pressed his hands hard on her head, forcing her to stay on him.

Zara knew he was tired. He'd had a long day. And no

sleep. Again, she thought about Verna. How great it would have been. "Think of when Verna comes," she said. He relaxed the pressure on her head, and she moved up to whisper in his ear. "Think of what she'll do to you. To me. Think of us all together."

Archer's breath came faster. It was helping. He was getting hard. "More. Tell me more."

"She won't be wearing many clothes. But she's not going to take them all off. She'll leave on a bikini. A string bikini."

"Go on! Go on!" Archer was inside Zara now. In and out. In and out.

"She's going to kiss me everywhere."

"Where?"

"Where you are now," she said, getting excited herself.

That was all Archer Blair needed. In one final thrust, it was over. In just a matter of seconds, it was as if it had never been. With a tired hand, Zara rolled from under him and reached for the champagne.

Maybe Verna could make it tomorrow, she thought hopefully.

10

Well past noon on the following day, John Kaplan sat in quiet comfort in Triomphe's new Gulfstream III, studying every last aspect of Wheaton Industries. J.K. had recently purchased the jet at a bargain $5 million from GE after they'd updated their mini air force with newer G-IVs. The $6 million difference in price, however, was hardly value received, since both traveled the same miles in the same time, burning the same amount of fuel. Not that J.K.'s board needed to be convinced. Use of corporate jets was one of the great directors' perks.

Although configured to carry as many as thirteen passengers, plus pilot, co-pilot, and flight attendant, J.K. not only had the interior luxuriously redone to accommodate only seven but had added a shower and an area easily converted into a bedroom. Even the oversized chairs, upholstered in soft desert colors with the Triomphe logo subtly woven into the fabric, tilted into sleepers. And under each seat were individual VCRs while screens lifted from the chair arms like small trays. Headsets, to avoid noise, were also provided.

Between the chairs, beige laminated-wood tables unfolded for work, food, or cards. Standard were comforts such as slippers, sweaters, and cashmere throws, as well as current newspapers and magazines. The kitchen was of closet proportions, yet it never saw the aluminum containers of precooked airline food. Special dishes were always brought aboard and always served on Triomphe's special Wedgwood. Kaplan rarely ate while flying, only drinking water to avoid dehydration. Although, while refueling and clearing customs in New York, he had a hearty tuna salad.

J.K. fit right into the elitist world of private planes, a world apart from public arrivals or departures, where customs officers come to you and the corporate hierarchy knows who's in town from a look at the call numbers on the tail.

J.K. took off his Cartier tank watch, a graduation present, to reset the time. It was hardly worth the bother, for the short time he'd be in Omaha, but he didn't want to insult George Wheaton in case he noticed. After moving the black steel hands around the Roman numerals, he smiled at the inscription: *Lost time is never found. Love, Mother.*

Time was the main reason J.K. had bought the G-III, and never had there been a better reason for the purchase than today. There was no nonstop commercial flight from New York to Omaha. And no way was Kaplan going to spend a night there. The place was nowhere. Omaha, he had been told, as if it had little else to recommend it, was exactly midway between New York and San Francisco. No, his meeting wouldn't last long enough to warrant staying the night. It was merely a courtesy call on his part.

J.K. had no doubt that he could steamroll right over George Wheaton. Not that he didn't anticipate the feisty little bugger's resisting his simple presentation, unable to believe it could be that easy to take Wheaton away. It wouldn't be long, though, before reality set in and Wheaton would see that what sounded like child's play could in fact become all-out war. It would be so clear, Wheaton might wonder why he'd been blind so long.

As they started their descent into Omaha, John Kaplan, freshly showered, stood in front of the mirror and, after brushing his hair, pushed the sides flat with his palms. Stretching his neck, he pulled his tie tight, turning it ever so slightly so the knot lay perfectly centered under the collar. His blue suit with its relatively slim white pinstripe was the reverse coloring of his shirt. Considering that he'd been traveling almost eleven hours, John Kaplan felt and looked remarkably fresh.

George Wheaton was tense as he stood before the huge picture window of his Omaha office. He'd been challenged before, but by people who worked for Wheaton, whose interests were the same as his own: a site that was too risky to build on, geologists' findings that showed insufficient oil to drill, airline routes that weren't adequately traveled. He always knew the hand he'd been dealt.

This was different. This was an outsider. Wheaton knew a lot about Kaplan, but then again he didn't. He'd heard rumors and he'd seen statistics. But statistics lie, and liars use statistics. And fuck Anglo-American reciprocity! He'd be damned if he was going to add Wheaton Industries to any Brit mega-deal buy-back of the colonies. Where in hell, he wondered, was Dellos? Why hadn't he come through?

Measuring not quite five-foot-eight, with short, straight-up brown hair "because it's easier," Wheaton looked more like the local high school coach than a top player in the hectic welter of takeovers.

As he gazed down at the muddy Missouri River from the jumbo skyscraper in the giant mall he'd built, sold at a huge profit, then leased back for Wheaton's headquarters, he wondered how much of the cargo on those heavily laden barges still belonged to Wheaton.

Though George Wheaton had had quite a selling spree, he'd kept other shopping malls, high-rises, and the undeveloped land in the Sun Belt. But many of the unrelated companies, such as the airline shuttle, the taco franchises, and the latex glove factories in Singapore, he'd sold. True, they were worth more now than when he sold them, but Wheaton was sure that with the coming downward spiral he'd buy back whatever he wanted at a fraction of the money he'd been paid.

There was one property, however, George Wheaton would never sell, no matter how much was offered: his ranch. Those two hundred thousand acres were sacred, his fortune's cornerstone, the first hundred-acre piece bought by his father years before.

George Flannagan Wheaton had grown rich from the fertile Nebraska soil, its cattle, beans, hay, oil, and minerals, and even richer from the empire he'd built on top of it. He was proud of his Nebraska roots and especially of his middle name, honoring the founder of nearby Boys Town. George's father, abandoned by his parents, had been one of its first graduates in the Depression. "Made the place as famous as Spencer Tracy," George Wheaton would brag. Actually, for Nebraskans, Duke Wheaton was more celebrated, having devised a unique system of irrigation by channeling Nebraska's untapped rivers and connecting them with the giant Missouri.

George Wheaton remembered thinking his father must be some kind of god when, as a little boy, he'd stand in the middle of the flat Nebraska farmland and, with the irrigation system going full force, watch daddy-made rainbows arching to the horizon. "Just want to leave the land a little better than when I found it, son," he'd say.

Close to the Boys Town statue of a young boy with a smaller boy on his back was a bigger-than-life statue of the Duke, erected by his son along with the Duke Wheaton Geology Center. It would be John Kaplan's first stop when his plane landed at Omaha's Eppley Airport.

"Downtown Omaha's only five miles from the airport, Mr. Kaplan," the chief pilot said, as the co-pilot lowered the steps to the runway.

Good-looking as well as skilled, Triomphe's crew were like movie extras in their forest-green uniforms, the company logo embroidered on their lapels.

J.K. insisted that Triomphe employ two sets of pilots for the jet and two for the helicopter, plus two flight attendants, which enabled the aircraft—but never the crew—to be in constant use. Another J.K. dictum was that the pilots be married, with children, to further ensure their sense of responsibility.

"Excellent. If all goes well, we should be wings-up by afternoon," Kaplan said, taking the stairs briskly.

Though J.K. knew Americans were famous for borrowing to the hilt to live beyond it, there was no way, with all the companies George Wheaton had sold off, that he could leverage what was left to get enough money to buy enough Wheaton stock to keep his company.

The narcotic thrill of the deal whipped through John Kaplan. As he had told his board, "This deal not only incorporates the glitz of the big name but the solidity of a Gibraltar."

The memory of those thundering words and the eager

looks from his board went through J.K.'s mind as he entered the terminal, almost missing the stocky man holding the sign with his name in bold, black letters. George Wheaton had spotted Kaplan the second his plane door opened. This was a favorite ploy: Catch them unawares. How do they look when they don't think you're looking? Is their walk aggressive? The stride energetic? Any mannerisms? A finger circling the collar? Perspiring? How will they greet the person they think is their driver?

John Kaplan approached the man with the sign. "I'm Kaplan," he said, in a cordial yet cool British tone.

The short, chunky man in the light linen-weave suit held out his hand. "I'm Wheaton. Welcome to Omaha."

John Kaplan, who had started walking ahead, halted abruptly. "Wheaton? George Wheaton?" He smiled uncertainly, staring at this unlikely fellow. "How nice of you to meet me."

"I know how you feel about time, with that jet and all, so I thought the least I could do was save you some at this end. Funny thing. TWA looked into putting nonstop service on from New York, but I guess not many people feel we're important enough to visit. Of course, silly as it sounds, there aren't many folks from Omaha who think flying nonstop from here to New York is worth it either."

George Wheaton's smile was as big and open as the prairie, though his slightly seedy look and that sign-holding business were rather off-putting. Nor did he seem to notice Kaplan's finely tailored pin-striped suit, his crisp shirt with the crest links, and the shoes still bright after all those miles.

"You're not carrying anything? No attaché case?" George Wheaton asked.

"No, nothing," John Kaplan said, riveted by Wheaton's hair, which his children might refer to as "spiked."

"You and Trump. Don told me he *never* carries anything. They say you're a big gambler like him, but I say that's what other people call smart people. Like they call them lucky."

Although George Wheaton's car was directly outside the gate, he preferred to take Kaplan through the airport's main terminal, through the countless "Hi, George"s and "Hello, Mr. Wheaton"s, past the advertisements and posters dominated by the name Wheaton that lined the walls: Wheaton Symphony, Wheaton Historical Museum and Park, Wheaton Civic Center, Wheaton Playhouse, Wheaton Bank and Trust, Wheaton cattle.

"You're quite a fellow," John Kaplan said, impressed.

"Hometown boy makes good," George Wheaton said modestly, knowing not a single Kodak blowup had been lost on his guest.

"*Does* good too, it seems. Must be very gratifying."

"It is, Jack. Sure is. Mind if I call you Jack? I hear that's what your good friends call you, and I hope that's what I'm going to be."

John Kaplan smiled again. Nobody had ever asked permission before; his good friends just grew into it. But then George Wheaton wouldn't have enough time, would he? "I'd be flattered."

"Anyhow, Jack, when they decided the Union Pacific Railroad should end here in Omaha, Nebraska's pioneer spirit was born. Nebraskans never saw it as a last stop. We saw these rich plains as a new beginning, a new frontier. I guess we still do. Tilling the soil, working the river. It's in the blood.

"My wife Erica's the one who's sensitive to the aesthetics. Not that she's not on top of an annual report too. Smart as a whip, she is. I tell you, it's the damnedest thing. Since Erica's taken on the theater and the symphony, they haven't had a losing season. She even imported one of your shows, *Oliver.*

But I can't say I care much for that Charles Dickens kind of English greed. Know what I mean?"

Wheaton's laugh was so hearty and his pat on the back so friendly, it took a second before Kaplan caught the innuendo. But by then Wheaton was back to his wife.

"She's damn pretty, too. Too pretty to be so smart." Wheaton took his wallet from behind the gold Cross pen in his inside jacket pocket and flipped it open to a snapshot. "That's our pride and joy with Erica. Named Georgette for me. Luckily, that's all she got from me. Here's one of the baby and Erica and my older boys. And this is Erica as Miss Nebraska. She'd kill me if she knew I carried it. Something, hmm?" He kept looking at the picture after Kaplan handed it back. "Truth is, she *is* something. Best thing ever happened to me. I never thought a man could get so lucky. There's nothing we don't share, and I mean nothing."

J.K. felt he should whisk out some family portraits from his own billfold, yet all he had were his calling cards from Smythson's. But then, that's all he ever needed. Even if he'd had a picture of Zara, it certainly wouldn't be in a swimsuit with a streamer across her body. Of course, she might be in a ball gown with a parrot, but that was different. Zara was, after all, Lady Zara.

"You must be very proud," J.K. said.

"I am," George Wheaton said as the terminal's electric doors opened to the snappy fall air. Indeed he was proud. And now that he'd established a thing or three with Mr. Kaplan, they'd be on their way.

"Top down bother you?" George Wheaton asked, as he opened the door of his new blue Mustang convertible.

"No, no. Fine," J.K. answered, annoyed as hell because he never carried a comb.

"Best way to see the sights without wasting time getting in and out," George Wheaton said, very friendly.

"Excellent." Sights? J.K. wondered what sights as he slowly moved his wrist to check the hour.

As it turned out, John Kaplan was absorbed by what he saw. He should have been. After all, it was going to be his—all except Boys Town, of course—the shopping malls, the land by the river, the real estate on the outskirts, which was fast becoming part of the town. They even saw the cattle yards and drove down to the river to inspect the barges carrying Wheaton produce to the rest of America.

"Anyhow, Jack, you see how the Nebraska soil's been good to me," Wheaton said as they headed to his office. "Enabled Wheaton to pick up those other little deals. You know?"

Did J.K. ever. Midland Airlines, Arctic Cola, Gold Crown Flower, Reggae Records, two Hollywood studios, twenty-eight McDonald's franchises, and enough Hawaii coastline to encircle Japan. Only by the skin of his teeth had Wheaton lost Beatrice to Kravis. Kaplan knew it all. He knew just as well what Wheaton had sold off.

"Stinger's still in my craw about Beatrice," Wheaton said, with a certain amount of wonderment but with more of a how-did-it-get-away-from-me? bewilderment. "They cleared about two billion on that buy-out, with hardly any of their dough in the six billion they put up. Henry Kravis told me he was in Kenya on safari and so bored out of his mind that he called the office, and that's when he heard Beatrice might be possible. Imagine! I'm *in* my office and I don't hear a thing! Didn't it make you crazy when Goldsmith bought *L'Express* and Cardin bought Maxime's right under your nose?"

Wheaton had sneaked in another right to the jaw. How

in the world did this nubby-suited Nebraskan know he'd been the underbidder? Even Mitterrand didn't know.

"You know, Jack, when I got over it?"

"Over what?"

"Beatrice." Wheaton was delighted to catch this poised, self-assured man off guard.

"Yes, of course. When?"

"When I got home and over the bed was a sign Erica had made. In big red letters, it said, *If you want billions through boredom go back to your first wife.*"

"She sounds quite extraordinary," J.K. said, his mind moving quickly.

"That's one word for her," George Wheaton answered. "There's not many around really care about you or are really affected by how you feel, especially when you're rich. But let me tell you"—and he took his hand off the wheel and pointed a forceful finger at J.K.—"you're not rich until you find someone who cares about you. Then you feel you've reached across the stars. . . . Matter of fact, there's a chance you might meet Erica—depending on how long you're here, of course. She'll be back this afternoon. Been in New York looking at apartments. We thought we'd get a real place there. It's tough going global from Omaha."

"Coincidentally, my wife's also in New York looking for a flat. I hope Erica is back in time. I'd be enchanted to meet her." Not that J.K. needed to. He pictured her precisely: a somewhat worn American hussy who'd done a beauty-queen con job, including getting Wheaton to sell off too much of his business in order to have her business of cash-on-the-line flourish. Once Wheaton woke up, J.K. was sure even more would be lost in a messy divorce. But then, Americans loved domestic calamities, as did their solicitors.

"Tell me something about your missus," George Wheaton said. "She's your second, too. Right?"

Odd, Kaplan thought, he'd never been asked about Zara before. Everyone he knew either knew her also or wasn't familiar enough to pry. How would he describe her? Somehow she was more an environment than a personality. It would be easier to depict boar hunting in Germany than to describe Zara.

"I would call Zara a free spirit, but also a rather expensive one, if you know what I mean." Kaplan laughed indulgently. He was pleased with his little sally, not knowing that Wheaton knew exactly what Kaplan himself didn't know: that his wife was the typical English floozy whose title let her do aboveboard what others did in closets, and who never would have married this Jewish gentleman without the pounds sterling.

"Tried to make a date with the governor," Wheaton said, changing the subject, having ascertained all he wanted about Kaplan's wife. "She was called to Washington, though. There's talk about her getting a cabinet post. But she's mighty interested in anyone as interested in our state as you seem to be. If my sources are accurate, you own close to five percent of Wheaton. And that's about as much as you can get without filing with the SEC."

J.K. was impressed again: the Wheaton billboards, the car, the tour, Wheaton's knowledge of the unsuccessful bids, which only J.K.'s lawyers knew about, and now of J.K.'s largely camouflaged Wheaton holdings.

"You and Zara have two children?"

Kaplan would have made book he knew their names. "Yes. A boy and a girl."

"Good planning, Jack. But then you *are* a good planner." George Wheaton slid his car into the reserved space marked

GW. Leading J.K. through the huge greenhouse lobby to the elevator, Wheaton looked proud and confident as he pressed the top button, WHEATON EXECUTIVE OFFICE.

From the moment J.K. stepped into the reception room, he was again taken aback. Like a World's Fair panorama, more blowups of Wheaton's world hung chockablock on the glazed white walls while the spacious office windows overlooked much of this world for real. The scene from George Wheaton's corner office, however, seemed to stretch as far as one could see across the heartland of America.

The view and the oversized ficus trees were the only live accents in an otherwise beige, glass, and steel decor. The leather sectionals, the Berber carpeting, even the marbleized walls were all the same monochromatic tone.

John Kaplan and George Wheaton sat in identical cane-back Regency chairs that faced each other across Wheaton's long glass-and-steel desk. "I usually sit where you are, Jack," said Wheaton. "Why look at a wall when you can see those great plains? When I'm entertaining, however, like now, I give my guests the view. They're not apt to see anything like it again," Wheaton added meaningfully.

Except for a picture of Erica and his children and a multiline beige phone, the no-drawer desk held none of the usual IN and OUT trays, papers, periodicals, and other executive clutter. It was another Wheaton ploy. He believed it made him look in control, ahead of the game. He liked seeing the look of disbelief that there wasn't even a trace of preparation or reference material.

J.K. shook his head. No ordinary dude, this Wheaton fellow. He was just about to speak when the intercom buzzed.

"Yes, honey?" Wheaton answered.

"A call on line three."

"Who is it?" George Wheaton asked, leaving the phone on speaker as if his life were as clean as his desk.

"Mr. Dellos. From New York."

"Good. Good. Tell him I'll be with him in a minute." George Wheaton turned to J.K. "Gary Dellos. Name mean anything to you?"

"No, can't say it does."

Wheaton wouldn't have put Gary Dellos above double-dealing them both, but he knew from the offhand way Kaplan answered that he'd never heard the name. When Wheaton found out about Dellos from a lawyer pal in London who worked for the royals and used hustlers like Dellos to blackmail those who were blackmailing the Crown, he got just the résumé he wanted. "If it's dirt you want, George, this Eurotrash wallows in it. Expensive, but he'll get it done."

George Wheaton pressed the hold button. "Excuse me a minute, Jack. Got to take this. I'll go in there so as not to bother you." Wheaton opened a connecting door into what looked like a rather complete gymnasium. "I should be using this room for a lot more than just to take a call." He laughed, patting his stomach before shutting the door.

"All right, honey. Put Dellos on." Wheaton sure hoped Dellos had something. Not that he was worried about Kaplan, but he didn't want to have to be a good sport about Kaplan's deal. He'd learned as a kid being a good sport only meant you'd lost.

"Hey, Gary. What's the bad word?"

Dellos knew Wheaton expected some good juice and that today was his date with Kaplan. Not that he'd promised specifically. "I just got in. My lead with Triomphe's MP board member is still hot," he lied.

"What do you have, Dellos? And make it quick. Kaplan's in the other room, and he seems cocky."

"I thought he was coming tomorrow." Another lie. "That's why I came today. I'm meeting her later." He couldn't even say Bettina's name. "Have you dropped the bomb yet?"

Pushing his hand through the bristle on his head, George Wheaton got hot just at the thought of having an animal like Dellos question him as if they were partners. Yet if this temporary liaison with sleaze would give him an ounce of prevention, he had no choice. "Just worry about your end, Dellos," Wheaton said, careful not to raise his voice.

"Okay. Okay. But I'm at her every minute about her old man. She's already asked me if I'm some spy," he lied again. "She's not dumb, just nuts. And Wheaton, I need more cash."

"COD, Dellos. That's the deal."

"What about the best places and the long limos?"

"Your expense account looks fat to me."

"Okay. But I'm keeping every tab."

"And I'm picking them up, Dellos. What's the beef?"

How Gary Dellos would love to have blown this mess, but he'd only be cutting off his own balls to cop out on Wheaton or Bettina when he had those two great chances to get out from under forever. The fifty thousand Wheaton had paid him already was just a drop in the bucket. "Look, Wheaton. You know I'm the best. Look at the bomb I got for you to drop today. Don't worry. I'll grab so much more stuff you'll have a hard time choosing. Okay?"

"It will be when I see it. Dig, Dellos. Dig deep. Open some drawers—only this time make sure they're not underwear," Wheaton added, before clicking off.

Yokel humor-failure! Dellos thought, slamming down the phone at his end. Just the idea of having to go back to that spoiled, sex-crazed bitch made him wish, for the first time in his life, he'd been born with a limp prick.

*   *   *

After he hung up, George Wheaton took a couple of deep breaths to clear his head. "Sorry about the call," he said, rejoining J.K.

"Perfectly all right. Say, what all do you have in there?" J.K. asked, fascinated by the equipment.

"Come take a look," Wheaton said, grateful to buy a little time to shift gears.

J.K. couldn't believe the assemblage of gleaming machinery was not, in fact, some exhibit of futuristic sculpture. Who on earth used it? Certainly not this pudgy little fellow. It was hard to equate his host with this war room of equipment. Making fiduciary sense out of the perverse disarray of Wheaton Industries was easier.

Wheaton smiled, interpreting Kaplan's look. "Mutual of Omaha gave me a helluva big policy after I put this in. Same premium, too. But I hate exercise. You do any?"

"Not on those contraptions," J.K. said. "I prefer my equipment live."

"A lot of people think this is goldenrod," George Wheaton said, as J.K. rubbed his hand across the shaft-of-wheat logo embroidered on all the towels and robes, "because goldenrod is Nebraska's state flower. Can you imagine England celebrating anything as dowdy as an allergy weed? I'm fighting like hell to have our legislature change the state flower to wheat. Makes a lot more sense. Wouldn't hurt Wheaton, either."

"Unless it's a rose, I'm afraid I'm hopeless."

"You know, Jack, 'hopeless' is not a word I would ever associate with you. I believe you live in constant hope. Hope against hope, one could say. Hope that you'll be able to take over Wheaton Industries. Hope that I'm living by some cracked crystal ball and that, by the time you're through, I'll have swallowed enough shards to kill a goat." George Wheaton's voice had a faint chuckle underneath, as he headed back to his office and sat down.

"You don't seem to miss a beat."

"Don't have time to miss a beat, with the amount of Wheaton stock you got. Right, Jack?" Wheaton scrutinized the cool Englishman's face.

It really irritated J.K. to keep hearing this man he'd just met call him Jack, especially under these circumstances. Wheaton probably knew more about J.K.'s affairs than most of his board did. But then, Wheaton had more at stake.

"Being a gambler," J.K. answered, pressing down the sides of his hair, "I'd be willing to wager you know to the share, the pound sterling."

"I've heard rumors," Wheaton said, liking the fact that Kaplan was beginning to appreciate him. Motioning for J.K. to sit, Wheaton picked up the picture of Erica on his desk and turned it around. "Double-sided frame," he said. "People always like to see a man's family, but they feel funny coming around the desk to stare. These double sides work wonders. Makes it easy." With the same avuncular voice, George Wheaton added, "But let me warn you, Jack, that's all I make easy."

For what J.K. considered an open-and-shut case, he found Wheaton quite aggressive. Maybe Wheaton's informants weren't quite as well informed as J.K.'s source, who just happened to be Wheaton's number-two man, soon to be number one—under the new owner, of course.

"So you're going to raid Wheaton Industries," George Wheaton said, getting up and trying to thrust his hands into his pockets, then pulling them free because there wasn't room.

"I don't think raid—"

"I don't *think, I know* raid's right, because Wheaton's not for sale! No offer, no tender, no anything would ever be considered friendly. So the word's 'raid.' Not that I'm not flattered. But as the Duke used to say, 'You don't fix it until it's broken.' And Wheaton's not even chipped. Only chip I see is on the shoulder of somebody getting a little jealous of what good shape we're in."

John Kaplan marveled at George Wheaton's belief in his own invincibility.

"George, you can see me either as the sick raider of a healthy company or as the savior of a company that is already badly chipped, one that soon will indeed be broken. Broke, if you will. And it won't be *if* inflation hits, it will be *when*. And when it does, it will be devastating."

George Wheaton now stood right beside J.K., making him look up as he spoke into his face. "See me any way you want, Mr. Kaplan, but in case you don't see too clear let me tell you I'm no folk hero, no immigrant's son who worked his way up the company ladder. I *am* the company. *And* the ladder. I built each rung. And I'm still building, and I'm still climbing. There's not the finest line between George Wheaton and Wheaton Industries. It was born from my rib, from this land, like me. We're one and the same. And we're going to stay that way until I die." Wheaton's voice cracked with emotion. His eyes looked tired under his shaggy brows.

John Kaplan tried to look away. He wasn't one for sentiment, especially where business was concerned. He also didn't want to detect any indignity in a man so filled with pride. "The thing is that Wheaton didn't need the money. A great cash flow was coming in from the companies you sold. I think you let your schooling interfere with your education. And because of it, cash flow isn't meeting operations and Wheaton Industries is living above its income. When the time comes, George, it's going to have to live within it. And Wheaton's time, I'm sorry to say, is here."

"I presume, Mr. Kaplan, you're betting you can convince the shareholders what a horse's ass I've been all these years that their stock's been doubling and tripling, sending their kids to college, themselves on vacation, and many of them to the Sun Belt for the rest of their lives."

"George, it's nice to sentimentalize about the loyalty of your little stockholders. I have a pretty good idea how many shares they own. But as you're aware, the dedication of the big boys at the bank and pension funds is fading." J.K. knew, too, that it was only a matter of time before Wheaton's faithful would stray.

"I guess you're pretty well up on *all* my facts and figures, not just those dealing with my 'little stockholders.'"

"That's one of the reasons I'm here. So you won't have to fight a losing war. And I don't mean a skirmish."

"Just how much cash do you think Wheaton has? How much do you think we've been squirreling away for that rainy day you believe will never come?"

"I have an idea," John Kaplan said, knowing to the penny.

"You do?" George Wheaton pushed a couple of buttons on his intercom. "Got a minute? You mind coming in?"

With the new arrival, George Wheaton was suddenly at a wonderful loss. He didn't know whom to watch, Jack Kaplan or Robert Ashley, his number-two man. "Rob?" he said to Ashley. "Good name for you: Rob. Of course, you know my pal Jack. Though maybe you don't call him Jack."

Ashley was about to smile when the ice pick hit him between the eyes.

"By the way, Rob, you're fired."

As cool as J.K. was, it was time for his index finger to

circle his collar. He'd obviously been right when he imagined this would be war. Yet if there was one casualty he hadn't expected, it was Ashley. He wondered how long Wheaton had known, how much of Ashley's information had been sabotaged.

He gave a small nod of defeat to Rob Ashley. What else could he do? Ashley knew Kaplan would be fair. That this was their deal. It wasn't Ashley whom Kaplan had misjudged. It was Wheaton.

Although Ashley had been All-American at Ohio State, he resembled an obsequious Oriental as he backed from the room. Almost on tiptoe and without a word, he closed the door.

"That's a skirmish," J.K. said to Wheaton, trying to recover, his palms moving toward his hair, "but well bowled."

"Like Hank Ford always told me, 'Competition's the cutting edge of business.' And if competition from the likes of you rids me of the likes of him, I've climbed another rung."

John Kaplan admired Wheaton's guts. Although Wheaton thought he had really nailed Kaplan, this high-risk game with its multi-billion-dollar pot was just starting to build.

"Why don't we go back to the ranch?" George Wheaton said. "I've had some tea brewed for the occasion."

It was as if the bell sounded and they were back in their corners. The round was finished, a decisive victory for the man in the nubby weave. Postmortems were unnecessary.

"Also, Jack, I want you to see what we call home. Who knows when you'll be coming our way again?" George Wheaton's laugh was affable as he gave J.K. a friendly slap on the back. Or was it a shove out the door?

Before they left, J.K. tried to call Zara. He was sure she wouldn't be there, but since he'd be back much later than he'd thought, he wanted her to know.

11

"*L*et it ring," Archer Blair said, tightening his grip on Zara's arm as she started to move away.

"I can't, darling. You know how persistent they are at the fucking switchboard. First they'll ring in here. Then in the bath. Then it'll be the other bedroom. The other bath. Then through the downstairs. It'll be ten minutes before those dreary operators are through. It's your wonderful American efficiency at play."

"You've mixed it up. I'm your wonderful American efficiency at play." Archer circled her mouth, her nose, her eyes with his tongue.

"Vy you can't just say no calls?" Verna asked, rubbing her own body with man-sized hands while taking a long drag on a freshly rolled joint.

"Right," Archer said, trying to get a firmer grip on Zara.

"Wrong. She's wrong. You're wrong." Pulling free, Zara leapt from the bed, an aura of sexuality belying her boyish build. She turned off the CD before picking up the phone, but Dinah Washington's sexy voice still kept swirling. "My yesterday was blue, dear, today I'm part of you, dear. . . . What a difference a day makes. . . ." And how. Yesterday, Archer had been in London. She'd had to cancel Verna. Today, Archer was here and Verna was free. What a difference!

At the sound of her husband's voice, Zara Kaplan pulled the loose sheet around her naked breasts. She then closed her eyes to make sure she wasn't dizzy. That was her trick to see whether she needed to be extra careful about her enunciation. Thank heavens she was still okay.

"John, darling!" The accentuation of "John" was for Archer and Verna's benefit as she mugged an "I told you so" toward them both. "What a lovely surprise. You're in Nevada? I've never had a call from Nevada before. . . . Oh, I'm sorry, darling, but you know what I mean." Zara giggled.

John Kaplan knew exactly. At the mention of business, she tuned out completely. Unfortunately, every now and then something relevant to her would come up, like yesterday's board meeting, but Zara would long since have gone on to something else.

"Does Mr. Nebraska have a wife?" Zara said, making sure "Nebraska" was clear. Though longing for another vodka, she was afraid her husband might hear the clinking of the ice. "She'd better not be pretty. You know how I am."

Had J.K. ever taken the time or truly cared, he might have discovered that Zara's "love" for him was a mixture of jealousy and pride. She loved it that this strong, sophisticated, brilliant man needed her. She adored showing the world that from all of them out there she was the one he'd chosen. If someone discussed his success, Zara would always bring up his "brilliant heritage" and, as a result, the "brilliant blood of our children." Though J.K. would wince when he'd hear her make the point, it was Zara's continuing attempt to be different as well as contentious. Zara hoped she'd be challenged. She wanted someone to utter the kind of anti-Semitic comment she had heard all her life.

That her enthusiasm for sex with her husband had begun to pall didn't bother Zara at all. She believed it a natural outgrowth of marriage. Not that he still couldn't please her. It was that her intensity was lower, as it was for "things." Her demonstrative energy had gone elsewhere—to Archer and Verna for now.

Just as curious was John Kaplan's obliviousness to their flagging sexual desires, unaware that what he now often did to produce the most potent erection was simply to shift his thoughts from percales to balance sheets.

"How late is 'very late,' darling? . . . But you promise you'll still see the flat tomorrow? . . . Say, 'I promise.' . . . Promise? Promise true?"

There she was, the little girl who'd been scooped up and whisked away, the toast of smart London, the "pretty please" Zara, devoted to her husband yet wanting and willing to do most everything with his best friend. "Me too, darling. And don't forget: you promised."

"What's this 'me too' business?" Archer Blair asked, when Zara hung up.

Zara meant what she'd said, but that had nothing to do with being crazy about Archer. Her husband and her children were what she thought of as her real life. Compared with her real world, Zara believed Archer was froth. He existed in order to keep her real world safe. What Zara couldn't see was that the true constant of her life would, ironically, always be the froth.

"Honestly, Archer. I've heard you be so soupy on the phone with Cornelia I could barf."

"But I don't mean it."

"That's what I mean. You're dishonest."

Archer had no recourse but to smile. Among Zara's greatest attractions were the things about herself she couldn't help, like her honest dishonesty, her jealousy, her prejudices.

As Zara laughed at herself, she let the sheet drop to the floor. Now only her sheer red stockings with black butterfly seams came between Zara and the sweet smoky air.

"I put zee music back," Verna said, having arrived only minutes earlier and having just finished lavishing her erotic-smelling European cream over her arms, legs, front, and back.

Seeing Zara and Verna naked, and knowing that both women were there for him, nearly drove Archer Blair out of his mind. This ravishing Scandinavian and his best friend's wife were the glamour he felt he not only needed but deserved. This was living!

As Dinah Washington wailed, Verna, in only the bottom of her string bikini, took Zara's gold-tipped cigarette from between her over-made-up lips and replaced it with the sweet-smelling pot.

After sucking in strongly, Zara floated to the bureau, lifted her Mason Pearson brush, and, without caring why, slowly began to brush, singing. "Was it in Tahiti . . . were we on the Nile . . . ?"

Lolling her head back, she brushed from her forehead; then, rolling her head forward, she stroked slowly from the back, her hair falling onto her nursery-pink nipples.

More than the pot, more than the vodka, it was Zara's bending over that aroused Archer Blair. Her smooth back with its well-delineated spine and her slightly rounded bottom made his mind explode. Draining the last of his drink, he pulled the joint from Verna's fingers, then lay back, waiting for the marijuana and vodka to rush to his brain. So absorbed was Archer with the magical transition in his head, he was unaware that Zara and Verna were dancing, Verna rubbing her wonderful cream onto Zara. All he saw were Zara's buttocks, bent over like a little boy's naughty behind.

"I'm very, very naughty! I've been a bad boy! A very naughty boy!" Archer Blair said breathlessly, his whole body hot.

Zara giggled as she stared at Archer. *"Je n'ai jamais* seen him like this. *Vraiment."* Zara's bric-a-brac French only appeared when she was nervous and giddy. That's when the desk became a *bureau plat* and the armchairs *fauteuils.*

Verna picked up the brush that Zara had dropped on the floor. In seconds she was over Archer, making oval red marks on the pale bottom of "zee naughty, naughty boy."

"Harder! Harder! *Harder!* You don't know how bad I've been!"

Verna amused herself by making a design on his tight white flesh before the red marks all became one. Zara, without taking her eyes from them, felt her way backward to the vodka, the thwacking sound of the brush pulsing in her ears. Finally, what sounded like a peacock in heat was followed by childlike sobbing as an exhausted Archer Blair fell onto his stomach.

There was something marvelously macabre and exciting, Zara thought, about Verna brushing her own short hair with the same brush. It was like eating with a fork you'd just used to poke someone's eyes. When Verna finished, she tossed the brush onto the pillow and, with the palms of her hands, made sure her hair was perfect. That excited Zara too, maybe because it was something that her husband did.

Taking the vodka from Zara, Verna shook her head at Archer Blair. "Ve got away easy." She laughed.

"Is he *fini?"* Zara asked hopefully. Barely having had

Archer the night before, Zara was much more interested in Verna.

"He'll be back in a vile. But that vill be a vile," Verna said, taking a last drag, then blowing it down Zara's throat. As they danced, the undulating rhythms of their minds matched the movements of their bodies as Zara slipped her hand into the tiny front of Verna's bikini.

". . . I remember you . . . you're the one who made my dreams come true . . . a few kisses ago . . . a few kisses ago."

12

As John Kaplan sat next to a humming, whistling George Wheaton, driving to whatever new surprise Wheaton called home, he felt as if Wheaton were more his size than when they'd first met. J.K. now expected his host to rev up, go through lights, do whatever it took to show how in command he was of any situation in Omaha, a kingdom where this little man could be as big as he wanted to be.

"We're about at the far end of the property line," Wheaton said, pointing to a well-tended split-rail fence running alongside the road. On the other side of the fence, pines and shrubbery provided a cover that made it impossible to see the vast acreage beyond. "It's a pretty fair patch," he went on, knowing from taking other people around that Kaplan would be thinking just that. "Been lucky to be able to add to it over the years. Sometimes it seems the land knows what you're up to and wants to help. It senses when you're going to be good to it."

When at last they reached the entrance, John Kaplan was amazed to see that there was no guard or elaborate security system, just a high, black electronic gate with two horseshoes formed from shafts of wheat linked in a large golden **W**. Inside the first horseshoe was a golden **E**; inside the second, a **G**. As George Wheaton pressed a button in his car, the heavy wrought-iron gates swung open. More immaculate green fencing bordered a mile and a half of gravel drive, so smooth it looked as if it had been raked with toothpicks. The rich plantings and old trees burned with the last fire of fall.

"Quite a spread," J.K. said respectfully in his best J. R. Ewing lingo.

"Got prize bulls in that field there. There's one now, under that copper beech. They can go two, three, sometimes as high as four million apiece. And when they say 'strong as a bull,' you better believe it! Ever see a bull mate? My God. You're talking an elephant's trunk and then some. My pal John Huston, at his farm in Ireland, used to take his guests to the breeding barns after dinner to watch the stallions cover the mares. Hell, I thought that was pretty big stuff until I watched these two-tonners."

Not only had George Wheaton never met John Huston, he'd never been to Ireland. But he did know Henry Ford II, and as his father said, "If you mix enough real with the fake, depending on who you are, it's all real."

"Yes, sir. This is a darn good working farm. Best in the state, I'd say. Wish I had more free time to spend here. We got cattle, quarter horses, even alfalfa. Our own dairy unit, too. Wheaton milk? Eggs? Got it all. Erica was even thinking to put thoroughbreds in that field there, but we just don't have the climate. Or we have too much, if you know what I mean."

Wheaton drove as slowly as if he were picking his way through a mine field. "By now you know I'm a proud sonofabitch, so you can see why I wanted you to see the place, and why I wanted to work out our little problems here. Besides, Jack, it's just us, and we already know what we got to say."

That was the first word of business uttered since they'd left the office. J.K. had wondered how long it would take Wheaton to bring it up and what his next move would be. But the ball was clearly in Wheaton's hands. After all, whatever it was they were playing, they were on his court.

"Very imposing," he said. "In our country, only land grants from kings approach this size. You should be proud." Although J.K. was used to people trying to impress him, Wheaton was definitely impressive. But sooner than Wheaton thought, J.K. would be handing him his wish on a silver salver: more free time.

"Wait'll you see my secret weapon, Jack. Then you'll see why I'm really proud."

As they approached the long white clapboard ranch, the outbuildings seemed to ramble on forever. What it was, in fact, was a long, luxurious compound consisting of garages, a huge main house, guest lodges—and even another gym.

George Wheaton left nothing to chance as they drove up, even to parking the car himself so Kaplan could see the two Bugattis, the black Aston-Martin, the Stutz, and the Pierce Arrow "given me by my old friend, Ed Harrah. Good as he has in his own museum."

The double horseshoes were everywhere: on doorknobs and mats, burned into saddles, and forged into weather vanes. The rooms in the main lodge were big and beam-ceilinged. The rough-hewn oak furniture, bright Navajo carpets, and Ultrasuede fabrics were all rich and comfortable. Above the fireplaces, oxen yokes, "used by my grandfather," spread their pioneer nooses, while Remington bronzes of cowboys stood on tables carved from whole tree trunks. The shocker to J.K., however, was two enormous picture frames stuffed with real money.

Although everyone was always shocked, George Wheaton especially appreciated J.K.'s surprise. "You know, Jack, most people don't give a damn about what they hang on their walls. It's just to show they're rich. So why not show people what they want to see and then some?" There was a mischievous sparkle in Wheaton's eye that Kaplan hadn't noticed before. "A million dollars in a frame. Saves everyone the trouble of pretending to know who painted it, and me the trouble of remembering."

George Wheaton looked at his watch, wondering what was delaying his "secret weapon." Suddenly, she appeared at the door.

Erica Wheaton wouldn't have stayed in New York longer even if George hadn't asked her to come back. Once fall comes, Nebraskans' devotion to football Saturday is inviolate. Overnight, the interstate turns into Cornhusker Highway as GO BIG RED stickers plaster the unbroken miles of cars. Memorial Stadium becomes Nebraska's third largest city when 75,000 loyalists, the Wheatons among the most ardent, rally to support their team.

John Kaplan could not believe his eyes. Wheaton had done it again. But this outdid everything. Erica Wheaton was an astonishing, raving beauty. Tall, exciting, alive, she burst into the room like an unexpected season. Christ, the contest picture J.K. thought was dated didn't do her justice. Though he'd always heard the phrase "all-American beauty," until now he had never really known what it meant. The great build, the undiluted colors, and the swinging blond hair personified health and glamour.

Erica and George kissed and hugged without embarrassment before saying a word to each other, before Wheaton introduced her, before she said, "Hi, Jack. Hijack. That's what I hear you're trying to do." Her husky, intimate laugh took away the sting. Her calling him Jack seemed as fitting as her husband's use of the nickname seemed inappropriate, especially as J.K. was sure her eyes hesitated on his for a split second more than politeness required.

While John Kaplan observed her unaffected ebullience, he was unaware that in the few moments she'd been in the room, he'd become quite undone.

"You've just come from New York?" he asked.

"Just."

"My wife is there. She's also looking for a flat." He liked the association.

"Large? Small?"

"Large. She's been looking a while. I think she's finally found one. Have you seen anything you like?"

"Not really."

"What about that fabulous one you were telling me ab—" George Wheaton began.

"Off the market. Damn it." Imperceptibly, Erica Wheaton closed the lid of one eye at her husband. It was sufficient. "But I saw a great play I hope will be right for our theater. Though it might be too rich for our blood, especially if 'cash flow' means money left over only after the bills are paid. But then, you boys know about that," Erica said, her eyes sparkling.

"She's being modest. She'll not only make it work but make a profit," George Wheaton said, grabbing a large handful of peanuts.

J.K. smiled at her. More Wheaton incongruence, he thought, in a woman who looked the way Erica looked.

"Honey pie," Wheaton said, patting her backside, "don't

go charging out before Jack explains what he's doing here, 'cause this is the fella whose generosity's going to relieve us of Wheaton."

Why were George Wheaton's stubby little fingers, with their pride of ownership on his wife's body, so annoying? J.K. wondered.

George had mentioned to Erica that an English company was trying to raid Wheaton, but he had convinced her that the threat was remote. Therefore, she hadn't paid much attention. But she would now. If he had asked her to be here, it must be important. He needed her.

"I wouldn't miss a word." Erica Wheaton's inviting smile made J.K. feel as if she were on his side. "And unless you want a sleep-over, you better get started."

J.K. didn't think she would understand, but he was glad to have her aboard. He was sure Wheaton brought her in as a distraction, but an audience such as Erica only sharpened his wits.

"Here we are. Especially for you," Erica said, as a proper English tea, with small finger sandwiches and pastries, was set before them. As the fire blazed, Erica poured, making polite conversation. J.K., who was not introspective, believed Erica was totally charmed by him as she complimented him on his energy after so enervating a trip and on the intelligence of owning a G-III.

To entice her and make himself appear all the more intelligent, J.K. outlined his plan for the "amicable and inevitable" transfer of her husband's company to his, as easily as possible. "As the maturing oil industry was ready to consolidate in the early eighties, now is the time for the consumer-brand companies to get together. And to get together globally. The world is small. It's getting smaller. We'll soon be one large consumer network. And before

Wheaton sells off any more valuable assets and becomes even less desirable, I intend to rescue it."

As Kaplan spoke, he stood with one hand behind his back. Erica sat on the sofa beside her husband, holding one of his hands between both of hers, in a husband-wife collaboration that was unheard-of in J.K.'s world.

Catching his breath, J.K. picked up his cup and began to stir, while looking directly into her eyes. Eyes that understood, if not every word, surely enough to know what her husband was doing to the company.

"Well, sweetheart," George Wheaton said nonchalantly. "What do you think of Mr. Kaplan's economics?"

"They're logical from his point of view." Erica's tone was equally unruffled but inside she was frightened, not for herself but for George. Kaplan made a lot of sense. Suddenly, Erica barraged J.K. with questions. Just how much would Triomphe offer over the market? Why wouldn't the banks lend Wheaton the money? What made him think he was the savior?

J.K. was surprised by Erica's aggression. Obviously she was worried that all the goodies were going, that being the wife of one of the most important men in America would soon be over.

"You're isolationists here," J.K. continued. "Not just Wheaton Industries, all the big ones that have fallen. You had it so good for so long, you never saw the ax. With Europe becoming dominant, America's only seen the beginning of its decline, in my opinion."

Erica Wheaton loathed the conceit and arrogance of this magnetic man. The way he thought he could swoop down and grab whatever he wanted with those all-encompassing claws, that scathing English cool! She hated his patronizing, condescending manner, although she knew in her gut that he was right, just as she knew that George didn't take him seriously

enough. There'd be no convincing him, either; George was too
American. He believed whatever buy-outs had been made here
were, for the most part, "temporary." And the idea that
America would let his company be bought out by the old
mother country made him laugh.

"No wonder you were the big debater," George Wheaton
said, cocking his head. "What do you think now, Erica honey?
It's not like you to turn so quiet."

Kaplan had noticed how Erica's attitude had changed as
he talked, how tense and taut she'd become. They're all the
same, that kind, he thought. They see the big picture. As
much as she wanted her husband to head Wheaton, she didn't
want Wheaton stock to go any lower. She didn't want to lose
another penny of her hard-earned money. George Wheaton
obviously wanted to put up a struggle. J.K. was sure Erica
would sell out now. He wished like hell he were up against
her!

How great being up against Erica would be! J.K.
fantasized, as he sat in the same Mustang convertible on his
way to the airport. George Wheaton had asked J.K. if he
minded if someone else drove him. J.K. not only preferred it,
he was relieved. He didn't want to hear about any more
Wheaton monuments or listen to any more Wheaton stories.
The only thing he would have preferred was to have Erica with
him.

Quite a piece of work, that Erica. As overt as she was,
there was something covert, too. Something he felt they had in
common. Maybe it was a ruthlessness, a love of the blue flame,
a competitiveness that was more sexual than sex. Not that she
didn't turn him on that way too. But there was definitely a
bond.

Wheaton obviously had taught her a bit about business,

especially as far as the company went. What she didn't know she seemed to sense. He wondered what they said after he left. He knew that, unlike her husband, she agreed with J.K.'s assessment.

Why shouldn't she go for the lion's share of what was still left?

Christ, J.K.'s lawyers and bankers were apt to end up with more than Erica would. In today's market, they *really* got the lion's share, taking cuts every which way. First they'd find the prey, then they'd produce the financing. After putting them together, these very same powers would construct the dissolution of the just-acquired company, finding parties to whom they could now sell off enough parts of the company until all that remained was pure profit, free and clear.

J.K. was sure Erica herself had a sizable amount of Wheaton stock; it certainly wasn't the warmth of family life that made her stick around. He was also sure she'd do anything to protect George's huge holdings. Very interesting, he thought. Actually, more than very interesting.

13

"*M*r. Kaplan, your plane is ready for takeoff," the chief attendant said as J.K. entered the private terminal.

"Well, I'm not!" Kaplan said hurriedly, racing to the phone. What was supposed to end with a single blow had suddenly become all-out war. But if Wheaton wanted war, J.K. wanted blood. He felt in his pocket for a quarter and the piece of paper with the number. It was only a local call. Very local. She answered on the first ring.

"I'm sorry I'm so late," J.K. said. "Obviously, it took longer than we'd planned, but I'm at the airport now." Much longer than I'd planned, J.K. thought, looking at his watch. Five P.M., Omaha time. What a day. He'd be lucky to make the Carlyle by ten. Not that he was tired. He was too revved up for that. J.K. required little sleep and resented even the little he needed.

"I guess you got the full 'how great I am' tour."

"All nine yards of Wheatonville," J.K. said. "How long before you can get to the motel?"

"Ten, fifteen minutes the most."

"Good. I had my pilot check me in. Room twenty-nine. Second floor. Don't worry. It's nowhere near registration. I'll be waiting."

What J.K. needed now was an office. Privacy. On his way to the airport, he'd mentally mobilized his army. Although Omaha wasn't Mayfair, power buttons worked anywhere. But J.K. didn't want to call from the motel, where numbers went through the switchboard. He wanted direct dial. Though he had phones on the plane, you needed to be airborne to use them, and killers like Kaplan didn't wait for altitude. He had to muster his minions now. He didn't care if he reached them in the middle of the night or the middle of a fuck. Wheaton's balls had to be squeezed until he cried "Kaplan!"

A dispatcher put J.K. in an empty office of a small feeder airline. Sitting behind the long metal desk heaped with resort brochures, Kaplan removed a plastic-coated card from his alligator billfold. The typed numbers were J.K.'s link to the world at the top. A world so widely scattered, yet so closely woven, that when called upon it moved as one. It was a merchant mafia as deadly and competitive as any Sicilian stronghold. It moved mountains, elected popes, started revolutions, even murdered world leaders. Its strength was stronger than organized crime because the havoc it wreaked was ostensibly within the law. Controlled by greed, its outstretched hands reached the loftiest haunts. When a billion dollars had vanished from the Vatican several years back, it was as if God himself had planned the cover-up, the way it disappeared from the news.

J.K. knew the greed with which stock ownership

changed hands when takeovers were announced. Arbitrageurs were the first sharks to take big bites for the short term. J.K. wanted in not only before them but before any new hot competition had a chance to push up the price. Also, Kaplan feared that Rob Ashley might join a clique of dissident Wheaton managers to take over Wheaton before J.K. did. That's what happened when Montgomery Ward's top brass got together and decided they themselves would raid and run the company out of the red before they were run out of their jobs.

Furiously, J.K. worked down the card, contacting Singapore, Hong Kong, Tokyo, Paris, New York, commanding his minions to amass enough cash to buy Wheaton the minute the market opened. As he hung up his last call, J.K. realized he'd better get over to the motel.

With an added spurt of energy, Kaplan took the wrought-iron steps two at a time. His urgency was not to get there but to get out. The fake grass carpeting, the framed Impressionist prints, cheap stucco walls, and chained TV made J.K. think that of all the places in the world he could be, this had to be the worst. Yet since he couldn't possibly chance being seen with her, it was the best.

Even before J.K. closed the door, he heard someone hurrying down the hall. "Mrs. Wheaton?"

"Hello. Yes. It's me," the woman answered breathlessly.

Kaplan judged Marian Wheaton to be about the same age as her former husband. Short and rotund, she and George were eerily alike, with their small, perky features. Although her light eyes crinkled like Wheaton's, they lacked his fire, and though the blue wool dress was expensive, the mink new, and the jewelry real, she looked dowdy.

"I didn't expect someone so attractive," Marian Wheaton said. "Rob never said you were so good-looking."

Or that you were so ugly, Kaplan thought.

When Kaplan first started buying Wheaton, Rob Ashley had informed him that Marian Wheaton controlled a large block of stock through her divorce and that she was crazed on the subject of getting back at George. If handled right, she would be a cinch to hand over her proxy. Her need for vengeance stemmed not so much from her husband's dumping her as from his making "that whore" the star in a town she'd once owned. What Marian Wheaton didn't understand was that, no matter what the town, homecoming queens change every second, depending on who backs their election.

Yet in spite of Marian Wheaton's bitterness, she had still remained in Omaha. Where else would everyone know who she had been? From time immemorial, insecure women have sacrificed possible future happiness for the glory of keeping past husbands' names.

"A drink? To celebrate?" she asked, pulling back the door of the small refrigerator.

"Celebrate what?"

"Us!"

The thought so nauseated J.K. he asked for something he knew wouldn't be in a motel fridge. "Why not? Champagne?"

"You've got it, J.K.," Marian Wheaton chirped, removing a split of Oneida Brut that looked as if it had been there since the place opened. "J.K. That *is* what they call you, isn't it?"

J.K. nodded, smiling at her missing the "Jack" that George Wheaton had appropriated so directly. As she darted busily about, tearing paper off the lavatory glasses, peeling foil from the bottle, working the cork to an amazing *pop,* she never stopped rambling about how horrible "she" was and how "whores who prey on family men shouldn't be allowed to work on airlines." After swirling some ice in the thick glasses, she poured the champagne as if it were liquid gold—which, in fact, Marian was sure it represented. After all, J.K. was there in order to dethrone Erica, behead the king, and return the kingdom to its rightful owner.

"Marian," J.K. started, pretending to sip the vile drink. "I hear you're not only a shrewd businesswoman but a member of a fine Nebraskan family. A welcome contrast, shall we say, to all the upstarts in the world." J.K. spoke in his best conspiratorial tone.

Marian Wheaton accepted flattery as her due, as she had during her marriage, never once thinking George Wheaton wanted her any more perfect than the day they married.

"A bright woman such as yourself must be sick at the drop in Wheaton's stock. After helping Wheaton become so successful, you must be devastated by what's happening." J.K.'s voice exuded sincerity. "But then, you were a helpmate. You encouraged your husband to mind the store."

"You're a clever man," Marian Wheaton said, her eyes on Kaplan.

"How do your boys feel about all this? They also have quite a lot at stake."

"They don't say much, but you can imagine what they feel."

"They'll be the big factors in Wheaton some day, Marian. That is, of course, if there's a Wheaton left." John Kaplan refilled her glass. "But until they're ready to assume the mantle, somebody other than George should be calling the shots."

"Odd you should say that, J.K. I always had a head for figures. Not that you'd know, but I was treasurer of my sorority."

"Then you can understand that with the shares you and your boys control, you'd be a fool to let what's happening continue. You're not even on the board."

"I don't have enough stock."

At least she knew that much, J.K. thought. "Neither do I, damn it." Kaplan looked at her quizzically.

Marian Wheaton swallowed it all. "I'll bet, J.K., between us, we could make the difference as to who gets Wheaton."

"Good thinking," Kaplan said, his best smile forward. "But you must decide soon. Wheaton could be up for grabs, with some real hustlers putting the bite on."

"Not on us," Marian said. "Here's to you and me as a team." Marian Wheaton drained the last of the wine and gave a repelled J.K. a peck on the cheek. In her fantasy she suddenly saw herself in a partnership with Kaplan that extended past Wheaton.

Not a moment too soon, Kaplan made a hasty exit and raced to the terminal. As he strode across the tarmac, his head buzzed with the day—Erica and George, the ranch, the tour, the funky airport signs, Marian. Christ!

But the biggest surprise was Erica: how she'd frowned that George didn't seem at all disturbed when he should have been. She'd even agreed with J.K.'s arguments that the monies J.K. could brandish were unimagined by her husband, not to mention unobtainable. She had seemed impressed as she returned his smiles with a subtlety he didn't expect. Damned smart, that Erica.

During the flight to New York, amid spread sheets and additional calls, J.K. kept wondering how his information could have been so wrong about George Wheaton. He was about as cozy as a drawn fist. While Erica, who he thought would be tough, was the one with the velvet gloves.

14

*T*urning his key quietly, J.K. entered the upper floor of his duplex in the Carlyle. The low lights and seductive scent reminded him of rum drinks in the tropics. The aroma drifted from the bedroom, where Zara had fallen asleep atop the fresh sheets, the lace of her gown draped over her breasts so just the right amount of flesh peeked through. Had J.K. known Verna had put it on her after she'd gotten Archer out and the maid in, it would have made a fittingly bizarre ending to his day.

John Kaplan had no intention of waking his wife. His shoes in his fingertips, he tiptoed to the bathroom, folded his suit to be pressed, put his laundry in the hamper, and took a quick shower. He wondered why George Wheaton, a man still in his early fifties, didn't keep himself more fit. Everything about him, except for his hair, wanted trimming. Strange, since all Wheaton's preachments were about protecting investments.

J.K. was pleased that Zara had arranged such a romantic

setting, even to wrapping herself in that delicious fragrance and sexy lace. He was sorry he'd arrived so late. Just looking at her, however, enabled him to put aside a day that had seemed like a year.

It flattered J.K. that people longed to be in the environment called Zara. And that she was his, all his, gave him a sense of power. Suddenly he needed to feel that power. With an impulsive swell of vigor, J.K. decided he was going to have her, do what he wanted with her, as others wished they could. Just the thought made him hard, even before he touched her.

Tossing his towel in the corner, he switched off the bathroom light. As delicately as his large frame would allow, he eased himself beside his wife, lifting her gown over her whip-thin body. Rolling her gently on her side, he traced the splendid curve of her spine with his tongue. Still half asleep, she flung her arms about his neck and wound her legs around his thighs. Holding tightly, very tightly, she kissed him as she had kissed Verna.

The hungry tongue, the greedy hands, brought it all back to her. Archer had passed out. Verna was still there. It had been wonderful with Verna, lying in each other's arms, doing everything to each other. Zara hadn't heard Verna when she told her she had to go leave for a booking in front of Trump Plaza. She didn't remember Verna saying, "I vill make Archer go out vith me."

Circling her legs tighter about the body she thought belonged to Verna, Zara squeezed her eyes shut, inhaling the lingering lust of the afternoon. Suddenly, she shoved herself away. Verna's cheeks didn't make hers burn. And Zara's arms and legs would have wound farther around Verna's body. Zara leapt from the bed, her heart pounding. Seeing her husband, his arms outstretched toward her, her eyes grew wide. Before

J.K. noticed her confusion, she'd fallen backward, over her own feet.

"Darling!" he cried, jumping from the bed. "Are you all right?"

"Fine, darling, fine." When did Verna leave? When did Archer leave? How did she get into her gown? "I was dreaming something awful. Whoever was here wasn't you. John, John, I love you so!" Zara wept softly, unable to saturate him with enough kisses, so grateful she hadn't made some dreadful mistake.

And he was so grateful she was all right that he held her almost as tightly as she held him, his lips caressing her shoulder points, neck, and cheeks, finally kissing the tears from beneath her eyes. Gently moving her away, he lifted her chin so he could look fully at this wonderful child who needed him so, who had never disappointed him in love.

Again, Zara pulled him close. She needed the warmth of his breath on her lips, the abrasiveness of his face on hers, his hands over her body. His large hands reminded her of Verna. She couldn't control her excitement. J.K. was ecstatic at how wet his wife had become.

"I need you," Zara whispered. "I need you so much. Don't ever leave me. You won't ever leave me, will you?"

"Never," he said, cradling her in his arms, his tongue opening her lips. Ever so gently he stretched her out on the bed. Kneeling above her, he watched her hips rise and fall. Zara reached her arms to draw him toward her. Instead, he ravished her with his eyes, aware that she was under his control, confident that he could do as he wished with her most private parts. As her thighs kept rolling and her moans sounded as if she were in pain, J.K. sat back on his haunches, moving his hands up and down the smooth sides of her body, over her flattened breasts, her stiff, tiny nipples. Taking both of her hands, he put them around his hard cock. Zara pulled one hand back to cover her eyes. J.K. forced it away. Even so small an action accentuated the pleasure of his being able to do what he wanted with her, just as he would do with George Wheaton. The more he thought of Wheaton, the more potent he became.

Rolling her nipples between his fingers, J.K. put them between his teeth and bit softly as she screamed and twisted until, at last, his large frame pinned her down. Shoving his hands under her buttocks, he slid one hand between her legs, his fingers moving along the feather-soft moisture. As Zara's body began to rock faster and faster, John Kaplan got set for the takeover. His sexual greed was reaching a new high. Abruptly his fingers left the slippery velvet. Zara was desperate for him. Squeezing her muscles as tightly as possible, she reached for her husband's hands, but they were already holding her thighs apart to allow him to thrust himself into her.

Forcing her legs wide, he shoved his knee between them until he could locate that velvet valley and maneuver himself inside. Once into her, he grabbed the flesh of her tight bottom, lifting it from underneath while thrusting himself in and out, deeper and deeper. As he grew bigger and harder, the slapping of his body became more and more intense. Gasping, she forced her hands into fists so she wouldn't scratch his back as he grabbed her hair, pulling hard, and plunged into her deeper than ever. Zara twisted under his weight, moving her clitoris under the base of his driving cock. Just as she was reaching the point of no return, J.K. emitted an ungodly groan and with one last lunge sank into the small pool of perspiration on Zara's chest and belly. He had never felt more victorious.

As he lay on top of her, growing limp, he wasn't in the least aware that she was still moving, trying to rub against what was left of him. Rolling away with a soft kiss to her cheek, J.K. went into the bathroom, happier than ever, making the Churchill V-for-victory sign in the mirror.

Once back in bed, he hadn't the slightest clue that Zara's fingers were busy finishing his work. As the rhythm heightened and her extended middle finger dug into the hardened, swelling center, she thought of Verna's fingers where hers were now. Her face contorted, her short sharp gasps almost drowned out J.K.'s noisy sleep.

15

*A*s usual, John Kaplan rose long before his wake-up call. The scent-soaked bedroom of the Carlyle seemed stale and musty. Throwing open the windows, he drew a quilt around Zara and stepped into the shower, his mind already in high gear.

It was a break for J.K. that Archer hadn't stayed in London for a few days, as he did after most Triomphe meetings. It meant J.K. could take him to lunch at Citibank to show those conservative stiffs that Blair was his great pal, not merely a boardroom figurehead. J.K. could use Archer to help pry loose the names of other big Wheaton buyers, if any. George Wheaton's long-wave theory, predicting a deflation that would make everything he sold worth less than when he sold it, wasn't working. Not only was everything Wheaton had sold much higher, but the price of Wheaton's stock had gone way down.

As far as John Kaplan was concerned, George Wheaton's

major asset at this point was Erica. Her sexuality was as magnetic as her mind, both of which J.K. thought had been grossly underrated by Rob Ashley. She seemed to grasp certain nuances and shadings that George Wheaton never saw. Of course, J.K. realized her sights were a helluva lot different from those of her husband. They weren't focused on the long haul. Erica Wheaton wasn't the type to watch her luck run out before she did.

"Darling?" Zara Kaplan called, still in bed, stretching her limbs like a puppy.

J.K. had just come out of his third shower in less than twenty-four hours. "Sweetheart. You're awake?"

"Of course, darling. I hardly slept. I'm so excited."

Whatever the reason, J.K. was delighted.

"Aren't you?"

"What?"

"Excited. Excited about the flat." Zara smiled at the realization that an eleven-million-dollar apartment wasn't uppermost in her husband's thoughts, although making the money to buy it would be. That's why Zara never felt guilty about her freeloving life. It kept her busy when he couldn't.

"Of course I'm excited, darling. Mostly because you are."

Clive van Arlyn laced his third cup of coffee with brandy in order to get up the nerve to phone Archer Blair. He should have done it yesterday. But he and Archer went way back together. They were both gentlemen. And this was blackmail.

He had finally realized that the man with Bettina was Gary Dellos. Although van Arlyn had long ago given up worrying about Dellos, he understood that Dellos's fear was the reason he'd never heard from him again. Of course, van Arlyn had been even more terrified of Dellos. Yet here was van Arlyn, about to blackmail his friend Archer. What else could he do? That commission was more money than he'd ever see again.

As Archer Blair spooned up the last of his oat bran and opened *The Wall Street Journal,* the phone rang. It was van Arlyn. "Up with the birds, Clive?" Blair said, checking the stock quotes.

"Like all big men, Arch." Van Arlyn forced a weak laugh.

"Aren't your rich clients up this early? From what they say, you're dealing with a lot of new billionaires." More and more, Blair was hearing club gossip about van Arlyn's unsuitable guests and his attempts to influence people into proposing them for membership.

"Actually, I *am* calling about a rich client." Van Arlyn was so hot he fanned his face with his hand.

"What about?"

"About Eight Twenty-three."

"Eight Twenty-three?"

"Yes, Arch. The penthouse. The Carnegie duplex."

"The one just on the market? Well, whom do you want to put in it?"

"Lovely people. Really, Arch. Lovely."

"I'm sure." Archer Blair's voice was flat.

In a few stumbling sentences, van Arlyn described the Wheatons. Of course, Archer knew Wheaton Industries, although he'd never met George Wheaton.

"They sound all right, Clive," Archer Blair said, relieved. "Fine, as a matter of fact. But I'm not the whole board. I have the same vote as everyone else. It just depends on the competition."

Fumbling for words, because there weren't any right ones, van Arlyn said, "I don't think there should be any competition."

"What do you mean?"

"The Wheatons are very good people." Van Arlyn paused and took a deep breath. "There's something else I want to mention, Archer. We saw a most unpleasant scene the other day, without meaning to. The elevator door suddenly opened at your floor, and there was Bettina with a very unsavory-looking man in a jogging suit. Bettina was undressed."

"What do you mean undressed?"

"Naked. And they were quarreling. I thought you should know, Archer. Fortunately, the elevator man was not in the car with Mrs. Wheaton and me. But he could have been."

It took a lot less time for Blair to take it all in than it did for van Arlyn to get it all out.

"I see," Archer Blair said, his voice lifeless. What he saw was that the price for van Arlyn's silence was to give the apartment to the Wheatons. "How sad. How very sad. After all these years we've known each other, lived in each other's pockets, and now we're reduced to being savage with each other. Is this what it's all about, this new-money world? Breaking up the old?"

"I know it's hard for you to believe, Arch, but I hate what I'm doing and I hate myself." It was true. He did. He knew Archer Blair was right. Not only was Plymouth Rock washing out to sea but he, Clive van Arlyn, was helping it crumble.

"Give me some time, Clive. I'll figure something out. I have to."

As Zara dressed, it made her feel sexy all over just thinking of running into Archer and Cornelia in the elevator of 823 on a night when she looked especially drop-dead, or having the Blairs up for a drink the evening of the day she and Archer had made love.

"Darling, didn't you almost die when I told you it was in Archer's building?"

"Only because we might have been able to buy it directly," J.K. said, only half jokingly.

"Then why, for goodness' sake, didn't you tell him we were looking?"

"I thought I had. Perhaps I didn't. Besides, he wouldn't think we'd want anything so major."

In all the years they'd been married, J.K. never remembered Zara getting ready so quickly. In no time she was bathed, dressed, and at breakfast. Because yesterday had been so wonderful, she even put on the same perfume for good luck. Watching her squeeze the last of the juice from her grapefruit onto the spoon, J.K. suddenly frowned. "Zara?" His tone was uncertain. "Is that new?"

"Is what new, darling?"

"I mean, is that right? What you're wearing?" Actually, J.K. had no idea what he meant. Everything Zara had on suddenly looked odd. The movie makeup. The crazy hair. The jewelry. The evening look at eight in the morning. Maybe that was it. At night it was courageous and different, eccentrically well bred, even endearing. The cold morning light made it look bizarre.

Zara glanced at her revealing Saint Laurent neckline. Had she spilled? She felt to see if the panther pin was hanging unlatched. Possibly she'd missed some of her hair; she could tell by a touch. No. Nothing.

Watching his wife's confusion, J.K. regretted what he had said. "It's the perfume, darling. That's what it is. The perfume."

Zara smiled, reassured. "I put on the same as last night, because last night was so wonderful. Remember?" She went around to her husband's chair and softly kissed his cheek.

Yes, J.K. thought, that must be it. "How could I forget?" he said. He put down his teacup and checked his watch.

Since the day was clear and bracing, they decided to walk to 823. Tall, dressed in the height of fashion, the Kaplans were a head-turning couple. Although J.K. usually delighted in the looks of envy and approbation, today the scrutiny, especially of Zara, bothered him.

Doris MacDonald was waiting in the lobby when the Kaplans arrived. After back-and-forth greetings, they began to speak as if the apartment already was theirs.

"Zara tells me we've got a winner," J.K. said, his stride brisk.

"There's not a better one in the city," Doris answered, keeping step with him.

Art Rooney, already at the elevator, beamed as Doris MacDonald introduced him. Rooney liked MacDonald. She brought in a darn sight more quality than that pantywaist van Arlyn. Sure, this Kaplan woman might look a bit far out, but that was the way with titles, especially in the royal circle, like he'd heard she was. The husband was certainly fine and prosperous-looking. The name Kaplan didn't have to be Jewish. The ones with changed names were worse. You never knew what was coming until you saw them. 'Course, that's why they changed them.

J.K. looked at his watch. "Tell me, Mr. Rooney, has Mr. Blair left yet?"

"Haven't seen him. You seen him, Pete?" Rooney asked the elevator man.

"No, sir."

"Good." J.K. turned to Zara. "After we look at the flat, I'm going to take Archer to the bank. And you know what, darling? Before we go would be the perfect time to tell him about our buying it. We can have Mr. Rooney pretend there's an emergency in the penthouse and ask him to come up immediately."

"Brilliant!" Zara said, tingling at visualizing Archer's shock.

"I'll call from the house phone upstairs," Rooney said, pleased to be in on the game and pleased he was right about Kaplan. After all, Mr. Blair was the best the building had, even if there was talk about the girl.

From the moment J.K. stepped into the spacious marble gallery, he liked what he saw. Zara, prone to hyperbole, had done her homework. Though J.K. fairly sprinted through its seven thousand square feet, he could already imagine himself in it.

"You girls did a superb job," he said, standing in the middle of the drawing room. "Doris, just let my office know about any letters, financial statements, other requirements that need to be handled. It'll be done in a flash. As they say, you can take this one off the market."

J.K.'s wide smile collided almost directly with Archer Blair's anxious frown as Blair walked into the joyous group. He'd hoped that whatever emergency Rooney had might prove a welcome distraction to van Arlyn's call about Bettina. Instead, as Zara and John shouted "Surprise!" Archer Blair suddenly realized what the surprise was, and his stomach twisted with a pain he thought was even more insurmountable than his problem.

Thank heavens J.K. and Zara smothered him with more cries of "Surprise!" It gave him time to come to, to react to their reaction. Beyond any reasonable doubt, Archer had to show he was thrilled beyond belief. After all, what could possibly make Archer Blair happier than helping his best friend and the love of his life get an apartment they adored in a building he controlled? Opening doors for one another was what their lives were all about.

How could the Kaplans possibly be kept out of 823? Incredible as it seemed, that's what Archer Blair had to figure out.

16

*A*s John Kaplan drove downtown with Archer Blair to Archer's office, J.K.'s headquarters away from London, he had every reason to be content with his world: the new apartment, Zara's renewed enthusiasm, and the great way things were going with Wheaton. Even now, as he spoke on the car phone, the figures were so good he kept repeating them for Archer's benefit.

"Thirty-two and a half? You're sure? To be up only two points after our buying a hundred and twenty-five thousand more shares is fantastic." J.K. tilted his pad toward Blair in case he'd missed anything.

Blair nodded without looking. All he was seeing was the disbelief that would be on his friends' faces when they learned they could not have the apartment.

"You know, Arch," J.K. said, still scribbling away, "that's no jump at all, especially since you can be sure Wheaton was in there buying after our meeting. In no time that stock will dry up and the price will soar, especially when those Omaha bankers who are beholden to Wheaton for business start buying to help him out. But we've got time. Even though we've hit five percent, we don't have to file our Thirteen-D for ten days, so that info won't be public for a couple of weeks. That means the arbs won't be buying big until they know for sure what they now only suspect. It's all so absurd anyway: everyone saying they're buying for the possibility of effecting a change in management and ownership, when everyone's out to skin everyone else alive."

"Right. Everyone," Blair echoed.

When the blue Corniche came to a halt, J.K., as usual, didn't wait for the driver to open his door. In fact, he was almost at the elevator by the time the man came around.

The Blair offices had changed little since Archer's grandfather's day. The carpeting, though replaced, was still a dull green, the walls the same stale off-white, and the secretaries still sat in cubicles with frosted glass partitions. Only the computers, with their bright flashing screens, added new life and color.

Archer's office also was almost unchanged. The old golf and sailing trophies, the mounted game fish, and the faded black-and-white family photographs were still in full array.

"Just give me a half hour," J.K. said. "Then we're off to the bank. Suit you?"

"I've plenty to do," Archer Blair said, just praying he could find a solution. He went to a little room in the back of his office, to the large armoire that hid two ugly steel cabinets, one with files to do with Blair family business and the other with business pertaining to 823—lists of employees, maintenance costs, tenant listings, board meeting minutes, and bylaws. Rifling through folder after folder, Blair hoped to come across something—anything—to make telling J.K. easier.

Not that Blair understood why J.K. even wanted such a huge place for the little time he spent in New York. As Blair dwelt on that thought, he was suddenly struck by another one. A great one. In a most uncharacteristic gesture, he brushed a bunch of the files from his desk onto the floor. Taking huge strides around his office, he rehearsed aloud how he'd announce his solution.

Jack, old buddy, I'm so sorry. Sorrier than you'll ever know. I can't believe it myself. It's nuts, I know. Crazy. But the Eight Twenty-three bylaws say you've got to be an American citizen to own an apartment in the building.

As he was about to burst into J.K.'s office, Blair suddenly wondered why in hell he should be the messenger. He wasn't the broker. Let MacDonald do the dirty work. He called her and explained.

"Yes. . . . Yes, Doris, I'm sorry for everyone." Archer Blair's words were quick. They had to be, because he *was* sorry and he was lying. "Christ, Jack's my best friend!"

But it was Doris MacDonald whose dreams were shattered beyond belief by that archaic clause. She begged Blair to amend the bylaws, arguing that the board would be fools to enforce such an obsolete law with a couple as suitable as the Kaplans. But then, as MacDonald well knew, like most of parvenu New York, 823 had its brutal nucleus of those such as J.K. who, once in themselves, made sure their counterparts were locked, sealed, and cemented out.

It was different from the days when WASP enclaves such as 823 were famous for their clannishness. People in those days had lived with each other because they were *like* each other, and they liked each other as well. Today's newly minted magnates and their newly minted wives seemed to possess an unparalleled self-loathing and an unnatural fear of their own kind. Architects of anonymous lives, they'd never accumulated any usable past to make their present worthy enough to carve a meaningful future.

"Doris, you don't honestly think, with Kaplan being so rich, Zara so beautiful, and America hating the British for owning more of America than any other country in the world, that the board would even consider amending the bylaws for the Kaplans, do you? Take it from me, we're lucky. Because if that rule weren't in place, the Kaplans would still be far from shoo-ins."

"What if the competition proves disastrous?"

"Doris, believe me, there's no way. None. You know J.K.'s dying to buy. He just can't have Eight Twenty-three. Call him now. He's here in my office. In fact, you might be able to show them both something today while they're hot. And Doris, again, I'm devastated for all of us." Before she had a chance to argue further, Blair hung up, grateful that by the time he saw J.K. the blow would be softened.

It didn't take long. "What in hell kind of idiotic rule is that?" J.K. barked, crashing into Blair's office.

"That's exactly it. Idiotic."

"Who knew it existed?"

"When I called Eight Twenty-three's agents to set up a board meeting, they reminded me of the French couple we turned down a few years back. Great people, too. Not like you and Zara, of course."

"Pardon my French, Arch, but bullshit! Not you, the rule. Amend it!"

Archer Blair shook his head. "I can't."

It was inconceivable to Jack Kaplan that his great friend couldn't get him into a building he controlled. Even if some newly discovered bylaw did say tenants had to be citizens, why couldn't this great social scion change it?

Long before J.K. had cut so powerful a figure, against all odds for one not born to the purple, even White's, London's most venerated men's club, had elected him. To be excluded from a building where half the tenants wouldn't even be allowed guest privileges at his London club was unthinkable.

Blair was a fool! Yet what would he know about struggling for acceptance when his very name engendered approval? Wasn't that why J.K. first befriended him at Yale? For his name and those splendid Gatsby vacations when J.K. couldn't afford the fare home and Blair would take him to his family compound on Long Island or in Maine, where the lawns seemed manicured by cuticle clippers and cares cleansed by the sea?

Though those holidays had much to do with forging J.K.'s resolve to become rich, after a while, for men such as Kaplan, the drive and the deal became the estates and the luxuries, while the status symbols were worn by new wives after the wives who helped attain them had been discarded. That was why, for J.K., this defeat was particularly insufferable. For the first time he was powerless to buy Zara something she truly wanted.

"Co-op! Brilliant name! Co-operative with whom? No wonder America's becoming Third World." J.K. was bitter. "Why would a bunch of losers want us to own any more? You know, Arch, I don't care about it myself"—J.K.'s jaw was tight, his hands deep into his pockets—"sure, I love the place; but Zara was really smitten. Until that flat came along, I was concerned about her lack of spirit. Then all at once, the old spark returned."

"I'm sorry it went so far, Jack. If there were anything, anything at all I could do—"

"I know, sport. I know. But then, so much for surprises and the best-laid plans, eh? Oh, well. Can't be helped. Many worse things. Suppose there were other companies as interested in Wheaton as we are. That would be *real* trouble. Easier to find another flat, old boy. Right?"

Watching the speed with which J.K. switched gears to what really mattered to him made Archer Blair doubly sorry for Zara. Sorry about 823, and sorrier that she was married to such a bastard.

17

*A*rcher Blair had been a perfect pawn for John Kaplan with the bank, just as Archer had been a perfect puppet for Clive van Arlyn earlier that morning with J.K. Little wonder his head was splitting, along with his world. Confused and angry, he could never have sat through a lunch with Jack and those bankers. Thank heavens he'd opted for home. The peace and civility would offset the greed he'd already been served.

Blair's apartment was a good deal smaller than the Carnegie duplex. Having belonged to Archer's parents, it was where he was raised. Between what he and Cornelia had inherited, they were surrounded by the same English antiques they knew from childhood. "Thank you. We are fortunate to have nice things," they would answer, each with the same self-effacing smile, as people admired the furniture and especially the paintings, most of them purchased by Blair's great-grandfather when he, like most of fashionable New York, relied on the expertise of Lord Duveen.

Archer Blair would have welcomed a lunch with J.K., had he suspected that, not long after he left, the sanctuary of his home had been invaded by Gary Dellos.

Dellos thanked heaven, since he knew goodness had nothing to do with it, that he'd finally decided to phone Bettina and make peace.

"You won't believe this! Where on earth have you been? I tried to call you all day yesterday. Wait till you hear!" She spoke as if there had never been an unpleasant word between them.

The shrill teenage voice so annoyed Dellos that his immediate reaction was to hang up, but this was business. "Hear what?"

"Well, just by chance I happened to hear my father on the phone. I didn't even know he was here. He never comes home so early. Anyway, remember how you told me to listen and everything?"

"Go on."

"Well, I heard him using that same voice I remembered when I was little, when I knew he was talking to some woman who wasn't my mother, when Mother would cry and everything. So I listened. Who do you think it was? You'll die."

"Who?"

"You're going to faint."

"Better than dying."

"Jack Kaplan's wife. Zara. I heard him ask for her by name: 'Mrs. John Kaplan.' I heard him say all love things. I heard him plan to meet her. I couldn't believe it. I still can't. I'm so excited."

"You did real good, baby."

"You happy?"

"You bet. Now you've got to help me put the screws to your old man. Think you can do it for me? For us, I mean?"

"Try me."

"Ten minutes too soon?"

Whisking past the doorman and that nosy superinten-dent, Dellos took a certain pride in the elevator man's not asking the floor. It was pride of ownership, if not of the apartment, at least of its tenant.

Aside from the dark glasses, Dellos thought Bettina looked surprisingly good. Even the wide, pleated pants and the underwear-style T-shirt looked good. Dellos would have liked to have joked that he was losing his punch, but wisely let a smile cross his lips instead.

"Bettina, let me say in person what I told you on the phone. I'm sorry." Hurriedly, Dellos took her in his arms.

"I know. Me too. I didn't mean to press. I just got frightened."

"Nothing wrong with honest fear, I guess." Dellos laughed, swinging his hand romantically in motion with hers as he walked her toward the library to get a drink.

For longer than Bettina could remember, the small library bar had been set with the same four cut crystal glasses, three decanters labeled WHISKEY, SHERRY, and GIN, and two bottles of Canada Dry club soda. Exactly at five-thirty each evening, a fresh lemon, a silver fruit knife, and a small sterling bowl filled with ice would be brought in. Over the years, the only change had been that the decanter labeled GIN was now filled with Absolut vodka.

"Do you mind?" Dellos asked.

"Do you want ice?"

"No. No," Gary Dellos said, pouring himself a decent shot of vodka. After one fast gulp, he shamelessly began to spin his heritage of straw into gold. Ingeniously, he fabricated a tale about how his family owned vast olive groves in Greece and how, after they'd refused to sell out to J.K., J.K. was poisoning the groves "so he can buy the land for a dime on the drachma."

"What a monster!" Bettina Blair cried, her love gushing out to this victimized man.

"Your father can stop Kaplan, Bettina. And you can make him do it." Dellos watched her eyes brighten as he explained about Zara and her father and what he needed her father to do as far as J.K. went.

So besotted was Bettina with Dellos that Dellos never needed the lie. Bettina never thought twice about blackmailing her father. Bullying either parent would be her pleasure. They'd never been there for her. Dellos had given her the only true love she'd ever known. Above all, he was the first controlling force in her life.

"You've got it," Bettina said. She threw her arms around him, feeling the thrill of a true partnership.

Since Bettina was hoping this reunion would include the bedroom, she was furious to hear her father's voice at this hour of the morning, although for Dellos the timing couldn't have been better. Blair was strung out, Dellos high as a kite on his own cunning, and Bettina wild at her father's intrusion. When Dellos suggested that she state the facts, Bettina began at once.

With a wink at her love, she stood brazenly before her father, her fisted hands on her hips, her chin forward. "So Daddy has a girlfriend."

Archer Blair's eyes narrowed. "What?"

"A mistress? No. It wouldn't be that. Daddy would have to pay."

"Bettina, get out of my way. You're crazy."

"Zara Kaplan ring your bell, Daddy?"

Archer Blair froze.

"As I said, Daddy has a girlfriend."

"What do you want, Bettina?"

"Aha! The doting father. Caring what I want."

"You're mad."

"Oh, Daddy. You told me yourself. Animals get mad. Humans get angry."

"This is your doing!" Blair said fiercely, his eyes shooting to a smirking Dellos.

"No, Daddy, it's both of us. He's my business partner." Bettina went to kiss Dellos full on the lips in front of her disbelieving father. "My partner, here, needs some dirt for his olive groves. We thought about fifty thou, right, darling?" Pleased with her cleverness, Bettina presented Dellos's case with gusto, stepping within a hair of her father.

"I'm right. You *are* mad!" He slapped her hard across the face.

Archer Blair couldn't believe he'd struck his daughter, hard enough to send her reeling. He'd never hit any woman in his life. And now he had hit his own daughter. Bedrock New Englanders didn't lose control. Lives could be strewn with calamity, yet outward emotion remained on hold. But Bettina had pulverized her father's already cracked composure. His baby was tough and hard as any streetwalker.

His mind whirling, Blair tried to extend a comforting arm to his daughter, to comfort himself as well. As he lurched toward her, Bettina, more defiant than ever, backed away. "Don't come near me," she warned, her lips tight.

"I'm sorry. So sorry, Bettina. What have I done to my baby? My poor baby?"

"Have a drink, Daddy dearest, while you mull it over," Bettina said. "And do try to restrain yourself from hitting me again. You know, until just now, you hadn't touched me for eighteen years. But I don't miss it. Gary, here, is my lover."

Things were even worse than Clive van Arlyn had

implied. Watching this changeling in his daughter's body, Blair slowly crossed the worn, flowered needlepoint rug for a much-needed drink. He tossed it down and then refilled his glass before turning back to her,

"Where's your mother, Bettina?"

"Not to fret, Daddy," Bettina mocked.

"I care for your mother, Bettina. Where is she?" Blair looked as if he could knock his daughter across the room. What had turned her into this harridan? It had to be this man.

Bettina liked seeing her father on the edge. It was easier to deal with him on her level. "She's in the country. A hard freeze is forecast. She must cover the chrysanthemums. Nothing is more important to dear old mum than her dear old mums, you know." Bettina looked at Dellos, who smiled appreciatively.

"You get the fuck out of here!" Blair yelled at Dellos, hurling what was left in his glass across Dellos's face as Dellos sat in Blair's favorite chair, resting his feet in their dirty sneakers on the ottoman.

"What a nice family trait!" Dellos glared at Bettina, who hated her father more than ever. She was terrified that her lover might leave. Dellos had to restrain himself from squashing Blair in front of her. Instead, he opened the humidor beside the chair and slowly and deliberately broke every cigar in two, thinking of each thick Havana as Blair's neck.

"Now, Mr. Archer Blair, we'll talk," said Dellos, and he filled Archer Blair's fogged mind with the details of Bettina's discovery.

Gary Dellos was acting more than ever as if he owned the joint. But then, Dellos did have America's finest on its knees. And to think that only this morning, when Dellos awoke, they had still owned the world.

"Archie, it's only because you've been such a first-rate

father that I promise you I won't marry your precious baby. My guarantee will cost a mere million, banked in Switzerland. Odd as it may seem, there are those of us who prefer the ugly oyster to your pearl. One tiny million, and I'll blow so fast even your new shrink won't believe it wasn't all a bad dream."

Hurriedly, Dellos gave the high sign to Bettina. He had to lie pretty good around this one. No one knew better than Dellos that you can't press your luck. At the moment he thought he detected a definite "maybe" in Blair and the understanding of an accomplice in Bettina.

If Dellos worked this sting right, with a million from Blair, another quarter-million from Wheaton, and no more Bettina forever, these moorings could be cut for good.

Not that Blair wanted his daughter back. Not *this* daughter. But with Dellos gone, Blair figured he might find the old one. But most important was saving Zara.

All at once, the entire room burned with fear. Bettina was terrified Dellos might blow. Dellos was terrified he might not get the chance. As for Archer Blair he was petrified that, whatever his decision, it would be the wrong one. It was a moment when any one of the three of them could easily kill the other two.

18

"**Y**es, Clive, your goddam commission is safe!" Archer Blair shouted into the phone and then slammed the receiver down so hard its plastic cover shattered.

The hysteria in Blair's voice stunned van Arlyn. He was so much more frenzied than this morning, when van Arlyn had first broken the news to him.

Though Archer Blair filled van Arlyn with both guilt and relief, the parts were hardly equal, and the guilt wasn't even worth van Arlyn's spinning his ring when he hung up. All van Arlyn had to do to change his mood was think of the call he'd received just before dialing Archer.

"Buy it!" George Wheaton had hollered from Omaha. "As long as she's happy, nail it!"

Clive van Arlyn knew George Wheaton would buy anything his wife loved. Still, he couldn't believe anyone would spend eleven million dollars without so much as a glance at what he was buying. That was another reason van

Arlyn was in a hurry, why he was anxious to arrange a board meeting as soon as possible. Luckily, Wheaton would soon be in town.

Three days later, in the living room of the Wheatons' suite at the Plaza where he had come to brief them on their application, van Arlyn finally met George Wheaton. At first he was aghast at this little powerball of a fellow in his sea-blue leisure suit garnished with a Boys Town tie clasp and monogrammed handkerchief of the sort van Arlyn couldn't recall having seen outside of an automobile showroom. However, like most car salesmen, Wheaton was eager and spirited, and the way he looked at Erica, in her clinging Christmas-red cashmere, was loving and nice. Really nice.

Van Arlyn was certainly a sharp contrast in his meticulous glen plaid with its subtle forest-green stripe matching the stripe in his tie and the lining of his jacket. However, if Wheaton had been asked later what van Arlyn had so painstakingly put together to wear, he wouldn't have remembered a single item.

Though it was still before nine in the morning, fresh flowers, fresh coffee, and even a butler to serve it were in the newly decorated suite when van Arlyn arrived.

Van Arlyn had noticed the new glitter throughout the lobby as he dashed to the elevator. Shiny gold leaf seemed to have been added to ceilings and moldings, while miles of new, too bright carpeting had been laid throughout. Once Trump took hold of the Plaza, van Arlyn thought, he had certainly over-gilded even the Gilded Age.

For George Wheaton, the views, the comfort, the instant laundry, instant cleaning, instant round-the-clock service with hot and cold running waiters, computers, and every variety of business machine "does me just fine," even at the almost million a year rent he'd have to pay. Thank God, van Arlyn thought, Erica disagreed.

As the trio sat before the newly enlarged window that framed Central Park, Wheaton looked at the time and patted Erica's knee. "Shall we?" he asked. He figured that van Arlyn would take five, ten—fifteen minutes at most.

When van Arlyn pulled out his sheaf of papers, Wheaton was shocked by its thickness. To the last scintilla, van Arlyn outlined each document the board members needed to receive before they would even meet the Wheatons. If, heaven forbid, any part of the package wasn't up to snuff, Archer Blair, who received all information first, could tell van Arlyn what wrongs to put right before anything went too far.

As van Arlyn began, Erica and George were horrified at the invasion of privacy they were expected to undergo before being permitted to plunk down eleven million.

Individual tax returns detailing every source of income had to be accompanied by a CPA's certified balance sheet listing their net worth, which had to be a minimum of ten times the cost of the apartment. In off-the-wall terms, they needed at least $121 million in assets to turn the key! And payment was all in cash. The very mention of the word "mortgage" would cause instant exile.

"Since money's not a problem in the cash-happy eight-ies," van Arlyn said, in his best throwaway tone, "today's sticky wicket has become those five letters of personal recom-mendation. An ideal one, of course, would be from someone who's lived in the building before the influx of . . . " and van Arlyn cleared his throat instead of finishing the sentence, as he perfunctorily read the roster of tenants.

"Tina and Hyatt Struthers are good friends," George said. "The best! Forgot they even lived at Eight Twenty-three. They're the sort who always think visiting firemen want nights on the town. Last time out, we had enough vodka to flood the pool at the Four Seasons. Fact is, Hyatt just loves being with Erica." George Wheaton's smile widened with pride.

Electrified, van Arlyn grabbed Erica's shoulders. "Erica, you've got to get the Strutherses. Tomorrow, first thing. At his office. What luck!"

Clive van Arlyn didn't have to shift his eyes to see George Wheaton's brows tighten into two sharp ridges.

"Relax, George," Clive said, his laugh just within control. "What's wrong with putting a little touch on somebody. We're not speaking 'make,' George. We're talking 'touch.'"

Erica shook her head at van Arlyn to drop it, knowing it was anathema for George to think Clive wanted him to manipulate his friends.

Unable to sputter an apology, van Arlyn twirled his ring, pursed his lips, and audibly blew the heat from under his collar.

"And, by George, George, for all our sakes, especially Erica's, no letters from names ending in vowels or from any flash trillionaires using their money to burn holes in other people's lives. Let's just play Eight Twenty-three till it's over."

Van Arlyn knew it was unconstitutional to turn down even the sleaziest applicant because of race or religion, but private boards, like private clubs, never need to come clean about their blackballs. Van Arlyn shuddered in mock disgust, praying Wheaton wouldn't turn into one of those asshole moralists fighting fire just to show his burns.

"Like Michelangelo, Plato, or Gandhi?" Wheaton asked, unable to suffer van Arlyn gladly. He was hanging in for Erica.

Forcing a weak smile, van Arlyn continued, "Another minor point could also come up, George," he said, knowing full well it would, though he sounded annoyed at having to mention anything so ridiculous. "About your boys. Naturally, all you would say is the truth: that they're grown and *permanently* in Omaha. You know how people think all college kids are just champing at the bit for wild city vacations."

Erica couldn't believe that she was hearing Clive correctly, after what they'd seen when the elevator stopped on 6.

"I'll say no such thing," George Wheaton said, about to explode. "My boys are—"

"George, sweetheart," Erica interrupted, "if Clive were as smart as you, *he'd* be buying the apartment."

"True," Wheaton said, relaxing.

Van Arlyn tried his damnedest to stay cool before the ugly finale. "The last report the board gets is this report you never see. It's a file going back as far as it can, trying to trip you as best it can. Let's say you—and you know I don't mean *you*—said something that could be labeled even the least bit fraudulent on your application, this'll pick it up: a club you weren't quite in, a degree not quite finished, a job you didn't really have. All anyone has to do is tap a couple of computer data boards, and your life's an X ray."

It wasn't only the Wheatons' silence that unnerved van Arlyn, it was imagining his own past revived for present approval.

"I guess by your book, van Arlyn, even Napoleon couldn't make it. He added inches to his height in order to join the army."

Again, van Arlyn forced a smile.

"In fact, sweetheart," George said, turning to Erica, "what Clive here is trying to say is it's like a Dun and Bradstreet report. Background material. Bank credit."

"Exactly. Just business as usual," van Arlyn said, further elated by Wheaton's quirky naïveté, for he didn't believe for a second that Wheaton could have come this far without a few skeletons.

Though Clive affected the style of a policeman reading a suspect his rights, he quaked at the thought of what he'd seen in some of those reports. The lowest down-and-out private eye couldn't dig dirtier.

Stretching and smoothing his permanent-press trousers, George Wheaton rose, kissed Erica, and shook van Arlyn's hand. "Gotta leave you all. Business is like a car. Only runs alone when it goes downhill."

"Sorry we couldn't talk more," van Arlyn said, relieved beyond euphoria.

"Erica, get Clive some lunch from room service," Wheaton roared. That was his idea of a joke. It wasn't lunchtime yet, but the last hour made it seem like it should be. Erica, in spite of herself, roared too, not only because it was a terrible joke but because she was thrilled George could still laugh after going through what she knew had been torture for him.

Van Arlyn, almost giddy, put his arm around George Wheaton and walked him hurriedly to the door.

"So, George, I'll put Eight Twenty-three into contract as soon as I get the ten percent deposit, which will be held in escrow until America's finest is yours."

"At least it's staying American. A lot more than I can say for a lot of our country's finest."

On that flag-waving note, as the elevator door shut on George Wheaton, Clive van Arlyn gave a little wave of his own. His gilt-edged future seemed secure.

19

*H*ours before the Wheatons' 9 A.M. appointment with the co-op board, pale with sleeplessness and unable to control himself another second, van Arlyn rang Erica one last time. "The beige Adolfo with the braided jacket and the skin pumps, *not* the slings. And call the minute—the split second—it's over." Since brokers weren't permitted at board meetings, van Arlyn hoped his excruciating tension wouldn't kill him before he heard Erica's voice.

Erica decided that slamming the phone on van Arlyn would only wake George up and make him even angrier than van Arlyn had made her. "Your faith, Clive, is underwhelming," she hissed softly, cutting van Arlyn short. Erica was fiercely protective of her husband, though only yesterday she'd bought George an Hermès tie, patterned with little H's, which she knew he'd wear because of her card: *Health! Happiness! Home!*

On the dot of nine, Erica and George Wheaton stood

before Archer Blair's door. It was difficult for Erica to look understated. With her dramatic coloring, her full hair swept from her face, in her hugging Adolfo and deliberate sling-backs, she was dazzling.

No sooner had Erica's finger left the bell than Archer Blair, in banker's gray, Racquet Club tie, buttoned-down broadcloth, and old-boy charm, thrust a hand and a smile toward the Wheatons. Blair personified the corporate scion—well-bred, well schooled, the "born executive" thanks to the family born before him. Though his eyes were clear and intense, they shifted uneasily in front of the Wheatons, never making contact with anything other than his familiar sur-roundings.

Erica Wheaton squinted at the bright shafts of sunlight bouncing from prismed chandeliers and polished woods as Blair led them to the library, aflame with the colorful chrysanthemums Cornelia Blair brought in every Monday from the country.

As the Wheatons entered, conversation stopped. It was as if they were parading before a tribunal rather than friendly next-door neighbors. Yet no matter how manufactured the smiles, the curiosity of the board was real.

Archer Blair first introduced Blanche Harwood, a widow for fifteen years. A walnut-faced woman, she carried her age and plump frame as if neither mattered. Long ago, she'd decided to accept change as if it had never happened. On the board for thirty years, she'd seen the best come and go, and with each arrival, everyone always believed the best had gone. After the First World War, her father had said, "The chaos of war always gives the lower classes a chance." After the Second, her husband had said the same. According to Blanche Har-wood, the battle of greed was no different now than it had ever been. For her and her ilk, "down to earth" was still the highest compliment one paid new money. Whether it would be bestowed upon the Wheatons was yet to be seen.

"Blanche, here," Blair said warmly, his hand resting on the familiar shoulder of the green comfort-zone knit, "was practically born in this building and—"

"Don't finish, Arch," she said, her cigarette voice becoming a crusty half laugh she tried to wash down with a gulp of coffee from what was obviously her own mug. "With what's being asked for the Carnegies', my heirs might decide to rush *me* out of this life and into the next!"

The mug fascinated Erica. Not because it was Mrs. Harwood's, but because she and her husband were offered nothing. For a building bursting with elegance, weren't manners necessary? Or was common courtesy just too common?

"Pretty, you are. Very," Blanche Harwood said, nodding approval. "Once you pass jealous, you want pretty around." Her eyes narrowed dismissively at the lumpy husband. Not that he mattered much, since he would never enter more than the lobby or elevator of her life.

As Archer Blair stood before Savannah Blakely, she raised her never-in-the-sun, perfectly manicured hand to Erica. "Lovely meetin' you." In her late thirties, her idiosyncratic good looks were what one immediately noticed; the sleek helmet of black hair, the white skin, bright almond eyes, tiny turned-up nose, and succulent bottom lip. Her safe business suit, however, hid the promise and threat of her full breasts and high, firm buttocks. A seemingly delicate southern transplant, Savannah Blakely never let you forget that her great-great-granddaddy's Civil War sword, used to cut her wedding cake, hung under his picture in the Union Club, while she conveniently forgot that there was never any ancestral dough to cut the mustard. Since childhood, she seemed always to know what life was worth and how to spend it. She was graduated with honors from every school she attended, including Columbia Business, where she maneuvered a meeting with and later a marriage to Todd Blakely. Both were twenty-seven when they met, and he was already a rising realtor.

Soon afterward, they joined forces to convert brownstones into condominiums under the shingle of Blakely Brothers. Though no brothers existed, the fraternal ring of Tishman, Fisher, and Trump exuded such power that Savannah believed a similar fraternity would open bank doors and buyers' wallets.

With Wall Street burgeoning with rich unmarrieds, Arab oil, and Far East silicon chips, their success was immediate. Unlike co-ops, condos have no boards to pass, making reselling as easy as buying. In less than a decade, the Blakelys had become almost as well known as their older "brothers."

Savannah, a talker and doer, was put on the board to do what she proposed. Not only did she spruce the uniforms and the men inside them, she persuaded even the old-timers into redoing the lobby.

Even after Savannah's efforts paid off, she remained a daily communicant in the sacrament of maintaining 823's superiority. And today she was hell-bent on giving the Wheatons her finest, steel-magnolia twice-over.

Seated next to Savannah on the sofa was Matt Thompson, whose physique reminded Erica of her first fifty-yard husband. He was a social staple like Blair, but younger and poorer, and had been, since boyhood, Blair's rubber stamp. What Archer said, Matt Thompson did. When real estate had started to soar, Thompson's loyalty had been rewarded. Archer Blair slipped Matt and his new bride, Carlotta, into 823 with a conference call to the summering board telling them that "the Thompsons, in person, are just like their reference letters say, 'the kind of people with whom you'd be comfortable.' So it's not really necessary to come all the way in from the country just to meet them. You can take my word."

That very afternoon a check from Carlotta's Colombian coffee empire was signed, hermetically sealed, and delivered to the powers of 823.

From the beginning, Matt had convinced Carlotta that, although he loved her, she had to understand that he'd had a long bachelor life without her, some of which must continue. He also made it quite clear that her present life without him would be impossible for an "exotic-skinned" Bogotá beauty, no matter how rich Papa's brew.

Archer Blair slapped Matt's banker's-gray back as Matt, displaying top manners, rose to the occasion. "Matt's one of us," he said to the Wheatons, not that Erica and George had any idea what "one of us" meant in this disparate group.

The final member present, Peter Walker, was a fifty-year-old matrimonial legal whiz for all except Peter Walker. His fourth and latest source of the erotic was a thirtyish French *fille de joie* who'd vowed to be Walker's last and would probably succeed, since Walker was, in all ways, spent, and there was no love for her to fall out of.

Francine de Chaumiand had met Peter Walker on the Concorde. Her trip had been paid for by Francine's old madam, who'd lost her license when Mitterrand decided decency would win France's presidency.

Maman, as Madame was called by the young, homesick girls who lived with her, backed Francine to the *chanson* of half a million francs to fly back and forth on the Concorde until she landed a big one—big enough to assure Madame *une bonne annuité* and Francine *une bonne vie.* Bribing the Air France agent by letting him undo more than her garter belt to put her beside *les grands riches* was Madame's final lesson. Until

Francine landed Peter Walker, there'd been sixteen round trips, eleven propositions, eight fucks, and two proposals of marriage.

The new Mrs. Walker was paranoid about Mrs. Wheaton. Judging from the "titles" with whom Francine had worked, including such notables as Miss Perrier and Miss Michelin Tires, a Miss Nebraska with Erica's looks posed too much competition. "Do not let those Wheatons in!" was her parting admonition to her husband as he left to join the rest of the board.

The only absent member was Burton Evans, a confirmed bachelor and head of an accounting firm who gave much of his free time to 823's finances.

"How about here?" Blair asked, motioning toward two straight-backed chairs that were already part of the circle.

Erica sat with her hands folded, her feet crossed at the ankles. She was surprised at how relaxed she was. She had that same naked assurance she had when she'd waited for the runway finals, except the judges here weren't as skilled at masking their emotions, such as relief, surprise, and even disappointment that she wasn't a fading tart.

Archer Blair pulled his chair next to the Wheatons. It was painful for him to face George and Erica, knowing that J.K. and Zara should be sitting there instead.

"Worst thing I seem to be able to say about the Wheatons," Blair began, his stiff smile directed at no one, "is that they know the Strutherses. Makes me think they may like a drink or two, which of course doesn't apply to anyone here." Blair's chuckle sounded more like a choke, though Matt Thompson did the best he could to echo each syllable, while wondering whether Wheaton was the kind of sport to give a pal a stock tip while riding to the club.

Expecting nothing unforeseen, since he'd already canvassed the board, Blair continued. "How much time do you expect to be spending in New York, with home being the heartland?"

George Wheaton shook his head. "Sweetheart?"

Erica laughed, threading her fingers through her thick hair. It was perhaps the only habit she and Zara had in common. "Why do husbands always defer questions about themselves to their wives?"

"She's right." Wheaton shrugged. "But who knows where we'll be? Today the market center's here, including, may I add, my wife's boo-teeks!"

Savannah Blakely's shudder was almost audible. Somewhere along the elocution trail, right alongside the route to the family fortune, Savannah had forgotten that her southern drawl was once worse than Wheaton's pronunciation.

Archer Blair saw her recoil. "Savannah? Is there something you'd like to ask the Wheatons that's not covered in the file?" Deftly, he rifled through the book-sized sheaf of papers.

"Indeed," she said, her finger lighting on her pad of notes. "I'm wonderin', Mr. Wheaton, about those boys of yours. You plan on them livin' here when you're not? What if . . . ?"

"What if what?"

"They party it up."

"You mean maintain the Carnegie tradition?" George asked. Van Arlyn had prevailed on Erica, "just for fun," to read George the history of 823 that van Arlyn had put together, pointing out how familiarity with this lore would impress the board. "Be great, though I doubt they'll bring live donkeys onto the terrace or smash fine crystal against the mantels or even hire rip-and-coke-snorting Dixie bands for breakfast. But then, nothing's like it was, Mrs. Blakely."

Savannah Blakely's finger slipped from her clipboard as

her eyes caught George Wheaton's calculated look of admiration, a look he seemed reluctant to release. Savannah Blakely was an easy mark for a George Wheaton.

"Mr. Wheaton," Mrs. Harwood said, her impatience like a tapping cane. "I want to know about construction. The hours you'll be banging over my almost dead body?"

"I'm a landlord myself, Mrs. Harwood. I never have men working unauthorized hours. Not that lengthening their day wouldn't shorten the job and the noise," Wheaton said as he turned his flattering gaze on her. Blanche Harwood swallowed a deep inhalation of Marlboro.

George Wheaton had mastered the art of two conversations at once, one with his eyes and one with his mouth. But, more importantly, George Wheaton had done his homework. Not that preparing for 823 was difficult, since the same moral voids and built-in hostilities made it business-as-usual.

The sudden silence gave Archer Blair the break to lavish compliments on the Wheatons' suitability and to wind down the meeting with his concluding rich-speak. "Now I know you know, but once more never hurts: servants use only back elevators; the doorman never walks pets; guests must always be announced; and the newest, most serious problem we have to watch for," he said seriously, "is limos congesting the entrance."

"We'll be careful," Wheaton said, trying to be just as serious.

When no further business seemed forthcoming, Blair shut his file with a satisfied look. Now, for the first time, he faced the Wheatons head on, his smile genuine as he led them to another room while the board voted. Since the raised hands would be a fast formality, he didn't bother with any "Make yourselves comfortable" as he left, only half shutting the door.

Gently, Erica put her arm around George's neck, proud of

his performance, her moist mouth lingering on his lips. "If there's a happier woman in the world, I don't want to be her."

"There'll never be one," George Wheaton said, his ears suddenly alert to the cacophony in the library.

"Out with it, Pete!" Blair barked.

From the open door, Wheaton watched Peter Walker get to his feet. Walker had done as much swiveling as his large frame could manage inside that upholstered cell. Perspiring freely, he kept visualizing a pouty, unhappy Francine. What gave Walker the balls to take this stand now was knowing that, if he didn't, his balls wouldn't matter.

"Look, Archer, I couldn't really say this in front of the Wheatons."

"Whatever it is, why, for Chrissake, are you saying this now? Why not last week? Even yesterday?" Blair demanded.

Walker couldn't tell him that Francine had only seen Erica for the first time this morning, just before he'd left for the meeting.

"Let's say I just discovered it."

"It? What?" Blair eyed Walker doubtfully.

George turned to see if Erica was listening, but she was riveted by some albums stamped *The Vineyard, Aboard the Blackthorn,* and *The Cornwall Shoot.*

Wheaton watched as Walker paced about, pushing his hands in and out of his pockets.

"There's a way a woman looks at you," Walker began uncertainly, "when you know you're being courted."

"You mean solicited, solicitor?" Savannah Blakely said, unable to resist.

Blanche Harwood, exasperated by such inanity, drummed the chair arm with her nails.

Archer Blair frowned with impatience.

Walker lowered his voice to a clubby whisper. "Look. In

my business I've seen enough women and dames to be a pretty good judge of both, and the few times I've seen Mrs. Wheaton in the lobby or the elevator, I've seen enough to know this dame's coming on. Obviously, she's planning to be here often without her husband. Not that I'm saying any of us are susceptible, but what about the element she could bring in? Even Francine mentioned it in passing."

Straining at the door, George caught only enough to hear "Mrs. Wheaton" and every now and then a disconnected word in a conspiratorial tone. Whatever it was, it wasn't good.

Oblivious to her husband standing at the door, Erica was still looking at the albums. "Look. Look here, darling," she called, her fingers tucked like markers into the pages. "Look at these pictures of John Kaplan. He's all over the place with Archer Blair."

George Wheaton was trying so hard to listen, he didn't hear a word Erica said except "Kaplan."

"Look, George. *Arch and J.K. sailing. Arch and J.K. shooting.* Arch and J.K. everywhere."

"Small world," George Wheaton said, wondering what connection there was between them.

Archer Blair, more than most of the board, was aware of the jealous fights between Walker and his wife. Backstairs gossip reached the parlors fast, but Rooney, the eyes-and-ears super, kept Archer "informed" fastest of all, especially about how "that Mrs. Walker never bothers to hold her robe tight around her." More than once, Archer Blair realized how lucky he'd been that the elevator man was off when the door opened on Bettina. He didn't want to indulge Walker in his domestic problems any more than did the rest of the board. Mostly, he wanted this procedural rigmarole to be over and done with. "Pete," he said, "that's all speculation. Speaking for myself, I find nothing nicer than a slight flirt. In fact, it sets me up for the day when I receive a come-hither look from your Francine. I know, as you do, nothing's meant for the long run, but for the short it's awfully pleasant. So why don't we put this case to rest?"

As Peter Walker took his seat, Blair smiled gratefully. "Now, if no one else has anything to say, I think we can bring back the Wheatons." Again leading with a handshake and a smile, he pushed wide the library door. "Congratulations, you two! And welcome to Eight Twenty-three!"

The circle of chairs was already empty when the Wheatons reentered. The board was just milling around, waiting to shake hands. Except for Archer and Matt, they had little more in common with one another than they had with the Wheatons.

When the formalities were finally over and the elevator had swallowed the last of them, including George Wheaton, Erica excitedly asked Archer Blair if she could use the phone.

"Of course," Blair said flatly. "Press the second line. I'll leave you alone."

Erica was truly elated. Before the meeting and Blair's congratulations it had been all fairy tale and silver screen. Now everything was real. The magnificence belonged to them, and they obviously belonged to it.

"Hello! Clive? Clive?" Erica said excitedly. "We got it! We're in!"

"Hold one second. My other line," van Arlyn said, his thumb victory-up.

"Hello, Clive?" Archer Blair said, his voice heavy. "Well, they're in."

"Good. Good job," van Arlyn said. "Let me call you back, Archer. My other phone."

Van Arlyn was aware how painful this had to be for Archer Blair, who still tried to live in a world where, by his mandate alone, cabbages never became kings.

20

"*D*amn sonofabitch! I can't believe that hayseed will be living there. It just can't be!" John Kaplan roared into the phone at Zara. It was eleven o'clock in the morning, and he was in David Rockefeller's office waiting for Paul Becker, Rockefeller's chief honcho at Chase Manhattan.

Hours before, in an early December snow, Zara and J.K. had arrived from London. Driving to the Carlyle, J.K. had been in great humor, even commenting on how peaceful and holiday-wrapped New York seemed. Now, as far as he was concerned, all signs of Christmas spirit had disappeared.

Zara had phoned J.K. right after hanging up from Doris MacDonald. Doris had called about a "spectacular townhouse" and then casually mentioned the George Wheatons and 823. Zara thought the name was familiar—George Wheaton was possibly the Wheaton of Wheaton Industries—but she wasn't sure. It was a name Zara hadn't paid any attention to until

recently, and then only because it had been snarled contemp-
tuously by Archer.

"Doris did say she was surprised the couple didn't seem
more suitable. Especially since so many people were supposedly vying to get in."

Though Zara's disappointment about 823 had been
profound when she'd first heard, like all her setbacks, it was
short-lived. Archer and Verna had been ample diversion.

"Suitable!" Just the word set J.K.'s body trembling. In a
most uncharacteristic gesture, he hurled his unlit twenty-
eight-dollar Davidoff against Paul Becker's pristine fifty-third-
story window. Had it been open, it might have fallen on one
of the peaceful skaters under the giant Rockefeller Center tree.
Pulling out a handkerchief, he brushed the tobacco from his
tongue and carried the phone with him as he wiped the
window. Suddenly, he wondered whether Wheaton might
have had an inkling that he'd wanted that apartment too. My
God! Now he was doubly frustrated. J.K.'s whole life had been
built on competition.

"You know, Zara"—J.K.'s voice was harsh and bitter—
"Archer's such a lazy lout, he probably took the first couple on
the list. Obviously, he hadn't associated Wheaton's name with
business, but then any business association for him is at best
difficult."

J.K. shook his head.

"Actually, lazy's too big a compliment. No wonder he's
been avoiding me lately. I can hardly wait for the day Arch
discovers good old suitable Wheaton is more buzzard than
canary." Especially unnerving to J.K. was having this setback
on the day of the Kaplans' big night with Prince Charles and
Princess Diana at the Royal Ballet at Lincoln Center. The
Kaplans were seated with the Waleses. What J.K. wouldn't

give to Charles's World Wildlife Fund for one shot at the human species endangering his personal world!

Kaplan was sure that Zara's renewed moodiness was due to 823. To think that a man like Wheaton could get it up where he couldn't made J.K.'s own mood black.

Actually, Zara's bad humor was due to her husband. J.K.'s fury at Archer was making everything unpleasantly sticky. It wasn't Archer's fault about Wheaton. Wasn't J.K. the big shot who could get everything fixed? Maybe Archer was even protecting J.K. Maybe the Kaplan name wasn't so great after all. Since J.K. knew how much she'd wanted the place, maybe the great J.K. realized it was he who had failed. Maybe that's what he was so wild about. "Don't you think you're a bit hard on Archer?" Zara asked. "He's not supposed to be a fixer, you know."

J.K. was too involved in his own feelings to notice the disenchantment in her tone. Fortunately, as he was about to resume criticizing Archer, Paul Becker came in and greeted J.K. warmly, restoring his composure as well as his confidence. Again, it was J.K's remarkable talent for shifting gears that made him hang up on Zara in good humor and hone in on Becker as if he'd never missed a beat.

"Listen, Paul, what I told David from London, and what I wish you'd reiterate, is what a charade it would be for the government to aid Wheaton in any way. His company's no Chrysler."

"David never mentioned it was on his agenda," Becker said, his owlish glasses making him look like a child genius.

"But it must be! David must press Congress to steer clear. Once the threat of a takeover is past, Wheaton will remain mismanaged until nothing's left to manage. Then where will the Wheaton workers be?"

"David will be back at his suite in the Watergate by seven. Call him yourself."

"Can't," Kaplan said. A lesser man might have said, It's our dinner for the Waleses, Charles and Diana. Kaplan only said, "We've a long-standing engagement." Whether he would have had such good manners if he thought it wouldn't appear in the morning papers, whatever he said, was another question.

Becker's smile was polite, nothing more. His was a fiduciary world.

Kaplan had gambled that Rockefeller would be in his office. But since he was unreachable, J.K. put Plan Two into play. Even with Becker in the room, J.K. called Jennie in London, who understood his cryptic verbal shorthand better than a Morse decoder.

"Get T.J. at S.M. Tell him about half."

The initials J.K. used were always scrambled. This time the first set stood for James Trotter. The second for Morgan Stanley. "About half" meant he'd be there in thirty minutes. However he coded his plans, Jennie would decipher all systems into go.

"If he can't make it, get me in the car. Not long. Good-bye."

Though Kaplan was a man in a hurry, he liked to leave the impression that his time was never too scarce for those who had time for him. Whenever a meeting ended, he'd take out the Churchillian cigar, though it remained unlit. While unwrapping, cutting, and licking, he'd make small talk.

As J.K. strode the corridors with Becker, he did just that, even bringing the cigar to his ear as he rolled it between his fingers, listening for just the right amount of crackle. The owlish Becker, nodding away at J.K.'s amiable chatter, didn't notice that Kaplan had pushed the elevator button three times.

The blue Corniche knew its way to Wall Street almost as well as J.K.'s black one knew its London route to the City. It was not nosing toward Jim Trotter's office at Morgan Stanley because Kaplan needed additional financing, however, but because he wanted assurance that the company would never help Wheaton.

How different the world was, J.K. thought happily, since Michael Milken's downfall. Sure, he was a crook, but junk bonds didn't deserve the bashing they were getting. Not only was their default rate almost the same as bonds with triple A ratings, but they paid two to three points more interest and allowed everyone to make it big: the bankers on their loans, the bond buyers on interest paid them, and companies like Wheaton to stay in business by raising the money to buy back enough stock to fend off raiders like J.K.

James Trotter, a Harvard MBA in his mid-thirties, was chief of Morgan Stanley's Mergers and Acquisitions group and had already accomplished what he'd been hired for: he brought in big numbers. Now, with England buying bigger and bigger U.S. companies, Trotter wanted a part of these deals. And what better wild card to have than J.K.?

Although Trotter had no trouble with Triomphe's financing, J.K. wanted Trotter to discourage any possible source Wheaton might contact for money.

J.K. rather liked the squat Italian with the alert chestnut-colored eyes and thick shelflike brows, who had been Tony Trotta after City College and before Harvard Business School. Kaplan enjoyed thinking a bit of the old Calabria ink still snaked through Trotter's veins, just as the old Courbeille fire still fueled his own engine.

"What do you hear about Wheaton?" J.K. asked.

"Just what I read," Trotter said. "You've filed and bought more."

Trotter knew Kaplan had come to play and, once in, would go pot limit. "I wish I did have something to report, but no one from Wheaton has so much as drawn a card."

"Look," J.K. said. "If Wheaton does decide to fight, he's going to have a tough time finding any backing. At the rate he's divesting, he'll have to change his terms daily, and from what I hear"—J.K. had heard nothing—"he's hurting big. To buy back assets he's liquidated, he'll have to put up a lot more than his smile for an umbrella."

Onto all of J.K.'s ploys, Trotter nodded as he ostentatiously fingered the Phi Beta Kappa key dangling on a slim gold fob between the pockets of his vest. "Had miniatures made into earrings for the wife," he said.

J.K. loathed the words "the wife."

"At first she was embarrassed, but when people thought she'd earned it herself, she never took them off. You figure women out, J.K., and we'll never have to do another deal."

Just then, Trotter's unusually plain secretary knocked. J.K. grinned as he remembered that Trotter had told him that "the wife" always hired his secretaries.

"Mr. Kaplan, your assistant's on the phone." She was even uglier when she smiled and flashed her gums.

J.K. always received calls from his "assistant" when out of the office. It made his business seem more urgent. It was not as if just any secretary had the liberty to interrupt.

"You want privacy?" Trotter asked.

"No, no," J.K. said, feeling sure it was some last social bit about the evening.

"Sorry to bother you, J.K.," Jennie said, "but a woman's called four times in the last fifteen minutes and refused to leave her name. Says it's a life-and-death matter. She sounds hysterical."

"Where's the call from?"

"Omaha."

J.K.'s mind raced. Erica? What would she want?

"She seems quite frantic. Weepy, too. Coherent, though barely," Jennie said.

"Right. Thanks. Give me the number."

After Jennie hung up, J.K. continued to speak on the telephone. "I'll call Sir James Goldsmith as soon as I get off." Not only did he want to impress Trotter and throw him off base, but to ensure that Trotter would leave him alone to make this call.

As soon as Trotter left, J.K. dialed.

"Thank God it's you. This is Marian," Marian Wheaton cried.

"What's the matter? Where are you?" J.K. was confused.

"At the hospital. It's George!"

"What happened?"

"A heart attack. I'm outside the ICU. She's inside and I'm outside. No one knows yet. I know because the boys had to be told. They're keeping it secret."

"How bad is it?" J.K. heard himself ask, wondering what he wanted to hear.

"They called Boys Town for Father Dunne."

21

J.K.'s mind was thick with confusion. The murky details of George Wheaton's attack whirred in counterpoint to Marian Wheaton's hysteria.

While he listened, Marian's words grew distant. Other voices began mixing with hers. "Marian! Marian!" J.K. shouted.

When a group of doctors emerged from the ICU, Marian Wheaton had run down the corridor, leaving the receiver dangling. John Kaplan, staring into his end of the phone, waited for answers to questions blasting through his mind. Had Wheaton died? What if he had? What then?

J.K. did not bear any personal enmity toward George Wheaton. He felt bad for him. Wheaton had everything to live for. Thanks to J.K., he would have had more than ever now. More cash to spend on his young wife and more time to add polish—to more than just those snub-nosed, rubber-soled shoes.

J.K. reflected that he should do more to stay in shape himself. He'd been lucky so far. But toting a Purdy or having a girl pump away while he lay with his arms folded behind his head wasn't exactly keeping fit.

Suddenly aware that he was holding a dead receiver, J.K. hung up. Now was not the time to be absentminded. Above all, he had to anticipate what Wall Street would do if George Wheaton died. Marian had left little doubt that this would be the case. Often, when chief executive officers go, either feet first or by other offers they can't refuse, the stock price plummets. But with Wheaton stock already low and the news about to break that J.K. had filed a 13D, were Wheaton to croak, the arbs would be killing each other over Wheaton stock. The takeover would be on.

Marian Wheaton had made J.K. privy to information she knew only because of her sons. J.K. was thus in charge of calling the market's shots. In doing so, how could he help but come out the winner?

As far as J.K. was concerned, even were George Wheaton to pull through, things wouldn't work out differently, they would just take a lot longer. The bottom line was dollars. The usual ways in which companies fight hostile takeovers—the typical "shark repellents" employed to deter raiders—did not appeal to George Wheaton. "Scorched earth" and "poison pill," while available as defensive strategies, were not tactics employed by a man who saw himself as the company and therefore unbeatable. It was lucky for J.K. that Wheaton's ego was so large.

J.K. was desperate to leave Trotter's office to buy as much Wheaton as possible before Marian's scoop became public. With every ounce of discipline, he bade Trotter a leisurely farewell and reentered his car. One thing was definite, he decided, stretching his legs sideways: after Wheaton he would give the Rolls to Zara and indulge in one of those wonderfully commodious "pimpmobiles" he only loathed from the outside.

"Chase it! Buy all you can!" J.K. said excitedly into the phone, knowing that after news of Wheaton's condition crossed the broad tape and people discovered J.K.'s buying spree, the price would spiral more. He wished there was a ticker tape in the car. He liked to see his orders executed, watch his power make markets jump along with his people.

When he had visited George Wheaton, J.K.'s 4.9 percent of Wheaton Industries' 30 million shares was virtually unknown, but now, with J.K. reaching for just under that 10 percent position when he'd have to file again, it would be just a matter of days before word would be all over the Street.

When that time came and Wheaton hit the high thirties, J.K. would make known his tender price. All along, he'd calculated it somewhere in the fifty-dollar range; all along, he knew Wheaton never had a prayer of raising the kind of money needed to meet such an offer. Also, J.K. knew that 40 percent was held by institutions who would find his offer hard to resist. Moreover, the Wheaton board, whose first responsibility was to its stockholders, would have no choice but to recommend that they accept Triomphe's offer.

As J.K. pushed his buttons, the medical team in the Omaha hospital ICU kept pressing theirs. Rigid with fear, Erica sat beside the oxygen tent, her hand reaching through the clear plastic slit to George's. Watching the tubes and monitors, she struggled to keep the tears from falling.

It had taken a lot out of George Wheaton to try and operate in Gary Dellos's underworld. Dellos's latest demand— for even more money—had made Wheaton slam down the phone. When his private number rang again, Wheaton knew it was Dellos, but the shooting pain down his arm and the weight on his chest was too severe for him to answer. As the weight grew and his breathing choked, his surroundings began to blur and darken.

While the paramedics adjusted the oxygen, Erica whispered, "I love you." She could still hear the heavy thud when George fell as she happened to pass his office. "Please hurry!" she'd screamed over the telephone. They had.

"You're going to be fine. Fine," she said, as she got up and stood directly before him, mouthing the words for him to read. "It's a blessing. A warning. I love you. I love you." These were the same words she'd cried when he collapsed, when the ambulance came, on the ride to the hospital; all the time she was kissing the icy hand that clung tighter and tighter to hers.

While the staff moved needles, adjusted IVs, and wrote, wrote, wrote on his chart, George Wheaton ever so slightly curled his lips upward.

Suddenly, the guarded quiet of the ICU turned to bedlam as Marian Wheaton burst through the door.

"Don't let him die! Don't let him die! George? George? Where are you, George?"

Erica looked around pleadingly for help. She didn't want to leave George's bed or have Marian Wheaton come any closer to it. A nurse and a young intern moved up quickly on either side of Marian, and as if she knew she had no choice she let them lead her away.

Thank God, Erica thought, reaching again for George's hand. "Darling, you're doing great. Really great."

Again, George Wheaton's lips curled. This time, though, he shook his head. Releasing her hand, he crooked his finger. Erica put her face into the opening of the oxygen tent. His lips made a rounded shape, but all he could manage was to blow a little air.

Erica put her finger to his mouth. "I know. I know," she

said, not knowing anything, just trying to save his strength.

As he coughed slightly, Erica motioned to Dr. Hartley, who'd been attending all along.

"It's all right," he said kindly. "Let him talk if he can."

"*You* talk!" Erica wheeled on the family physician and friend. "Tell him he'll be fine!"

Hartley stood beside Erica, aware of her strain as he faced Wheaton's tired eyes. "It's going to be fine, George. You'll see. It's going to be just fine."

"Not 'it's'! You! *You!*" Erica whispered angrily. "*You're* going to be fine. Get in front of him so he can see your lips. Tell him." Erica's tears poured forth. "Please," she sobbed. "Please tell him he'll be home soon. Make him believe it. Please!"

George Wheaton seemed to understand. Gently, softly, Erica put her lips to her husband's ear. "You'll be home for the pony show, for caroling, for Christmas, my darling. We'll get a big blue spruce. Bigger than ever. Bigger than last year. And this year we'll trim it earlier. As soon as you're home. Next week. Tuesday. Yes, Tuesday. Tuesday will be our good news day."

Dr. Hartley's final entry on George Wheaton's chart was made while Erica continued her fantasy, chattering as if she knew that when she stopped there'd be no need to start again.

Hartley had just replaced the chart when Father Dunne rushed into the unit. Holding up his hand, Hartley pointed to the monitor. From either side, they knelt by Erica.

"Darling, remember when the top star fell? You were taking the ornaments off. You bent the branch to reach the star. So we have to buy . . ."

Father Dunne took Erica's hand and patted her shoulder. As she turned toward the priest, the tears rushed from her closed eyes. Parting the plastic, she put her head inside and kissed her husband's lips. Then without a word she sank to her knees next to the good father.

22

Gary Dellos strode grandly about the hi-tech bachelor pad Bettina had rented for him. She'd found it on the bulletin board at the United Nations where short-term sublets were always posted. It was certainly a better place for Dellos to do business than the lousy salesman's digs Wheaton had provided. Actually, the surroundings suited him perfectly. The black-and-white decor, with its stainless steel and glass, was cold and unyielding. And for a man who loved creature comforts, the way everything from curtains to coffee worked with buttons was almost baronial.

Although his flight had arrived earlier that morning, it was nice that no one knew he was in town. He could have this time without Bettina. He was still in khakis and a navy pullover. His stubble was dark, but his skin felt great from not shaving. He was more relaxed in New York after his sojourn in Athens and London, a hiatus from Wheaton and his mano-a-mouse dealings with Blair.

Flipping the apartment key from one finger to the next, a skill he'd perfected as a boy along with the lifting of wallets, Gary Dellos felt he'd finally unlocked the big one. Pretty good angling for a fisherman's boy. With that kind of haul he could parlay drachmas to *Dynasty*. He could buy his own island. Call it Dellos. Marry Jackie O. Make her Jackie D. D-lightful! D-licious! D-ellos! Big D-little-E-double-L-O-S.

With his shoes on, Gary Dellos sprawled across the down comforter, swilling Amstel Light from the bottle, pressing the remote to see whatever TV battle of the sexes was dulling the senses of America. Christ almighty! His eyes popping, he bolted upright, unaware that his beer had spilled as he pressed the volume to high.

"—of a heart attack late yesterday afternoon at Saint Joseph's Hospital, Omaha. George Wheaton, fifty-three, was the embodiment of the American dream. Founder and chairman of Wheaton Industries, this maverick entrepreneur and humanitarian rose from . . ."

Gary Dellos gasped as he took a breath. The more he tried to relax, the more his breath caught. After Wheaton had slammed down the phone, Dellos had decided to give him time to cool off before calling back. Cool off, yes. But cool altogether? Christ!

". . . seen here with his devoted wife, Erica, a former Miss Nebraska, opening the Wheaton Museum, for which he . . ."

Dellos was frozen with shock. He sipped his beer to ease his parched throat, his eyes bonded to the screen.

"Among the all-Nebraskan pallbearers at tomorrow's services will be talk-show host Johnny Carson; Warren Buffet, one of America's seven self-made billionaires; Pete Peterson, former Secretary of Commerce, son of Greek immigrants . . ."

No, no! That little SOB! How could he die? Dellos smashed his fist into the pillows. Shit! Today was the day he was to get the money on account. Two hundred thousand big ones buried!

Dellos paced the black rug, his shoes disappearing in the thick nap. Think, Dellos. Think. One ticket's gone, but one's still left. One ticket can still collect a helluva lot of shirts. Use it, Dellos. Run with it! Blair hates you. Scare the shit out of him, and the bucks will follow. You saw the way he looked in 823.

"Go, Dellos, go!" he yelled, giving the air a swift middle finger.

He picked up the phone to call Blair. He would wear his nipped Italian suit with the padded shoulders and a supple black silk shirt. And his thick ribbed silver tie. The kind of dude dressing Blair would hate.

Archer Blair had purposely chosen the Metropolitan Club for their meeting. Its membership was large and varied, and the two men would not come under the same scrutiny as they would at the Brook or Links. Also, he knew its marble halls and grand staircase would impress Dellos.

He waited at the bar, every inch the conservative multigeneration clubman. The black who brought Dellos over, himself a thirty-year man at the club, had his own opinion of Dellos. "Mr. Blair's right there," he said, omitting the "sir" and not moving until he was sure Dellos really was expected.

Archer Blair had been chatting with Old George, the bartender, who used to be Young George when his own father worked behind the bar. He greeted Dellos much more charmingly than when last they'd met. "Mr. Dellos, this is

George. Makes the best martini in town. They're lethal but great. What'll you have?"

"The same," Gary Dellos said, thrown by the "Mr." He didn't quite know what to call Blair.

"How are you?" Blair asked, his smile massive. "Not that I have to ask. You look like a million dollars!" His laugh was hearty and unsettling as he slapped Dellos's back, on the way to their table. "Yes sirree! A million bucks if I ever saw it. Which I never have. Have you, Mr. Dellos?"

The tables in the bar were starting to fill with members, many of whom preferred to continue working in a more convivial atmosphere. For others, it was a painless way to turn day into night and earning to spending.

"Sit down, Mr. Dellos," Blair said deferentially. Before sitting himself, Archer Blair took a handful of nuts from the small crested bowl.

"Used to be a lot more cashews than peanuts in this mix," he said casually. "But even here, lower standards can slip in. What do you think?"

Gary Dellos stared—not at the bowl but at his nut-case host. Whatever he was on, he wanted some.

"I'd like to get them to eliminate the ashtrays, along with the peanuts. Not that smoking's forbidden. But if a man has to get up to get an ashtray, he'll be embarrassed, and men hate to be embarrassed in front of other men, don't you think?" Blair took a sip of his drink while carefully keeping his eyes on Dellos. "By the way, weren't you in Europe longer than planned?"

"I hadn't planned."

"It's so expensive in Europe for Americans, with the current exchange rate," Blair said, his features as forbidding as his native New England coast. "Luckily, my travel's deter-mined by my board meetings." He peered over the rim of his martini. As people passed and said hello, Blair responded with his usual charm. Never once did he introduce Dellos.

"Like you say, Arch," Dellos said, "depends on who's paying the bill."

"I don't believe those were my words," Blair answered, his look mock-quizzical. "Doesn't sound like a Blair comment. A male Blair, anyway."

Blair's voice bit deep. Dellos wiped the tumbled hair from his brow. He wasn't prepared for tactical warfare, and he couldn't understand why Blair was so cavalier. Why did he seem to believe he held the upper hand?

"You know, Mr. Dellos," Blair said, straightening his already perfect tie, "as they say in some circles, you're a curious chap. In town since early this morning, and you haven't as yet called your true love. She *is* your true love, isn't she? I mean, she must be, for you to be carried away with—whatever—enough to propose marriage?"

Archer Blair speared the olive from his glass, his eyes constantly on Dellos, his Yankee Clipper meanness coming to the fore.

"Let's say I wanted to rest up to be at my best."

Defiantly, Dellos threw back his drink, staring Blair down as he'd learned to do on the docks when bigger kids bullied him.

"Listen, Arch," he said, in a loud voice. "Don't bullshit a bullshitter."

For the first time, Archer Blair took his eyes from Dellos and looked around to see who might have heard.

"And don't look as if you think these lightfooted freaks haven't heard the word 'bullshit,'" Dellos said, even louder. "Got it?"

Archer Blair stared at him. "Got what, Mr. Dellos? What

am I to get? I thought *you* were here to get something. Frankly, no. I don't get it."

His third martini arrived. Blair was surprised the others hadn't had more of an effect, but he was so charged up, the gin had become a chaser to his adrenaline.

"Before your trip, Mr. Dellos, you made me an offer—or should I say offered me a swap—for things I already own. My money and my daughter. You generously offered to forsake Bettina—or should I say jilt her?—for a million dollars. Though you and I know very well what you are, my daughter doesn't seem to have the slightest idea, even though she heard your proposition. She's still at the stage of, shall I say, rebelling against her parents. But let me assure you, Mr. Dellos, her independence is in thought only." Blair crossed his arms as he leaned toward Dellos.

Dellos leaned back, feeling baffled. He wasn't supposed to be against the ropes. He'd expected Blair to be docile and frightened, with his hearth and home in danger.

"You're right. She's a pussycat with me," Dellos said. He reached into his pocket and took out the key. "See this? It unlocks our love nest. Paid for by your daughter."

Blair's expression became icier, if possible. "Enjoy it, Mr. Dellos. At least for today." He loved seeing the beads of sweat pop around the roots of Dellos's curls. Bully a bully, and the bully backs down. Isn't that how it always goes, Blair thought. With each handful of nuts his strength seemed to grow.

Dellos lifted his glass but resisted the temptation to throw it.

"Let's hear it, Mr. Dellos," Blair said. "Not too loud, but clear."

"Arch," Dellos began, his mind racing, "we both know why I'm here. The same thing will make me go away. A mere million dollars. After all, what's a million to you, compared to your only daughter?"

Blair waved toward the paneled walls, hung with formal portraits of the club's founding fathers. "See those men? The only reason they're hanging here and not on the gallows is that they got the enemy before the enemy got them. The world, Mr. Dellos, has always been won by the fastest gun. Mr. Dellos, I'm about to pull the trigger."

Gary Dellos began to pick cashews from the bowl, one by one. Exactly how much sting had filtered down to this WASP from his ancestors?

Suddenly, Blair loosed a sneer worthy of a Mafia don. "Take her, she's mine. Go ahead and marry Bettina, Dellos. I don't want her around anymore. Maybe I'm—we're—to blame. I don't know. I just know I don't want her."

"That's really smart, Blair," Dellos said, stalling. His napkin was in shreds, his glass empty, toothpicks broken.

"You see, Mr. Dellos, I don't like blackmailing daughters or their blackmailing boyfriends. And if you're thinking trust fund, don't. By the time I lose control of it, you'll be too old to splash at those elegant watering spots."

Dellos was sick. Wheaton gone. Bettina gone. What now? From the corner of his eye, he saw Blair snap his fingers for another drink.

The click snapped Dellos's self-control. He mustered all his saliva and let it fly in Blair's face. "Fucking bastard!" Dellos shouted. He smiled into Blair's shocked eyes. Then, with a sort of primal satisfaction, he upended the table.

Dellos took the marble stairs two at a time and, once out on the street, headed blindly uptown. By the time he came to, he found himself across the street from the Carlyle. Spotting a phone on the corner, Dellos figured it would be justice for

Blair if Bettina believed her lover had deserted her because Daddy had threatened to kill him. Why not make the call?

"And that's why I gotta scram. And alone. Your old man's a maniac. He'd as soon murder me as buy me a drink. But I'll send for you in a couple of days. When I do, make sure you don't get him riled up. You know, sweetheart, when these uptight blue bloods crack, they splatter."

As Dellos hung up, he thought, Why not make another call to see if the John Kaplans were in town? The elegant Lady Zara and her mass mergerer. Either one would do. He could tell J.K. about Zara and Blair or tell Zara he'd tell J.K. about her. First home, first served. His battery recharged, he gave himself a high five.

23

Archer Pierpont Blair was visibly shaken. The waiters scurried en masse to remove the debris and reset the table. When Blair came back to the bar after washing Dellos's spittle from his face, he could hardly keep his fourth martini from spilling. Nearby club members were in shock, not only at the outburst but at Archer Blair's being its object. Blair wanted desperately to vanish from the scene, but instead he stayed at the bar, to give George the explanation Blair wanted to get around to the other members. It would be too embarrassing to explain to them himself. As Joe Kennedy said, "Never complain, never explain."

George kept wiping and rewiping the same glasses so it wouldn't seem as if he were waiting for Blair to speak. The last thing he would ever do would be to volunteer an opinion. Experience had taught him unsolicited advice was not what confidants needed. They wanted ears and expiation, a confessional replete with booze, devoid of penance.

"Cornelia fired that bum in the country," Blair said, stabbing an olive. "I'm stunned he came here. I never thought he'd have the nerve . . . but servants are the most ungrateful beasts going. Mother always said, 'Archer, the loyalty of old family retainers went out with high-buttoned shoes.' "

"Right, Mr. Blair."

"Did you notice what he was wearing?"

"Sure did," George answered noncommittally.

"He probably thought he looked like me. They get ideas from living in your house. Know what he had the gall to ask?"

"No, sir."

Blair wasn't sure what lie he was about to plant, but he did know whatever it was it would take root quickly. "First, he said his father died in Greece. That bastard never knew his father! Then he said he owed the Mafia and they'd kill me if I didn't pay. I said, 'There's no Mafia in Greece.' He said, 'The Hand's everywhere.' Then I said, 'Greedy, slimy hands like yours.' Then he said if I didn't pay, they'd get Bettina too. That's when I called his bluff. That's when he said he'd kill me. That Greek crook, who'd be shot on the next block, threatened *my* life. I can have him deported with less trouble than it takes to squash a piss-ant." Blair took a handful of nuts to absorb the gin. His mother had also told him that canapés were served with cocktails for just that reason.

Through the years, George had seen most of them in their cups, heard most of their dreary wife tales, mistress tales, business bummers. But Archer Blair had always been truly old guard, tight-lipped even when he was tight. To see him this undone, undid George too.

Still playing it cool, Blair decided to hang around for a while. He went over to some acquaintances who'd witnessed the commotion and started a conversation, even tossed off a couple of remarks about Dellos. With those members he knew better, Blair pulled up a chair and chatted at length about the market and their respective families. Surely his unruffled composure would dispel any thoughts that a bum like Dellos had any place in Archer Blair's life.

Suddenly, Blair looked at his watch. Christ! It was almost eight o'clock. Zara would be at the Carlyle already. She said she'd call if J.K. was working late, but Blair hadn't been where he could be reached. He'd better rush home and change.

As Blair raced into 823, Mike held the door with an oddly sheepish "Evening, Mr. Blair." The reaction of Pete, on the elevator, was the same.

Archer didn't have to go far into his apartment to understand. The havoc, the wanton, willful way things were thrown and strewn about, looked as if madmen had ransacked the place. Drawers were pulled out, paintings torn from the frames. The place was a shambles. Even Cornelia's jewelry pouch, unzipped and empty, was thrown into a corner.

How in hell did Dellos get in? Blair wondered. Raging, he ran to the kitchen to call the super and interrogate the maids. The maids had the same sheepish look as the men who worked in the building.

"How'd he get in? Who let him in?"

Rooney rushed into the kitchen and motioned Blair to the hall. He stared patiently at the parquet floor as Blair ranted about security. "This could mean your job, Rooney!"

"Pardon me, Mr. Blair, but—"

"But what?"

Rooney shook his head. "Excuse me, Mr. Blair, but—"

"Excuse you, hell! Look at this place!"

"Miss Bettina," Rooney said softly. "It was Miss Bettina," he said, still unable to look at Blair.

Archer Blair's eyes blazed. "It can't be," he said softly. But he knew it was true.

212 ————————————— JUDITH GREEN

Why, Rooney thought, couldn't it be one of the new ones? Why did it have to happen to a fine gentleman like Mr. Blair? "Pete was on the elevator, and he called me. She—Miss Bettina—was in a terrible state. By the time me and Pete came to have a look, things were already bad. There was no way we could stop her. She was thrashin' around, draggin' suitcases and pictures. Wasn't our Miss Bettina."

Archer Blair never looked up. He just nodded. Rooney left without another word.

24

Confident about his mission, Dellos felt much more at ease this time as he rode up in the Carlyle elevator. He was lucky to find m'lady in residence. But then, it was time he won one.

"Penthouse," he told the elevator operator calmly. Obviously his call to Zara had been sufficiently intriguing—or frightening. Dellos didn't even have to look this time as he flipped his key between his fingers. Instead, he watched the numbers. They seemed to take forever to light up.

His hair flopping, his black eyes snappy, and his step jaunty, Dellos looked more like a gigolo than a con man.

When the elevator stopped on the living room level and Lady Zara opened the door, Dellos stepped back, stunned. Her eyes, as green as island waters, and her rapacious mouth, drawn wide and shimmering with gloss, was a triumph of lust, while the wild wired hair, tight skirt, and leopard blouse only enhanced the impression of a jungle goddess. It was hard to believe she had a title so close to the Crown.

Dellos couldn't help asking himself the crucial question: Why Archer Blair? Had Dellos met Zara under different circumstances, on a different day, near the island seas that matched her eyes, her feelings for Blair would have washed away with the tide.

"Come in please, Mr. Dellos," Zara said, her voice cool.

As he entered the large living room whose thirty-third-story windows overlooked the tops of much of Manhattan, Gary Dellos caught the lingering scent of sandalwood. The sexy whine of Gershwin seeped from speakers hidden in the corners of the room. There was a silver tray littered with food. Tiny sandwiches were picked apart, the buttered slices of bread remaining, and miniature pastries had little bites in them and berries plucked from their centers.

"I've just had tea," Zara said, in clipped upper-class syllables, in answer to his stare. "I'm afraid the remnants are a bit unsavory. But they're not contagious. If you're hungry," she added, with the faintest smile.

Dellos was complimented that she wanted to share the leftover food with him, not realizing she was offering him scraps as she might to a dog. "No. No, thanks," he said.

"A drink, then?"

"Gin and ice," he said. "It will make it easier to say what I have to say."

Dellos watched her move to the bar. Nothing about her was neutral or soothing. Her coloring, her hair, her lipstick, and her nail polish made her look as if she were bathed in neon. Oddly transfixed, he wished his call were anything but business.

After handing him his gin and pouring champagne for herself, Zara curled on the round ottoman, her long legs beneath her like a gangly cat. "I'm breathless," she said innocently, taking a slow sip.

Since he had already mentioned Blair on the phone, her ingenuousness and detachment were incredible.

Zara didn't think herself incredible. She was being what she was born to be, the controlled lady, although the act was killing her.

Dellos's hot Mediterranean blood would never understand such contradictions. He was so confident he was going to shatter her, he even considered softening what he had to say.

"So, Mr. Dellos. Has the gin sufficiently freed your tongue?" Her tone held a slight taunt, but Dellos caught only its benign quality. "You seem to be having a hard time of it."

Not even for a split second did those brilliant eyes betray the tense interior feelings. As Zara placed her gold-tipped cigarette in her gold holder and then held it, as if he were a servant, for him to light, she willed her hands not to tremble.

So what if she wasn't quite human and a bit dumb, Dellos decided. There's no time like the present. But the more he thought, the more jittery *he* became. Since he'd learned nothing calms the nerves like starting a performance, he quickly began.

"The fact you asked me to come here says you're guilty."

"Says it to whom?"

"To me, Socrates Garapoulos Dellos."

"Guilty of what?"

"You know."

"No. You do."

"Why *are* you seeing me?"

Zara inhaled deeply. Even with someone like Dellos, she instinctively turned her head away from him to exhale. "Curiosity."

"Curiosity killed the cat, but it can save Lady Zara."

"Out with it—or with you, Mr. Dellos."

"You're having an affair with Archer Blair." Dellos spoke

slowly in order to watch for the slightest sign of betrayal. "I know everything."

Zara swallowed air, wishing it were straight vodka. "Everything?"

With satisfaction, Dellos watched her hand now tremble as she brought the cigarette holder to her lips. "Your lover confessed everything to his daughter, and she told me. She's my girlfriend. She wants to marry me."

Suddenly, this bizarre conversation—a common stranger telling her about herself and Archer and Bettina—was too much. Stubbing out her cigarette, she went to the bar. This time, however, Zara's good manners did not extend to offering Dellos anything.

"What is it you're after, Mr. Dellos?" she asked.

"Look," Dellos said. "I'm not a guy to keep coming back, the kind who gives the pictures and holds the negatives. Anyway, I like you." What a stupid thing to say, he thought. He didn't like her. He wanted to be in her, wanted to be where Blair had been to show her what she could have had, because she was an animal, weird and wild, like him. Even the way she was acting now was crazy.

"I can't give what's not mine."

"But you can get it. If you don't, you might have to give up a lot more. Like those," he added, pointing at the jewels crowding her knuckles and wrists.

Lady Zara seemed unruffled. "You're being quite preposterous."

"Look, Lady Zara," Dellos said, slightly unnerved. "No matter what kind of outer-space freak you are, the possibility of a divorce and front-page scandal should make you more cooperative. Perhaps you don't realize that I'm about to blow your affair to your husband?"

"And tell him what?"

Dellos jumped at the voice coming from behind him.

"My dear Dellos," John Kaplan said, standing at least ten feet tall, broad and brilliant and fearless. "You don't think I've come this far without dealing with scum, do you? I cut my teeth on bastards like you, and they all have scars to prove it." With a gallant flourish, he went to his wife. Her eyes were filled with emotion. "Hello, my darling," he said, his lips brushing hers. Then he went to the bar and poured himself a whiskey, neat.

"You know, Dellos, your kind are easy marks, because you believe we're idiots."

The spark in Dellos's eyes was now a glaze. His head pounded with the jackhammer of Kaplan's voice. "I'm not one of your hirelings, Kaplan."

J.K. sneered at the ridiculousness of such a possibility. "I don't solicit trash, Dellos."

"What about your wife? She's a fucking—"

"Watch your mouth, Dellos."

"—whore! And you talk morals!"

"Of course I do. And I talk of family and home and, yes, I'm patriotic too."

"I can go to the press."

"My dear fellow, the press and I are old friends, though I doubt you'd understand that, any more than you'd understand any loyalty, mine to my wife and hers to me. She called me, you see."

Dellos's breath came hard. "The loyalty of the press is to its readership, Kaplan. They topple bigger ones than you every day. The only morality they know is circulation."

"True," Kaplan said, nodding, looking at Zara. How fragile she looked! Thank heavens he'd been in New York to get her call, to advise her what to do.

"I'll tell you one press who's not old friends with you—or

with anyone. It's the *National Enquirer*. When their flashes go off on me with Bettina at my side, you won't be so high and mighty." Neither would he, Gary Dellos thought, with the paltry amount the *Enquirer* would pay. "I'll give you tonight to think about it."

"Don't bother," J.K. said, before Dellos slammed the apartment door.

25

*A*s Gary Dellos entered his black-and-white parlor, he almost fell over a heap of luggage. Suitcases. Rolled canvases. What in . . . ?

"Darling? Gary? Darling?"

Dellos stood transfixed in the midst of half-closed baggage crammed with a jumble of shoes and dresses and lingerie. All at once he began to laugh wildly, doubling over on his knees until he stumbled and fell among the garbage of his ungodly day. Lying amid the debris, he didn't even have the strength to pull Bettina's arms from his neck.

"What is it, darling? What's the matter?" Bettina sounded almost as hysterical as he did. "Are you okay? You sound weird." She tried to kiss him. "You smell of liquor. Father got you drunk! But don't worry. Just look what I've done to him. To both of them. For you. For us." Bettina reached toward a pile of rolled-up canvases. "This is a very early Gauguin. It's small, I know, but it's of Gauguin's daughter, and the Met—"

"I'll take it," Dellos said, his eyes popping as she switched the Gauguin for a Renoir.

"This is a Renoir drawing of two women."

"I'm hep, baby. But where I come from, we don't paint naked women. We take real pictures of them." Again, Dellos started to laugh, but this time because he thought he was funny.

Bettina followed the Renoir with a Mary Cassatt baby in a lace bonnet and a small Cézanne of a peach and a plum. "These are worth much more than photos. They're worth enough for us to live on forever." Nervously, Bettina pushed them at him. Anything, so long as he didn't leave. Or, if he did, he'd at least have to take her with him.

By the time Bettina pulled out the double strand of pearls, the Cartier dragonfly of diamonds, and the Van Cleef clips with their fat emerald centers, Dellos was into high multiplication. This was serious money.

He knew few dealers would want the paintings. Not that they cared whether they'd been looted, just as they didn't care about art that had been stolen by the Nazis. They cared only if they were too recognizable, too traceable, too hard to sell. Like these. Yet whatever Dellos could get would be a windfall. And he knew just the guy who'd cut the deal.

"I have a perfect outlet for these in London," Dellos told Bettina. "Kevin should give me—us—top dollar. But first we have to get there, and the sooner the better. Come here," Dellos said lovingly. "You did a good job," he whispered, holding Bettina and the jewels.

"I'm so happy," Bettina said, a brave woman who had defied her world.

Gary Dellos was a new man. With this hand he was

suddenly back in the game. As he went to call British Airways, his swagger was back as well. "Two, please. On tomorrow's Concorde." He winked conspiratorially at Bettina. "D-E-L-L-O-S and B-L-A-I-R. . . . Yes. . . . No, we'll pick them up. . . . No problem. None whatsoever. . . . By credit card. What time do you close?"

"Darling, darling, I love you so!"

"You have American Express, don't you, my pet?" he asked.

"Yes," she answered eagerly.

"I'll need my cash for when we land, so let's put the tickets on your card. The bill will go to Eight Twenty-three anyway, and then your father can pay. It's the least he can do to get rid of us both."

"You're brilliant," Bettina said, beaming.

Dellos nodded as he stuffed the jewelry in his pockets and looked again at the paintings. This was more than just run-of-the-millionaire walking-around money. It was riding-around money, in Ferraris and Porsches and Jags. London, Paris, mother Athens, dear sweet world, here I come! he thought excitedly.

Yet no matter how excited Dellos was, Bettina was more so. She'd not only done it to her parents, she'd made her lover more in love with her than ever. She'd managed to kill both birds with one stone and keep the stone besides! Again, she hugged Dellos.

"Sweetheart," he said slowly, as if mentally mulling over the details, "*you've* got to pick up those tickets. I have to find us a place to stay in London. And, most important, I've got to make the contacts to convert our present stash to future cash."

"I'm on my way," she said blissfully, grabbing her purse.

"Hurry back so we can celebrate. We won't even sleep. Just a little you know what."

"I really did good, didn't I?" Bettina asked with disarming candor, kissing him again as she flew out the door.

"Real good, baby."

Dellos went to the window and watched Bettina get into a taxi before he dialed Tom Wheelock of Barton Wheelock Sons, Dealers in Fine Art since 1910. Wheelock was an old acquaintance dating back to what Dellos called his Monte Carlo days. That's how Dellos preferred to think of his time with van Arlyn. Wheelock had marketed many "wartime" old masters to rich bargain hunters. It made them feel they were getting the better of a world they knew was always trying to get the better of them. Luckily, when Dellos called, Wheelock was still at the gallery.

"I'll be right over," Wheelock suggested.

"No. I'll come to you," Dellos said. "It's better."

As soon as Dellos hung up, he dialed Olympic Airways. "Athens. One seat. First class. Tonight's flight. Dellos. . . . D-E-L-L-O-S."

Pulling a thick sisal rope from Bettina's pathetic accumulation of luggage, Dellos tied his new paintings tightly together before slamming the door on the Big Apple.

26

*E*rica Wheaton clutched little Georgette's hand as they hurried through the Wheaton Mall, searching for a star to put atop the blue spruce. At every bell-ringing Santa, Georgette tugged at Erica to stop. "You're mean!"

All at once, Erica's patience snapped. Shaking loose the little hand, tears welling uncontrollably in her eyes as she grabbed the tiny shoulders, she cried, "You want no Christmas and no tree as well as no daddy?"

Georgette's eyes widened in fright and she began to cry. She squirmed to get free, but her mother wouldn't let go, though all she was holding were the shoulders of the snowsuit. Suddenly, the panic in her daughter's sobs created a panic in Erica.

Releasing her hold, she sat on the stone floor and rocked Georgette in her arms. "Darling, Mommy isn't mean. Mommy's just tired. Very tired. Mommy loves you. Mommy loves you the best. And Mommy's sorry. Sometimes mommies make big, big booboos, too."

Georgette had never seen her mother cry, but once she had stopped, Georgette wasn't frightened. Making two tiny fists, she rubbed the leftover tears from her own eyes. And when Erica stood up and reached for Georgette's hand, they went quickly to the toy store.

If only it were this easy, Erica thought, as she paid the clerk for the teddy bear that Georgette was soon scolding for "nagging and being naughty."

Two weeks had gone by since the funeral, and Omaha was still reeling from the turnout. The night before the service, Eppley Airport had been clogged with private jets and every available limousine had been pressed into service. Mourners had braved the winter cold to wait in front of the church. World-famous dignitaries, little people, football heroes, and any other part of Nebraska that could fit inside came to pray and give thanks for a man who'd given so much to them.

After considerable thought, John Kaplan sent a red carnation replica of the ranch's entwined horseshoes, with tiny white roses forming the initials.

Flowers had filled every room at the ranch and filled the church too. The idea of asking that contributions go to a charity in lieu of flowers would never have occurred to Erica. George's funeral was a time for everything to be beautiful, for the altar to be resplendent with the colors created by God, and for the myriad fragrances to waft like a new spring through the chill of the day.

What Erica did not like was a church organ. Since childhood, organ music had depressed her. Instead, the University of Nebraska band played Christmas carols as the children's choir sang. There was no chance for gloom. Even the eulogies were upbeat—not the usual list of achievements but humorous, heartfelt stories of kindness and generosity. People spoke without notes, words coming in torrents, words that would have embarrassed George Wheaton.

"If ever a man could be called shyly beautiful," Father Dunne said, "it was George Wheaton."

Both of Wheaton's sons recounted loving memories. Their mother had chosen not to come. After George had left her, Marian Wheaton never really accepted the fact that they'd been divorced or that he had married again. When he died, she wasn't able to accept that loss, either.

After the burial at Boys Town, Erica threw open the ranch for a barbecue for George's friends. Never once did it occur to her to defend the lighthearted mood with "It's what George would have wanted."

When Erica and Georgette had finally found their star for the Christmas tree, Erica rushed home for a meeting with Hong Kong's Peter Chang; Nils Nordstrom from Oslo; Dan Aaron, her lawyer; and Tom Platt, her accountant. It was the first time they'd all been able to meet.

Chang and Nordstrom had been selected by Jack Dowling, George's pal at Lazard Frères, to be Erica's partners in her fight for Wheaton Industries. Lazard's bankers had dealt successfully with them in the past, helping to enlarge their position in America by finding situations needing immediate cash. Since the long-range promise, rather than the fast buck and the quick turnover, was their goal, they were ideal partners for Erica.

The tiny Mr. Chang, in his vested black suit with only the smallest bit of white shirt and burgundy tie peeking through, seemed even smaller than usual standing next to

Erica. Nordstrom, however, because of his broad build looked taller than his six feet. Both were a good deal younger than Erica had anticipated, probably because, in middle America, corporate success and middle age are usually synonymous. Chang and Nordstrom were just as surprised by Erica's glamour, revealed to its fullest in white stretch pants and clinging cashmere.

After exchanging greetings, Erica led them to the big beamed room with the great fire and magnificent tree.

"My daughter and I found that lucky star this morning," Erica said happily.

"The tree must be Norwegian," Nordstrom said, moving back to get the full breadth and height of the majestic spruce.

Mr. Chang tilted his head upward as if taking in a skyscraper.

Erica was pleased at the easy manner of this pleasant although odd couple. "Do you want to tour the ranch or have some food first?" she asked calmly as if she were addressing a garden club instead of the two men now most important in her life.

"Maybe tour the ranch first so we can talk at lunch," Dan Aaron suggested.

"I'm eager to see the cattle. We don't have too much grazing land in Hong Kong," Peter Chang said with a twinkle.

Selling the land was Erica's only way of getting enough money to participate equally with Chang and Nordstrom in the buy-out of Wheaton. Imagining John Kaplan at Wheaton's helm overpowered any regrets she might have.

George Wheaton had been lucky to keep control of Wheaton Industries after he started selling assets. The financial world believed he controlled 23 percent rather than the 18 percent he actually owned, because they assumed the 5 percent he had settled on Marian when they divorced still remained under his control. Furthermore, since the small shareholders and the Wheaton workers, to whom options were consistently offered, always made money, it was as if George Wheaton himself had owned their stock as far as voting was concerned. But with Kaplan's tender offer of fifty dollars a share coming through the front door, the small stockholders' loyalty would soon bolt out the back. Even the banks who'd always supported George Wheaton had a fiduciary responsibility to sell at such a price.

Erica knew that J.K. expected her to sell. She had known it the day of his meeting with George, when he was so sure he had her ear but in fact had only her practiced eye. Long ago, Erica Phelps from upriver Bellevue had vowed never to go backward, and she was sure not going to let any limey raider change her plans. She knew, too, that he believed the reason she did not answer his calls was that she was holding out for bigger bucks. The real reason was that she had nothing to say to Kaplan until this meeting was over.

Not that Erica wasn't frightened without George, all the more so in his arena. In the middle of the night, as if a bomb had exploded, Erica would jump out of bed, terrified at what she was doing, and scream, "George! George!" She knew George would have fought too, but he would have hated these foreigners. What did they know about Wheaton? About grass-roots America?

Half crazed, sometimes she didn't even know what winning was. Assuming she got the backing, how far would it go? What if Kaplan went higher than she could, and she lost? And what if she won? Wheaton in debt and no one to run it? Was that winning?

Selling the ranch was the only way. That's why George

was buried at Boys Town instead of at the ranch. She had tried to explain this to him when she went to his grave early that morning. She told him she wanted an American buyer, but no one came up with the right kind of numbers to compete with Kaplan. Chang and Nordstrom planned to build a town called Wheatonville, where businesses and shopping and housing would make money for everyone. "And, George," she said, "that means Wheaton will stay with us forever."

Naturally, rumors about Wheaton's future were flying in Omaha. Wheaton-watching had become a big sport. The melodrama was made even juicier by Marian Wheaton's vicious mouth.

Erica gave Chang and Nordstrom boots and parkas before the tour, knowing how often they'd be getting in and out of the Range Rover to visit the barns, silos, and stables as they trekked over the property.

"It's got to be the most beautiful piece of land ever to draw life from the Missouri," Erica said. "I wouldn't bet against planting a sawed-off shotgun in these fields and having its muzzle grow back," she added, unconsciously quoting George.

Although Chang and Nordstrom had been pretty much convinced buyers before the trip, their conviction was confirmed when they saw for themselves the ranch's proximity to downtown Omaha, the pristine condition of the outbuildings, the fitness of the horseflesh and the cattle.

"Our work is cut out for us, but it will be easier than yours," Nordstrom said sympathetically.

"It's unusual for a woman to take on this kind of fight," Chang said. His British accent made him sound eerily like J.K.

"I can't wait," Erica told him, her eyes narrowing and her

mouth set. "It's like the coach said. 'If you aren't fired with enthusiasm, you'll be *fired* with enthusiasm.'"

By the time they all returned to the Christmas tree indoors, the nip in the air had made the fire welcome. Along with the logs, the partners were glowing as they looked forward to a hard-won victory.

27

*O*n the same day that Erica made her pact with Chang and Nordstrom, John Kaplan met with his board in Archer Blair's office to determine how much higher Triomphe would go over its initial offer of fifty dollars a share. Kaplan intended to compliment his board members on the brilliance of their previous plans so they could again "help" him plot the moves he'd already decided on. Though J.K. was extraordinarily prescient in targeting vulnerable companies, even he was not clairvoyant enough to have predicted George Wheaton's death.

For a brief moment it crossed J.K.'s mind to hold the meeting at the Carlyle, to torment Archer and watch him squirm. Though Blair knew he'd been caught, he had no idea how deep the hook was set, or what effect Zara's frightened confession had had on J.K.'s usually unshakable composure.

Zara's disclosure to her husband had been complete. "It's over forever," Zara swore. "It was only for the excitement. Archer knows I mean it; the real excitement of it all, darling, was, believe it or not, you. I was dancing around your discovery, your anger, your jealousy."

J.K. had been devoted to Zara's caprices and whims, but infidelity with his best friend was more than a charming eccentricity. It was tawdry, especially when Gary Dellos turned up, hoping to turn blackmail into a blood sport. Suddenly, the give-and-take had become too much take on Zara's part.

J.K.'s perennial willingness to forgive was not forthcoming this time. As Zara wrapped herself about her husband, J.K. was unable to take her in his arms. For the first time he decided not to be indulgent toward his wife. In his craw he felt she'd been tainted by Blair and Dellos.

Dellos was a slimy creature, but, after all, he was only a mercenary. Archer was the real betrayer. What J.K. really would have liked was to oust Blair from the board. But that particular move would have to wait until the Wheaton deal was done.

As J.K. stood in Archer Blair's office, waiting to welcome the rest of his peripatetic board, he looked at picture after picture on the walls and on Blair's desk: snapshots of Cornelia, of the children, of holidays. J.K. marveled at the manifest happiness of the family. The one he picked up, however, was a large blowup of Archer's wedding on that long-ago day on that long Long Island lawn. J.K. had been the bachelor usher and Blair the doting groom.

"Things rarely turn out as we think they will, do they, sport?" J.K. said to Archer, holding the picture between them.

Bet your ass they don't, Blair thought. Zara gone, Bettina back. It was supposed to be the other way around. The one he wanted was lost. The one he was too tired to control was home.

When Bettina realized Dellos had skipped for good, she had no place to go but back home to her old bedroom, with her collections of tiny glass animals, horse show ribbons, school pictures, and her faithful panda propped on the mound of pillows on her four-poster.

Bettina's "momentary insanity" in the theft of the paintings and jewels was rationalized by Archer and Cornelia as a severe teenage aberration. What it really meant, of course, was that once again the Blairs avoided dealing with their daughter directly.

As Triomphe's small but powerful contingent sat at attention, J.K. mapped the scene in swift detail. "The numbers haven't changed, gentlemen. Since interest rates haven't risen, we'll still be coming away with five hundred million. And knowing, as we all do, the banks' willingness to lend eighty percent on assets, our five hundred million is actually a whopping four billion in buying power."

Heads nodded and smiled as J.K. smoothed the sides of his hair and grinned back at them—at all but Archer Blair.

"The one man who could have stopped us," J.K. continued, "is dead."

"It would be unconscionable for anyone controlling even a share of Wheaton stock not to advise his clients to sell at fifty," Gunther, the Swiss banker, said.

Again, heads nodded.

"At that price no one should hold out," Aumont, the Frenchman, added. "Especially since Triomphe started buying at thirty. We alone pushed it to the high thirties even before our tender. Without Triomphe, it could fall back below where we started."

"Listen, Jack," Archer Blair said, staring at J.K., "there's a lot more loyalty in what you call the sticks than you think."

It was as if J.K. had been thrown an across-the-plate pitch with bases loaded.

"Think that's true, Arch?" he asked. "What about you? Has your loyalty ever been tested? I'm asking Arch," Kaplan said to the others, "because he and I go back the farthest." J.K.'s laugh was nostalgic as he patted Blair on the back. "Has it ever been tested, Arch?" J.K. asked again, fixing Blair with a stare.

"Of course not," Blair said uncertainly.

"Loyalty?" J.K. mocked, astonished the word could even pass Archer's lips. "What makes you think the sticks are more loyal than right here? Do you think that conscience varies with geography?"

Though Archer's control was just short of breaking, this time his New England restraint saved him.

"We'd kill for a Wheaton buy-out in my country," Aki Yoshoto said, knowing full well that the Japanese don't give a yen about book value. The worth of their companies is realistically based on replacement costs and cash flow. That's why no one raids Japanese companies. After all, where's the profit in a company already selling at its true value? Little wonder, then, that Japan can hold on to its own while gobbling up the rest of the world.

"If we thought our opportunity good before, it's golden now," J.K. said, smashing his fist into his palm inches from Archer and making him recoil.

As some calculated on yellow pads, others sipped water; rarely did anyone look away from the fire in J.K.'s eyes, unaware that the sparks were caused as much by Archer Blair as by Wheaton Industries.

"So, gentlemen, what might have seemed a high flyer months ago has dropped like a pheasant at our feet."

Seconds later, Jack Minton made a motion that, if

necessary, Triomphe tender at sixty dollars a share for the common stock of Wheaton Industries. Gunther seconded. All those in favor were all those present.

"Thanks so much for the use of the hall, old buddy," J.K. said icily to Archer Blair, when the others had left. "But then it's really just quid pro quo. Right?"

Blair didn't answer.

"Pussy got your tongue, Arch?"

Blair was too unstrung to answer.

"Look, Arch. You use my place, I use yours. I use your things, you use mine. I use your secretary, you use— Anyway, thanks." With a broad smile, Kaplan picked up a little-girl photograph of puff-sleeved Bettina. "Chip off the old block, don't you think?"

28

Erica Wheaton had scheduled her trip to New York even before Chang and Nordstrom came to Omaha, betting on her hunch that they wouldn't travel so far without wanting in. Happily, they seemed to be the ideal long-term investors. They made it big by building big and creating big. They also made bigger profits, in the long run.

The joined forces of Peter Chang, Nils Nordstrom, and Erica Wheaton were a mighty phalanx, especially once Erica authorized the old-school firm of Lazard Frères to make the move. Lazard had been George's investment bankers for years, and continuing to use them was like dealing with friends.

Even Lazard's offices were warm, although to some they might appear dowdy. Compared to others, their space was small, including that of their most notable partner, Felix Rohatyn. Everywhere one looked there was nice, safe beige. The stains on the conference room wallpaper had been there so long they looked as if they were part of the pattern. In a way they were: the pattern of old money, played to the hilt.

Over the years, Lazard had taken as much pride in Wheaton's growth as had George Wheaton himself and had, in fact, found many of the companies that made Wheaton such a huge force. Though they'd been opposed to George's selling of assets, their arguments were not sufficiently convincing for him to listen.

Ironically, however, people like Chang and Nordstrom, who were putting their money into the sort of hard assets that George Wheaton had sold, kept the dollar strong.

Ever since Triomphe had tendered for Wheaton, Kaplan had tried unsuccessfully to reach Erica on the phone. Even though he thought Erica was on his side, there was no way he could have informed her before the tender, or before it was announced to the public. Though there was the off-chance she'd be difficult, he wanted to confirm that she was an ally and tell her that, if necessary, Triomphe could even consider sweetening the proposal.

Several times J.K. had thought about the Sir Galahad scenario he'd enact, envisioning Erica's excitement when he told her the high multiple of his offer. He saw himself winging his way to Omaha to have her sign over her inherited stock, then taking her for an intimate lunch where he'd go over perks such as a half-million-dollar consultant's fee, a river-view office, a downtown apartment, and the use of the company plane. None of this, including his trip, was necessary, but having her support was smart business. Besides, he liked her. He knew, too, that she was attracted to him. After all, they were a lot alike.

When Archer Blair called following the Triomphe meeting, even before J.K. was in the elevator, Erica was in Omaha, in George's office, interviewing still another candidate for the

CEO slot. With eighteen percent of the company, she had an important say about who would fill her husband's chair. Immediately after George died, Erica had called in a top New York headhunter, who sent her a stream of well-qualified candidates.

Excusing herself from the latest contender, Erica took the call in George's pristine gym.

"Hello there, Mr. Blair. I hope there's no problem with my apartment."

Archer Blair hesitated. "No. No," he said. Given everything that had happened since Erica and George's meeting with the 823 board, he'd momentarily forgotten that Erica had also bought the penthouse. "Nothing like that. Not at all. Of course, we were all so sorry. I trust you received our flowers. And anything, of course, we can do when you're in town, before you move in . . . just call. Please."

"You're sure nothing—"

"No, nothing."

"You can understand that I haven't had a chance—"

"Yes. Perfectly. That's not why I'm calling. My call has nothing to do with Eight Twenty-three."

All at once, Erica caught the tightness in his voice. Actually, it was more like anger, but what could that have to do with her?

"I'm calling about Wheaton."

"Wheaton?"

"Wheaton Industries. I'm on the board of Triomphe."

"Yes, of course."

"A few minutes ago, Triomphe concluded a board meeting here in my office where we voted to tender fifty dollars a share for Wheaton." Archer Blair lowered his voice with each word.

"That's quite a multiple," Erica said. "You must want it badly."

"John Kaplan does. And what he wants, Mrs. Wheaton, he gets."

Blair's tone was icy. Erica could imagine his thin lips tightening into a minus sign. She wondered what Blair was aching to reveal.

"I've no quarrel with the multiple," he continued. "It's what Kaplan plans after he gets the company that I worry about. He plans to skin it alive. Sell off what he can. Leave bones so bare a dog would pass them by. And after taking off with Wheaton's five hundred million in cash, he'll never look back."

Erica's head was spinning. "Why are you telling me this? Even as a good neighbor, aren't you going a bit overboard?" Erica laughed that husky laugh Blair remembered from the meeting.

Nervously, Blair cleared his throat. "Like you and your late husband, Mrs. Wheaton, I believe in roots and in America. Maybe I'm sick of seeing our country eaten alive by foreigners. I may be on an English board, but my loyalty's here. I don't know if you will see me as a turncoat or a patriot, but I had to warn you about what lies ahead."

Erica was more surprised by Archer Blair's call than by his warning. "I don't see you as one or the other, Mr. Blair, but I'm sure I should thank you. So, thank you. But to get back to the apartment for a minute. When I've decided on any work I'm going to have done, I'll submit it to the board right away. I do love it, and rest assured I'm keeping it. It's going to be a great retreat from everything that's evidently about to explode." As she spoke, she realized her group must act fast. She immediately scheduled a meeting with Jack Dowling at Lazard Frères in New York.

*   *   *

Dowling's own beige office at Lazard was as impersonal and businesslike as he was warm and familiar. A short, bespectacled man of forty, Dowling was quite a contrast to the flashy Erica, in her white fur boots and turquoise coat. Dowling's clothes were colorless except for his wide Harry Truman tie, which he wore just so everyone could say it was so unlike him.

"The battle that is to come," Dowling explained to Erica, as they sat side by side on the sofa, "represents the classic confrontation of immediate versus long-term goals. Obviously," Dowling continued, "J.K. believes there's no way you have the muscle to compete. And he wouldn't understand why you would want to. Erica, you'll see in a minute what's basically going to happen."

"I will if it's not too technical." Although Erica had canny business sense, she had to be spoon-fed spread-sheet talk.

"Wheaton could cost up to two billion. With your money from Chang and Nordstrom for the ranch, you'll all three be putting in the same equity. You'll be partners, putting up what could amount to seventy-five million each, but with one very important difference. If you succeed in getting Wheaton Industries, George's estate, which you control, will have to guarantee portions of the bank loans. This makes you, Erica Wheaton, controlling partner in the deal."

"Right." Erica nodded and inched forward on the large cushions, as if leaning closer to Dowling would make his words clearer.

"Lazard's job is to raise the remaining one point eight billion without overloading the package with junk bonds. The egg is only as good as the goose. And though those interest rates can look great, the companies paying them are often luring buyers into firms already teetering on disaster."

Erica smiled at this genius's benign little face.

"Anyway, let's say we've got the money. Next, you three musketeers make your own tender for Wheaton, obviously higher than Kaplan's. The bidding war will begin. He'll offer more, then you, then him, then you. During the war, the stock goes up. Not only because of you but because the Street and the arbs are buying big. They know the battle's for real. But not to worry. You've got it over Kaplan."

"Where? How?"

"Because you *are* Wheaton Industries, Erica. You're part of what's made it and what's going to make it live, not die."

"What if J.K. offers more than we can go?"

"Blackjack Kaplan is not about to lose his shirt. No way does Kaplan want to go for broke or for ego. And with your bids so close, those Wheaton investors whose stock grew annually at twenty percent for years aren't going to sell to someone about to sell out."

"They don't know that."

"They will. And when those little old ladies who've come this far with their annuities find out, they won't be moving those nest eggs anywhere."

"You make everything sound so hopeful."

"I try, but it's far from clear sailing. And I wouldn't be doing my job or acting as your friend and George's if I didn't again tell you that the only clear sailing would be to sell out. You'd be a very, very rich woman, Erica, with nary a care."

"You know, Jack, I would have a care. Wheaton."

"Putting up George's estate and selling the ranch is a huge gamble. And even if you do go ahead, it's not going to be that easy. You'll be so leveraged that before you get back a dime, Wheaton not only will have to make substantial payments on its debt but will have to be in the black. It could be a long pull. And, of course, you might lose. . . . However, your ace in the hole is the over three hundred million in George's estate, which you can always use to pay back debts."

"Jack, I'm literally betting the ranch. But thanks. What would I do without you?"

"You won't have to, Erica."

"I know," she said. "More than one pillow talk with George included you."

"I do manage to get into the bedroom one way or another," Dowling said, patting her hand. "Where was it you said you were going so I can't show off my only gorgeous client?"

"I'm meeting my decorator and becoming one of those ladies who lunch."

"Good for you. And please don't worry. When Kaplan finds out you're his competition—and who's going with you—he may think again about raising the Union Jack over Omaha."

"Never," Erica said. That's where her gut had it over any hardened power broker. She'd only had to meet J.K. once to know he was in for keeps. And once he was in, he never folded.

As Erica entered the tiny French bistro across from the decorator and designer showrooms, the first person she saw, to her delight, was van Arlyn. Although they'd spoken frequently, she hadn't seen Clive since before the 823 board meeting.

"Let Oldfield come without me? Are you mad?" Clive asked, rolling his eyes, looking Erica up and down before hugging her. "Merry Christmas! I see all we need is the sleigh."

"Same old Clive." Erica laughed.

"Same young Erica."

Brice Oldfield joined in. "Same me, too."

"Who asked you?" said Clive, taking Erica's arm proprietarily, hustling her to their table.

"Who asked *you* is more like it," Brice said, trying to grab her other arm.

Erica laughed. "To borrow a word, 'pul-eese.'"

After ordering two Perriers and an Absolut on the rocks for Clive, Oldfield looked earnestly at Erica. "My dear Mrs. Wheaton. I hope I'm correct in concluding that you've been sufficiently infected by the city's urgent vulgarity to glut every parlor with the glitz of a mogul's paradise."

"Taught him all his eloquence," van Arlyn said, reaching over to puff up Oldfield's foulard.

A faint wave of happiness swept over Erica as her mind eased from the fight ahead to the froth at hand. "Gentlemen, I have only twenty-five million to spend, and I don't mean per room!" she said, drumming her nails on the table.

"Can't possibly do it. You'd need at least that much to acquire a single major work of art if you're considering having any social status on the street of dreams. And that's major with a capital M. M-anet. M-atisse. Or just Money with a *y* instead of the *t*."

"'Twas always thus. As the last century turned, the nouveau raced to Paris and London to be properly gowned by Molyneux and Poiret, fed by Fortnum's, and decorated by the galleries on the rue de la Paix," van Arlyn said, purposely blasé, showing off for Brice and Erica.

How George would have appreciated this, Erica thought. He had surpassed them all with his simple frames of money.

Brice Oldfield looked into Erica's eyes. "What can one

possibly do when today's arbiters of elegance are yesterday's mistresses!"

"Too true," van Arlyn agreed, feeling weak as he patted his brow with the overstarched napkin.

Van Arlyn actually had almost fainted earlier that day, at the sight of the morning headlines and photographs in all three papers:

GREEK PLAYBOY SOUGHT IN PAINTING HEIST

SOCIALITE MILLIONAIRE ROBBED BY GREEK GIGOLO

HIT MAN HITS SOCIALITE FOR MILLIONS IN ART

With every word, van Arlyn's knees had grown shakier until they'd finally buckled. Dellos! After reviving with a couple of Valiums and a tumbler of Absolut, van Arlyn had wondered if Erica would remember Dellos's face from that morning in the elevator and make the connection. He wondered, too, where Dellos was hiding, knowing how terrified he must be.

29

*S*auntering along the docks of Piraeus, Gary Dellos had never been happier. He had a pocketful of money and a tankful of gas—a Ferrari tank at that. The hometown-boy-made-bad was about to spend even more of Blair's hard-inherited dough on a yacht, onto which he would now invite those he'd once served.

Passing a newsstand, he whirled as his eye caught the front page. Shocked, he gave the dealer the change, staring him straight in the eye, but the old man had a white cane with a red tip.

All at once, Dellos's bright demeanor turned to pitch and the boulevardier's strut became a slouch. Before reading any further, he quickly bought an oversized pair of mirrored aviator glasses.

Crossing the square, he sank onto a hard metal chair outside a café and ordered a double brandy. His world, having just fallen into place, had fallen apart.

Did Blair really think he could get away with this shit? That Dellos would sit back and take the rap? Didn't Blair know Dellos would drag Bettina over every fucking coal? Or didn't Blair give a damn? Again, he read the front page.

GREEK PLAYBOY WANTED

LOVER OF BETTINA BLAIR MASTERMINDS THEFT

Dellos couldn't believe it. Bettina admits taking the paintings and Dellos is blamed. Blair must've flipped all the way. No matter what lies that little bitch told her father, no matter what he had swallowed, Dellos was not losing those paintings.

The rich were a helluva lot worse frauds than he was. How about that lying bitch! He'd thought she'd be too scared to tell her cocksucker old man, and he'd be too scared of damaging his name to go to the cops. But if they dragged Dellos back to trial, the world would soon know about the elegant Blairs. He'd smear slime from every sewer in New York onto their precious name. Wild with rage, he threw down another double.

Maybe he should call Blair now. Tell him he'd make him more notorious than a post office pinup. Him and Zara, as well as his nympho-klepto daughter. And tell him, too, there was no way Gary Dellos would hide his face so the press couldn't photograph him. He'd be proud to pose for the truth.

The more Dellos thought about it, the happier he became. Taking off his glasses, he smiled drunkenly at passersby, especially Americans. "Hello! You know Mr. Archer Pisspot Blair or his whore-thief daughter from New York? From Fifth Avenue? Very, very, very rich. Very, very, very social."

They walked swiftly by, looking anywhere but at him. Maybe they'd have stopped if he'd shown them his picture in the paper. Americans love celebrities. He'd show them a real star.

Dellos watched the activity along the wharf. Suddenly his eyes were drawn to a dark, sullen boy in a fishnet shirt, sweating in the chilly air, loading a big motherfucker of a yacht with champagne. Dellos wondered, if he were that boy, whether he wouldn't just shove those cases in the sea and take his chance with what was below in the main stateroom.

Probably he would. The overconfidence of youth had never left Dellos. He was still a kid with a dream to be rich. Shit, he was like the rich in other ways. He was even a better cheat. Just not rich enough to get away with it.

After draining his drink, he went inside the café. Laughing loudly, he showed the owner his picture.

"What do you think? Famous, huh?" Turning to the morning stragglers, he held the paper over his head. "This is me. I'm famous all over the world. The great Dellos. Like the great Santini, Houdini, Mother Cabrini. And now I'm gonna nail that bastard. Nail him to his empty picture frames. Change for the phone, please, my good man," Dellos said, slurring his words as he shoved a wad of bills across the bar. "No collect calls for Gary Dellos. Not for a man of means who's gonna mean a lot more!" Staggering to the wall phone, Dellos got Blair on the first try.

Too stunned to speak, Blair muttered, "Call me back in two minutes. Two minutes."

"Sure, Archie, old sport. If you're sure that's enough time for everyone to tap in. Just make sure my beloved Bettina is on."

Dellos was right. Blair wanted time to get the law *and* his lawyers on the line.

"Everything in place, Mr. Pisspot, sir?" Dellos asked when he called Blair back.

"Everything's fine, Dellos." Blair had recovered some-what.

"Hi there, Bettina," Dellos called. "How's that cute little black hole of Calcutta?"

"Dellos, for God's sake!" Archie Blair's voice pulsed with tension.

"It's *my* drachma, Archie."

"Say what you have to say, Dellos."

"Well, you just heard part of it. But I can understand your not wanting to waste time on your daughter." Then, as soberly as possible, Dellos told him that, as far as who took the paintings, it would be his word against Blair's. "In fact, my own attorneys are this minute readying a defamation suit against you. Or are those my tailors?"

Dellos roared.

"Just dust the walls for fingerprints, Arch. You'll see how innocent I am. Look, sport, I know since the lady's left you've got sex on the brain. And I know that's no place for it; it's causing a lot of damage. Ever hear of Sophocles?"

"Wait a minute," Blair said, pressing HOLD. He wanted to think a minute. Not ask anyone. Just clear his head.

"What in hell's going on?" Dellos yelled. "I don't have all day."

Archer Blair was angrier with Bettina than with Dellos. Releasing the HOLD button, he said, "Call me in ten minutes."

"I'm not made of money, Blair, like the black sheep who took the goods off your walls or the lady who just took you period." Dellos didn't want to hang up. He was having fun. He had a pocketful of change.

"Then I'll call you back in ten minutes," Blair said. "What's the number?" His hand shook as he wrote it down.

"Make it five, blue brain."

It didn't take three for Blair to call back, but the man who answered said Dellos had gone to the bar.

"Dellos! Dellos!" Blair yelled. All he could hear was music, a blur of voices, and noises that sounded like boat horns. "Dellos!"

Gary Dellos smiled at the dangling receiver as he threw down another double. "I'm having a drink to celebrate!" he shouted in the direction of the phone. Finally, he condescended to pick up the receiver. "What did the gentlemen of the jury tell you, Mr. Nice Guy?"

"Dellos, I swear, if you ever come—"

"They advised you to threaten the peaceable kingdom?"

"Dellos, you're filth all over the world."

"If I'm filth, what does that make you? Anyway, sport, how are you settling my slander suit? Should we meet at the Metropolitan Club? Have George make another martini?"

"All right, Dellos," Blair said, about to break. "I'll drop the case."

Dellos could hardly believe it. "What about my good name?" Now he was really having fun. "I want a retraction, so you and me can meet like gents in the same parlors."

"There'll be a retraction, Dellos."

"Make sure it's on the front page. Your money can only buy so much, but I suggest you let it buy that." Dellos slapped his fat wallet as he strained to see if his Ferrari was still parked at the end of the square.

"Okay, Dellos." All Blair wanted was to get off the phone. He never wanted to hear Dellos's voice again.

Not only would Archer Blair have to drop all charges against this swine but all insurance claims as well. Millions of dollars down the manhole. Millions! He rubbed his head. Every muscle ached. Every artery throbbed. How would he explain it to the police? This was a serious investigation to call off so suddenly. It was a manhunt. Bettina suffered from temporary insanity! That would do it. It's what it was, anyway. They could deal with it. They'd find the best rest home there was, with the best doctors and the best care. Bettina would be taken care of in the best Blair fashion—by somebody else.

"Okay what, pisspot?"

"Okay, fine. Is this the end of it, then?" Blair had to ask. He was desperate.

"Sure, Arch. But you got to promise to punish the real thief," Dellos said, rubbing the whole Aegean into Blair's open wound.

"Don't worry," Blair answered. "This *is* the end?" Again Blair had to ask. Actually he was pleading.

"Thieves' honor!"

For whatever remained of his own sanity, Archer Blair had to believe Dellos. If the money he'd get from the paintings and jewelry wasn't sufficient reason to stay away, maybe his never having to deal with Bettina again would be. Suddenly horrified, Blair realized he and Dellos did have one thing in common: Bettina.

30

*T*he following morning's headlines stunned van Arlyn as much as had those of the previous day.

BLAIR DROPS CHARGES AGAINST DELLOS

WRONG GREEK WRONGED, BLAIR ADMITS

What in hell did Gary Dellos have on Archer Blair? Bettina? Judging from the scene van Arlyn and Erica had witnessed, she must have been seriously involved. Even with today's retractions, van Arlyn knew yesterday's papers had told the real story. Though the contrived explanation about a Barry Dellos read legitimately, it didn't fool him one bit.

Van Arlyn was sure Blair's deal had to do with getting Dellos out of the way, or he would never have gone so public. Blair's sudden reversal had to mean Dellos had enough goods on Blair to drop recovering the paintings along with the case.

In fact, when van Arlyn realized it was Dellos who'd surfaced at 823, all his hidden fears about exposure had surfaced too. Van Arlyn was thrilled that Dellos had extorted some really big money. Now Dellos wouldn't be coming after *him*.

Again, van Arlyn wondered if Erica would make the connection with 823. It would be easier this morning, with all the photographs. Yet if Erica's head was anywhere like it was yesterday, she'd be too distracted to focus on much besides Wheaton Industries. Though she'd been the old carefree Erica during lunch, in the showrooms she could barely concentrate on fabrics and furniture. The conversation always seemed to revert to the fight for Wheaton.

Clive had taken Oldfield aside to assure him that it wasn't Brice's taste that was causing her distraction. Since this was to be Oldfield's signature job, Clive didn't want Brice to lose his cool and he didn't want to lose his cut. Van Arlyn felt no compunction at all about getting in on the action, since it came out of Brice's third. After his commission from 823 and his slice from Oldfield, van Arlyn could easily switch his life back from trade to leisure. But he'd grown accustomed to the pace—and he still fantasized about growing more accustomed to Oldfield.

After yesterday, Erica realized that until Wheaton was settled, nothing else in her life would be. The jousting of Clive and Brice, the trekking through chintz, and the pursuit of gossip were not for now. Her place was in the eye of the storm.

And so it erupted that very evening, with the early edition of *The New York Times,* hand delivered by Jack Dowling, who opened to the front page of the business section. There she was, pictured alongside John Kaplan.

Although the possession of almost any form of inside information had become a felony on Wall Street, it still seemed that secrets were known to outsiders before the inner doors had even closed. In the walls, in the machines, through the furniture and carpeting, little bugs had to be sending

signals to the outside. The buzz the *Times* printed was that
Erica Wheaton wasn't going to sell:

> George Wheaton's widow,
> with an influential consortium,
> has enlisted Lazard Frères & Co.
> to help finance her fight with
> John Kaplan, Triomphe's man-
> aging director and, until yester-
> day, the lone wolf on the Omaha
> trail. Responding to the news,
> John Kaplan said yesterday from
> his New York office, "It's as if I
> were the steak and she were the
> peas and we were on the same
> plate. When I start to carve, the
> peas shall disperse all over the
> plate."

"They couldn't reach you for comment," Dowling said.
"It's good you were where you were, buried in carpet and
chintz. Not that you couldn't have handled it, but it's better
to be prepared. Anyway, nothing is final until we raise the
money. If you're pressed, all you have to say is that the
thought of selling never occurred to you. Wheaton's American, and that's how it should stay. Let that wonderful voice
float with charm and double-talk."

The morning sun flowed through the living room of the
Carlyle. J.K. felt full of vigor. Looking at Zara's undisturbed
half of the bed, he felt a sense of relief at being alone. No
temperament or moods to worry about. Having spoken to the
children last night, J.K. didn't think of calling home this
morning as once he would have.

As J.K. opened *The New York Times* he turned immediately to the business section. In a second, his sense of well-being disappeared. Dumbfounded, he read the piece and scrutinized the pictures. Instead of Erica and him smiling side by side in the same photograph, there they were—formal and serious looking, in different pictures, as if they were the antagonists the article portrayed them to be. Kaplan was bewildered by what he thought an odd turn of events. He had thought she would sell Wheaton. He never imagined she would put up a struggle. Why in God's name would she do that?

Kaplan wondered who'd gotten to her. Who was behind this stupidity? Did she really want to stay on the banks of that sludge-filled river and rot? No one needed the frenzy of a bidding war. Everyone would win once J.K. cut his deal.

Even if she was silly enough to have been devoted to that husband, why would she feel the same way about a business? It wasn't even a glamorous one.

Straightening his tie and throwing back his shoulders, he knew one thing for sure: he had to give it the old school try. The dazzling Kaplan footwork had to be displayed before this round was over. Not that he felt especially encouraged by the fact that she never returned his calls.

J.K. patted his hair with a few choice words to the mirror. "I do believe, old chap, that in this battle you have even more to offer than 'blood, toil, tears, and sweat.'"

With a keen sense of excitement and confidence, J.K. strode down Fifth Avenue to the Plaza. Passing 823, even more energy possessed him. Although he'd lost the apartment, there had been no battle to wage because the winner had been declared without a contest. But Wheaton was different.

Although the Christmas lights and decorations inside the hotel were festive, J.K. didn't notice. He raced to the front desk.

"No, Mrs. Wheaton is not in her room," the rosy-cheeked Frock Coat told him.

"You're sure she hasn't checked out?"

"It would have come up on the screen."

J.K. turned his wrist. Only eight-fifteen. Maybe she was doing that jogging Americans do.

"You might try the Edwardian Room, sir." Although Frock Coat wasn't supposed to relinquish information about guests, this fellow looked richly legitimate. In fact, Frock Coat even decided to call the dining room. "We're in luck, sir. She's having breakfast. Sitting alone. Expecting you, perhaps."

"Thank you," J.K. said, handing him a twenty.

"Oh, no, no, sir. Thank you. Mrs. Trump doesn't allow gratuities."

Kaplan smiled to himself, wondering what the turnover rate was among the staff.

Passing the newsstand, J.K. suddenly had an idea. Buying another *Times,* he took it over to the gift shop and had the pictures of Erica and himself cut out and taped together inside a silver frame. Not a bad calling card, he thought.

J.K. watched from the entrance of the Edwardian Room as the captain handed the frame to Erica Wheaton. Running her fingers through her hair, she looked toward the door as she watched Kaplan come toward her.

"What a coincidence," he said, his eyes their most flirtatious as he stood beside her. Remarkable, he thought, how sparkling she looked so early.

"Indeed." She smiled, a bit embarrassed yet pleased by Kaplan's staring.

"May I?" J.K. asked as he pulled a chair from her window table. It faced the horses and carriages waiting for winter's slim pickings.

"Anyone this inventive is always welcome," Erica said, looking at the frame. "Obviously I didn't expect you, but now that you're here I'm not surprised."

"Thank you," J.K. said, wondering why, since their thinking was so alike, she would take the position she was taking. But then, that's why he was here. "A direct approach seemed the only way. You're a difficult lady to reach, Mrs. Wheaton."

"Not where there's a will."

There it was, J.K. thought. That come-on intonation. The very essence of what had given him hope in Omaha. "It's more amusing that way," J.K. said.

"I hope you won't be disappointed," Erica said, thinking of Wheaton.

"I hope not too," he said, as the come-on began to come off. "Do you mind if I have some tea?"

"Forgive me. By all means."

Unconsciously putting her on an equal footing, J.K. sat back, thinking she would call the waiter. Realizing at the same time that both of them were waiting, they laughed as J.K. finally made the motion.

Amazing, J.K. mused, that someone so fuckable in clinging red jersey could have the mind of a gray flannel suit.

"I understand you're in New York shopping," he said, propping the frame between them.

"'Tis the season."

"I tried doing mine earlier. Then I liked what I bought so much I bought more. Now I'd like to buy every bit that's still available. But you know the minute something is hot, it doesn't last long—usually because people don't want anyone else to have it."

"I disagree," Erica said, nodding at the waiter to remove the last bite of what had been eggs Benedict.

J.K. couldn't help comparing Erica's breakfast with Zara's grapefruit—and comparing Erica's figure as well. Both were a helluva lot more appetizing.

While the waiter cleared the table, Erica picked the yellow rose from the glass vase and smelled it. "I don't know what's usual, but I don't want Wheaton because it is or isn't hot." Her eyes were wide and guileless. Although she looked as if she belonged in a room ringed with college pennants instead of jousting over a power breakfast, she sounded like George Wheaton's ghost riding through town in vengeance.

J.K. looked into his tea, as if the answer to Erica could be found in the leaves. As if he could find the way to turn this bull-headed woman into a grateful widow by offering her the life most women would die for.

Like Zara, for instance. "*Toujours gai. Toujours riche.* The best. *N'est-ce pas?*" as Zara said.

Erica ordered more coffee and J.K. poured the last of his tea. He wondered how he could make Erica see the futility of her fight. All those lawyers and bankers were advising her to stay in so they could extract exorbitant fees. There wasn't a chance she could win. Not only were his pockets deeper, his pride wouldn't allow defeat.

Pulling a petal from the rose, Erica rubbed its softness between her fingers. "I hope your coming to New York wasn't just for this meeting. I'd be wild, having made such a trip, to go home with what you're taking back."

Although J.K. felt patronized, her voice was so ingenuous he again felt sorry for her. Did she really believe he'd come all this way on the chance of breakfast?

"Not to worry," John Kaplan said coolly. "I often crave the Plaza's tea. Sometimes I make a round-trip just for a pot. At least today I can write off my crossing." What irritated

Kaplan most was that she made him uncomfortable. He couldn't just write *her* off.

"I'm sorry," she said. "I didn't mean that the way it sounded. I'm not a pro at this."

"No, you're not," Kaplan said with a nip in his voice. But she was better than she thought, although he didn't say it. "That's why I'm offering you the opportunity to be done with it."

"I'm sure I should say thanks, but no thanks."

J.K. winced at her sophomoric response. "You're making a mistake, Erica. I'm saying this as a friend."

She knew he was, in his way. But his way wasn't hers. "I couldn't live with myself if I didn't fight for what George built, or if I put people on the street to put money in my purse."

"I have no thought of doing that," J.K. said indignantly.

"'Asset-stripping' is a term I'd never heard until I'd heard of you." Erica's voice was passionate.

"'Efficient operation' is the correct term. And when one is efficient, one must cut dead wood away to make room for new growth. For the short term it eliminates jobs. But in the long run, the dying grove becomes a forest."

"But everyone knows J.K. doesn't stick around for the long term."

"The world has your ear?"

"Of course not. But it knows your reputation."

"Wheaton's shareholders are grumbling about undervalued stock. The option I'm offering is best for them. My base is bigger than George Wheaton's ever was. And that's before he began his *own* asset-stripping. In fact, if he hadn't done what you accuse me of wanting to do, we wouldn't be here."

"His way was different. He was selling for the long term. You want out."

"Don't be sure. And how do I know that you and whoever is behind you won't do what you *think* I'm going to do, given the opportunity—which, by the way, I'll never give!"

"Give what you don't own?"

"I don't yet, Erica. But 'yet' is a temporary state."

"Everything is," Erica said nostalgically. "Like all these beautiful decorations. I love Christmas. Don't you?"

"I do. Yes. Very much."

"I wish it were snowing."

J.K. stood as Erica rose, unaware that she had signed the check, unaware, too, that she was feeling the same gnawing discomfort he had felt.

"Will you be in England for Christmas?"

"No, Switzerland. Skiing." Right now, J.K. wouldn't have minded a little ride with Erica in one of those horse-drawn carriages.

"Good-bye for now," Erica said, extending her hand as they reached the lobby. "Have a wonderful holiday."

"I'm sure we'll be in touch."

"I'm sure," she answered, slowly pulling her hand free.

31

*J*ohn Kaplan was delighted that Zara and the family were going without him to Saint Moritz after Christmas. Philip, who'd remained Zara's great friend, would be the perfect companion. He was still enough of a child himself to be good fun for the children and, like Zara, he could stay up all night and party. But most of all, he loved to create Zara's fantasy outfits for the myriad balls at the Palace Hotel during this, the height of the winter season.

However, J.K. was surprised at how relieved he was not to go. True, he would be swamped with business. With Lazard behind Erica, he knew her financing was assured and fast moves would be in order. Yet it wasn't the freedom to attend to Wheaton that gave J.K. the lightness he felt. It was his freedom from Zara. Even before Archer, had J.K. taken the time, he would have noticed that his existence had less and less to do with Zara. If no disguise can conceal love, the opposite is equally true. Also, their lack of sex had become embarrassing and their silences were no longer those of comfort or understanding.

Christmas Day was spent at the country house near Chartwell, much as it always was, with long walks, leaping fires, and plum pudding. And, as usual, Zara's parents, with their equally freeloading friends, arrived early. It suited J.K. to have the lord come to *his* manor.

When everyone gathered, the first activity after brandy had been to follow the caretaker to the far end of the estate to select the tree. Later, those still steady on their feet helped the children hang the delicately carved angels given to Zara's grandfather by the Cornish nuns for rebuilding their war-torn convent. Each year Zara's father would go on about the family's donation and each year the amount he named would rise, along with his wrath that the money had gone to the church instead of to him.

Zara always adored Christmas, but this year had been special. Her affair with Archer had begun to pale even before the mess with Dellos. Therefore, her newfound freedom from him, as well as J.K.'s all-out dedication to that Wheaton business, was most welcome. The omission of J.K.'s usual sentimental card with his gift of a lavish ruby-and-diamond bracelet under the tree went unnoticed, and any lingering disappointment over 823 had totally disappeared.

So far as J.K. was concerned, not getting 823 was the same as escaping a bullet. Not that he had given up wanting a grand city apartment. The time had come for a substantial base in the States. New York was as close to Omaha as he wanted to be to a company whose days were numbered, especially when he would be responsible for the countdown. Yet he felt no guilt. He'd given Erica fair warning and a fair shot.

* * *

Erica Wheaton couldn't have had a better Christmas present than Jack Dowling's call. The financing for her group was definitely in place. "Erica, Merry Christmas."

"Thank you, Jack. I know George is thanking you too."

"I just want to hear from you, not George quite yet, if you don't mind."

Erica laughed. "How could I mind anything this morning?"

Although Erica understood LBOs, Dowling wanted to spell out the deal as it applied to Wheaton. "Lazard and its network are going to raise roughly eighty percent of the secured debt. It works like a mortgage, only this money is against Wheaton's assets instead of against a house. Then you, Chang, and Nordstrom are in for ten percent. Okay?"

"Right."

"The last ten percent will be financed by junk bonds. But you have to come up with as much cash as possible to make this deal work, and the only reason you can is because what George left of Wheaton is of such top quality. Why do you think J.K. is so hot for this deal for himself? What's important is you've got the money, and let's hope you get Wheaton."

"It's *we*, Jack. I never could have done it without you."

"Thanks, Erica. How have your holidays been?"

"Much better than I thought," she said honestly. "George's boys were here a good deal. Marian's taken to her bed."

"Alone?"

"With a bottle. They're going to do something about her after the New Year."

"Letting her toast it in first."

"It's sad."

"Sad, Erica, is when you don't go around hurting others. Let's forget Marian."

"Fine, but let's stay on bottles and New York for a second. You want to hear something really kind Archer Blair did? He's the head of the board at Eight Twenty-three."

"I know." Dowling smiled, thinking how Erica referred to Blair.

"He sent me a magnum of Dom Perignon. There was nothing on the card about having-a-merry or even about Christmas. He just wished me happiness and success in the New Year. Considering his own mess with those paintings, it was so sweet. It made me feel good about where I'm going to live." Erica had been stunned when she'd read about the theft of Blair's paintings. It was not only Blair's loss that upset her, but the security of 823.

"I'm glad for you, Erica, but also a little surprised, considering Blair's going to be an archenemy."

"He obviously keeps business and pleasure separate."

"He's Kaplan's closest pal."

"Then it was doubly sweet," Erica said. Actually, something Erica couldn't put her finger on had disturbed her about Archer's gift and the card. Maybe it was the very thing she was trying to find so thoughtful, the no mention of the holidays, yet it was clearly a Christmas gift. Possibly the words "success for the New Year." Erica couldn't help feeling that some warning was packaged along with the champagne. After all, he *had* called her about J.K.

32

*T*here had been no doubt in J.K.'s mind about Lazard's ability to come up with the financing Erica needed. And after their breakfast, he knew nothing would stop her. Wheaton was one of the last great takeovers of the eighties. It was too bad, J.K. thought, that he and Erica couldn't be on the same team.

Needless to say, the gluttons of Wall Street feasted on Erica's war with Kaplan. When her fifty-three-dollars-per-share comeback flattened Triomphe's blockbuster offer of fifty, the Street was stunned and shares traded with lightning speed.

With stocks rising, taxation on buying *and* selling surging, and the default rate on junk bonds soaring past thirty percent, the takeover climate, as Zara would say, had gone from *très chaud* to *très froid*.

Through it all, the Wheaton momentum continued, each genius on the Street sure his prediction was the right one.

What was unique was that the Street's prophets applied the same theories to both bidders.

"Erica's team will pay anything!"

"For Kaplan the sky's the limit."

"Like Goldsmith with Goodyear, Kaplan will get gold from greenmail."

"She'll throw in her hand when she sees what she's dealt."

"Kaplan will fold before attrition begins."

"Erica will never let Wheaton go!"

"Triomphe's got Wheaton cold!"

The week that Erica tendered her group's bid of fifty-three, she made two round trips to New York. She felt safer nearer the action. With Hong Kong and Norway at such a distance, Dowling was her only flesh-and-blood contact, although they conferred daily.

One of J.K.'s biggest pluses was that, with Triomphe's powerful board, he could summon the elite of international corporate hierarchy by flicking his finger. "Wheaton should welcome war," John Kaplan told London's *Financial Times*. "Without a fight, mismanaged companies stay mismanaged forever. Like bad politicians who remain unchallenged."

The more J.K. smeared Wheaton, the more everyone waited for Triomphe's answer to Erica's fifty-three. And within seventy-two hours, the Mayfair lion had roared "Fifty-five!" across the broad Atlantic.

As the market tried to predict what would happen next, analysts stayed glued to the ticker as if watching a giant chess game on a global screen. Sooner than expected, Omaha shot back: "Fifty-seven!"

J.K. became more and more frustrated. Phones rang at all hours. Misinformation was rampant. The board was at odds. Still, the final decision was his. "Yes, of course you heard correctly," he shouted into the receiver. "Sixty! I said sixty! Shall I say it again? Sixty! Sixty!"

When J.K. had first started to buy Wheaton, less than a month before his trip to Omaha, the stock had been thirty, half its present high. Now, at sixty, the tape was starting to melt.

Erica couldn't believe it. "George, I hope you're watching," she whispered, "because this isn't practice. It's a real game with real points. But it's funny, George. So far only the people on the sidelines are winners. And the score is higher than any player ever dreamed. And I'm frightened. I wish you were here."

Though some stockholders had tendered their shares at fifty and more, most of them held tight, though during the seesaw, some had also switched when one offer or the other seemed unbeatable. However, to refuse J.K.'s bid of sixty now seemed next to impossible. It was as if this was the close-out figure for which everyone had been waiting. Not that one couldn't always withdraw his tender from J.K., were Erica's group to do the impossible and go higher. But what was great to know, barring the deal's total collapse—sixty was in the bank.

In what seemed like an eternity but in reality was only ten days, the time desperately needed for Wheaton's board to confer and for the banks to rethink and redo their numbers, the impossible happened.

"A new economic superpower, Erica Wheaton, George Wheaton's widow, has bid sixty-two dollars for Wheaton Industries," boomed a financial telecaster on the evening news. "The new offer more than doubles the price of Wheaton shares before this war began. Stay tuned for the sixty-four-dollar question!"

As the days flew, so did more rumors.

"Erica's strung out."

"Kaplan's backed away."

"The deal's collapsing."

"Man and superwoman."

Shareholders were worried. Erica hadn't slept in days. Only J.K. knew the answer. And then he told them.

"Sixty-four!" His voice was cool and crisp before the barrage of press. The price was higher than he'd intended, but thank goodness it was over. In a few days he would even call Erica himself. As Sir Winston said, "In victory, magnanimity." No one would understand more than Erica the difference between college and the majors.

When J.K. called Erica about what a fine offering she had at sixty-four, he realized it must be obvious even to her that the fight was over. Before hanging up, she thanked J.K. for his call and, in her coolest manner, allowed as how not only was the fight not finished but the last round had not yet begun.

One day later, Erica's group responded. *Their* matching sixty-four-dollar offer was composed of fifty-nine dollars in cash and five dollars in ten-year interest-bearing debentures. Following on the heels of that announcement came a second bombshell. A special meeting of Wheaton shareholders had been called.

When the notice of the special meeting arrived, J.K. believed this could only be Erica's lunacy at work. Somehow she had managed to get the board to consent to this preposterous idea. J.K. was a businessman, an efficient operator. This subterfuge was about as unprofessional as one could get. But then, again, why should he be surprised by what Miss Nebraska did? Pretty didn't mean clever. And no one should ever confuse ambitious with smart.

Of course, there were shares still not tendered, still out

there to be counted, shares that could swing the vote, but that was to be expected. Owners of those shares were just waiting to make sure that J.K.'s bid was the best and no new players came in at the last minute. As soon as that was definite, they would tender in J.K.'s direction.

It infuriated J.K. that this battle was to drag on unnecessarily. It wasn't as if the bids were equal. What idiots would accept junk bonds instead of cash? The only difference J.K. could see was the added expense, especially to Erica and those dummies backing her.

To make a public plea for shares was for J.K. the same as begging. In England, when the king dies, it's over. "The king is dead, long live the king!" And who but J.K. was going to reign over Wheaton? Erica should have kept her crisis to herself, Kaplan thought. Why pull in the whole state, especially all those good folk about whom she pretended to care so desperately? If she were truly interested in the people, she'd let them get their money and get out.

Maybe Erica just wanted center stage. Maybe that's what this exercise in futility was about. She wanted glamour. This would be her last hurrah. What do they say about the boy and his farm? J.K. shook his head. Whatever it was, the same held true for the girl and the runway.

Suddenly, J.K. remembered the last half of Sir Winston's quote: "In defeat defiance."

To the shareholders of
Wheaton Industries

You are hereby notified that the
directors of Wheaton Industries
have called a special shareholders' meeting on February 29 at
11:00 A.M. at the Wheaton
Conference Center in Omaha,
Nebraska. The purpose of this
meeting is to evaluate the out-
standing offers to purchase the
company, as well as to consider
any alternatives that may be
appropriate and to transact any
business that may, at this time,
be lawfully brought before the
board.

Sincerely,
James G. Clausen, Secretary

The notice was published in *The Wall Street Journal* and sent to all stockholders by Mailgram four days after John Kaplan's sixty-four-dollar tender for the company.

The morning of the meeting was crisp and clear. The sky was a deep winter blue, and the ground was covered with a light snow. John Kaplan certainly never thought he'd be flying back into Eppley Airport except to shake hands with *his* new board of directors and to meet whatever management was left in *his* new company.

Although he'd considered bringing one of his associates along, when he thought about it again he decided against the added bother of conversation. "Don't go too far," he had told his crew. "This won't take long."

As J.K. walked through the airport he felt the ghost of George Wheaton everywhere. Those same posters stared down even more convincingly now that he was gone. That's what it's like, J.K. thought, to be a big fish in a small pond. There was no way one could leave that mark in London or New York.

J.K. was still thinking about George when he heard his name. Had the voice not interrupted his thoughts, he would never have seen the chauffeur holding the sign. Again, J.K. felt strange, remembering George Wheaton and a similar sign.

"I've been saying 'Mr. Kaplan?' to all the big-city types I've seen," the uniformed driver said, happy he hadn't missed J.K. "I'm Cal. You have any luggage, sir?"

"No, none," J.K. said quickly, shaking his head. Though J.K. didn't know where he was going or where the limousine was parked, he walked on ahead, used to being in control, leading the way.

The driver had to hustle to keep up. "This your first trip to Omaha, sir?"

"No." Americans really have no manners, J.K. thought irritably. Always butting in.

"Left the motor running so it would be warm," the driver said, pulling open the limousine door. "Not that I thought anybody would come to Omaha on a day like this without a coat. George Wheaton never wore a coat either."

"What has Mr. Wheaton got to do with it?" J.K. asked.

"Aren't you here for the meeting?"

"Actually, yes."

"That's what. Mr. Wheaton was a big man here, and the meeting's a big deal. Looks like Wheaton's going to be sold."

"Is that good or bad?"

"Depends."

"On what?"

"On what the new owners are going to do with it."

"You're well informed." J.K. was grateful to find the button to close the glass partition between himself and the front seat.

Sunshine washed the Wheaton Mall in a glow of well-being as J.K. drove up to the high glass doors of the entrance.

"I won't be too long," J.K. said curtly.

"I'll be waiting, sir."

Inside the huge lobby, a festive atmosphere seemed to prevail, possibly because of the massive pots of forsythia planted along the tall windows and banked next to the elevators and seating area. Clean and impeccably maintained, not so much as a cigarette butt lay on the highly polished travertine marble floor.

All over, signs and arrows pointed in the direction of the room where the meeting would be held. With every step, John Kaplan became part of a larger and larger group following the arrows. Outside the huge meeting room, pretty cheerleader types handed out copies of a brief agenda.

J.K. accepted the paper coolly. Once inside, however, he was stunned by the size of the crowd already gathered. Row upon row of seats were filled, by people of every description: young and old, well-dressed professionals and dowdy farm types, sophisticates and a surprising number who'd obviously taken time off from work. Some women had brought their children, and a few even carried babies. There were probably enough votes here to swing the tide of General Motors. The shouting back and forth, the laughter, the two wagons set up for soft drinks reminded J.K. of a political convention, the kind he'd watched on TV. It was so . . . American.

On the dais in front of each place was an acrylic name plate used at Wheaton's annual stockholders' meetings, but those meetings had never drawn a tenth this many people.

It didn't take long for Erica Wheaton to spot John Kaplan. Even through the swarm of people it would have been difficult to miss the pinstripes and that towering presence. Although Erica obviously hadn't invited him, she kept watching for him without realizing what she was doing.

It certainly wasn't necessary for J.K. to come. His money usually did the talking. And he wasn't there to gloat over the inevitable ending. This time he just thought it would be the decent thing to congratulate his new stockholders personally, especially after his first big American triumph.

Erica looked quite wonderful, Kaplan thought. True, this was her day to shine, but shine she did. Nothing was overdone. There was nothing offensive. Bright colors suited her. Needless to say, he had no idea she wore the vibrant red for the Cornhuskers' winning team.

Not to be ungracious, J.K. threaded his way through the crowd to greet her.

To make it easier for him and to be a good sport, Erica met him halfway. "Hello." Her smile was tentative. "I can't exactly say Wheaton Industries welcomes you."

"Wheaton will," J.K. said forcefully but not unkindly, "once this little game is played out."

"If it's so little, how come it's brought you so far afield?"

"The stakes are big." He also wanted to add, After today this will be a large part of Triomphe turf—but something stopped him. Maybe it was her reckless loyalty. Maybe he wanted to protect her.

"I must go," Erica said quickly.

"Good luck," J.K. said, not only because he was sure it wouldn't help.

Promptly at eleven, Tom McKnight, acting head of Wheaton's board, took the microphone. Looking about the room, McKnight asked in his flat midwestern voice that everyone be seated. J.K. couldn't believe it: there wasn't a spare chair; people were standing around the sides and in the back of the auditorium.

In seconds, the din, the ice cubes, even the children on laps were silent. But it was a heavy rather than an expectant silence. As is customary, someone preselected from the floor made the motion for the meeting to come to order, someone else seconded it, and since all were obviously "in favor," the meeting began. Also, since there were no alternative bids, and since the only business on the agenda was Erica's, McKnight called on Erica to speak.

From her midstream location on the aisle, Erica Wheaton smiled in response to the scattered applause. An usher, posted by her side, handed her a portable mike. Erica Wheaton rose to present her case for her company.

Not to interfere with any of Erica's final theatrics, J.K. stood far back. He was already sorry for her after the uncertain applause, though not sorry enough to want her to score any sympathy votes.

"Good morning and welcome—fellow Wheatonites, Nebraskans, and, most of all, friends. From the bottom of my heart I thank you for coming." Her head high, her smile wide, she waved to them all, giving special nods to those she was able to recognize. What brought a catch to her throat was seeing a smiling Clive van Arlyn, thumbs up, only a few rows away.

The audience, a mixture of curiosity and compassion, was mostly composed of people who had already made up their minds but were here as honor-bound, decent citizens to hear her out. So sure were the big institutions of the outcome, their representation, if any, was minor. Even the financial press, except for Omaha, was sparse. Too bad, Jack Dowling thought, his heart breaking for Erica, the clock couldn't spin ahead to show the destruction J.K. had planned.

Without notes, her voice filled with passion and conviction, Erica continued. "I understand the confusion many of you have about which way Wheaton is going and which way your votes should be cast. We must unscramble that confusion to understand fully what's ahead before it's too late. Maybe Mark Twain said it best." Slowly, fervently, Erica read aloud to her people.

" 'Tom appeared on the sidewalk with a bucket of whitewash and a long-handled brush. He surveyed the fence, and all gladness left him and a deep melancholy settled down upon his spirit. Thirty yards of board fence nine feet high! Life to him seemed hollow, and existence but a burden.'

"One time or another we've all stood with Tom Sawyer. I was there when George Wheaton died, seeing Wheaton Industries about to be torn apart and destroyed. But as my anger and sorrow turned to strength, the gloom lifted.

Suddenly, I had the power to fight, to be able to get enough backing to call you all together to help me win. Believe me, we're not here to present an alternative to Mr. Kaplan's offer. We're here as the *solution,* to save Wheaton from being stripped to the bone and at the same time to give it a rebirth.

"We all know Wheaton Industries came on hard times, just as we all know promises can't turn it around. If John Kaplan is his own country's most ruthless raider, why would he be a builder here?"

In as little detail as necessary, Erica Wheaton explained Kaplan's all-cash offer versus her group's fifty-nine dollars in cash and five dollars in bonds.

"Unconscionable as it seems, even at the inflated price of sixty-four dollars, Mr. Kaplan will walk off with Wheaton free and clear, since the actual cash he puts up amounts to just about the cash in Wheaton's reserves. Delivering Wheaton today to some opportunist who doesn't care past tomorrow— and couldn't care less if we become a nation of renters to the great products we've created—would be a tragedy. After selling off what's left of Wheaton's assets, he'll have enough cash to cover what he borrowed in order to pay all you folks, plus the half billion he put up as collateral. The half billion that Wheaton has in cash reserves will then be his, scot-free, and back to Britain he'll go, half a billion American dollars richer, with the once-great Wheaton Industries nothing but history. By accepting an immediate five dollars in cash you'd also be accepting the immediate extinction of Wheaton."

Erica stopped to catch her breath. Running her fingers through her hair, she looked squarely at the strained, questioning faces, knowing that the confidence radiating from her face was as important as the expressions of confidence from her lips. Gathering every last ounce of energy, she went on, stronger than ever.

"I'm not a gambler like Mr. Kaplan, but I've always been a winner. When we win Wheaton, I will turn the tables on Mr. Kaplan by adopting England's own Thatcher plan. I will offer each and every worker a huge discount to buy Wheaton shares, so no thief can ever threaten us again. I'm aware that institutions greedy for the buck would seesaw their vote for the last nickel. But I also know that you stockholders who've been with Wheaton from the start, been part of its growth and collected its dividends, know that Wheaton's not only a part of our lives but a part of America that we cannot afford to have meet a quick death for a quick buck. For those of you not yet with me, I am begging—I am pleading for your votes!"

The more impassioned Erica became, the more the crowd did, too. Once again she surveyed her audience. The clock was ticking. Or was it her heart?

"In conclusion, let me say this. We all know human beings are not immortal. But we know, too, that their souls and deeds can live forever. And that, ladies and gentlemen, is why we are here today. Not to carry on one man or one company, but to perpetuate the hopes of George Wheaton, whose spirit is woven into every star and stripe in our flag. Let's be proud the world over that we're Americans: still building, still producing, still making this the greatest country in the world."

All at once, tears filled her eyes and her voice became tender.

"For all of you out there, and for you too, George, the Big Red is going to do it once more. Thank you. And may God bless you all."

As Erica sat back down next to Jack Dowling, she felt exhausted, with no real sense of victory, even though the resounding applause and cheers were genuine.

"Your chances are a helluva lot better than when we started," Dowling said encouragingly.

J.K. also felt she'd been great. However, it was impossible for emotion to overcome dollars for long. When the final vote comes, business always wins over bullshit. But she sure had whipped them up. The little lady certainly deserved a big hand.

Erica felt so spent she never even heard McKnight ask if anyone had anything to add "before we move to close the open forum." She did, however, sense some new excitement. Someone was shouting. Heads were turning toward a tall figure racing down the aisle.

"Indeed, I have something to say," the man called out as he reached the dais. Before addressing the meeting, however, he looked toward the back at John Kaplan.

"Hello, Blackjack," he said, loud and clear into the mike. His eyes were like blue steel. "And hello to all of you. My name is Archer Blair. I am a member of the board of Triomphe Limited, and have been since the company was founded. But more than a member of its board, and more than an old classmate of John Kaplan's, I am an American."

Archer Blair took a proud breath.

"What Erica Wheaton has told you is true. No matter the consequences, I couldn't live with myself a moment longer if I didn't expose this charade in which I'm ashamed to have played a part. It has given me sleepless nights and tortured days."

The room was hushed and expectant, as if whatever force charged the air would also permanently change its composition.

John Kaplan couldn't believe his ears. It was impossible. This wimp, this frightened fool making a fool of him? Had

J.K. thought Blair had the guts, he'd have—God knows what.

"Ever since John Kaplan bought his first Wheaton shares, he's been planning its destruction, so that Triomphe will bail out with a cool half billion."

Jack Dowling squeezed Erica Wheaton's hand so hard she actually gave a small cry.

Clive van Arlyn, twirling away at his ring, would not have missed this for the world, although the more he kept putting two and two together the more he came up with five.

Only J.K. knew where Archer Blair was coming from.

"I, too, am a generation builder. My family, like George Wheaton and his father, helped build America, and there's no way while I'm breathing its free air that I can sit by and let it be destroyed. Damn 'fiduciary responsibility.' Damn 'breach of boardroom morals.' And damn people trying to tear our country apart!"

Archer Blair dabbed his brow with his handkerchief.

"Thank you all for listening. In conclusion, let me just say, God bless America and, please God, may it always remain one nation indivisible."

McKnight's closing statement was completely obscured by cheers. Emotion rocked the room as Archer Blair strode up the aisle, shaking as many outstretched hands as possible, until he saw J.K. Then Blair defiantly held up his fingers in the Churchillian V-for-victory sign, savoring his own finest hour.

J.K. watched transfixed as the shouting grew more intense and Erica was surrounded by well-wishers.

"Keep the Wheaton name in Wheaton, Erica! You run it!"

"Erica, you're our man!"

Erica was desperate to thank Archer Blair for his courage,

but Blair had left as soon as he'd seen what he'd come for—shock and fury on the face of the unflappable John Kaplan.

Although it would take at least until the next day for the final vote to be tallied, there was no doubt in anyone's mind that Erica Wheaton's group would be victorious.

The journey from Bellevue, Nebraska, had been a long one for Erica Phelps. Over the years her native intelligence had ripened, and during her marriage to George Wheaton her strength had freed her from being merely a rich man's beautiful wife, the kind of wife who would have avoided today's battle and the struggle ahead.

When the loudspeaker announced the governor had arrived, and the excitement grew to fever pitch, John Kaplan again tried to maneuver his way to Erica Wheaton.

Amid her dazed joy, Erica never saw J.K. coming toward her, although she turned quickly when she heard the unmistakable accent.

"I didn't want to leave without offering my congratulations. And although this is not exactly in the Kaplan tradition, let me add that, even without my good chum's help, I do believe the best person won."

"Thank you," Erica said, stunned as much by J.K.'s words as she'd been by Archer Blair's.

"Before they devour you totally," J.K. said, smiling, "I'd like to say one more thing. Please realize that because I've lost Wheaton, I have some extra cash to buy a bit of time for you. May I?"

Erica nodded, deeply touched, unable to speak, and held out her hand, but security guards intervened in order to make way for Erica to greet the governor. As she looked back at J.K. and ahead at the governor, a wave of euphoria swept over her. She felt like a quarterback floating on the shoulders of victorious teammates as they moved downfield past the clamoring fans.

*F*rom the heavy glass doors of 823 Fifth Avenue, Art Rooney watched the brisk October wind swirling leaves high above the lamp-lit night sky of Central Park. Suddenly, his usual scowl turned to a grin and he hurried to pull the door open while Mike went to help Mrs. Wheaton out of her car. Rooney smiled broadly. His father would have called her "the fourth leaf on the clover."

By now Rooney had forgotten his first reaction to Erica Wheaton, and especially to her wardrobe. He'd swear she had always dressed in those expensive European clothes: colorful, sure, but always elegant and refined. Everything about her was wonderful. Even Clive van Arlyn was wonderful, for bringing her here that morning a year ago. It had nothing to do with her money. It was her manner: the way she talked with him and the other building men, what her help said about her. It wasn't that she was familiar. It was that she always had time.

She looked really, really pretty tonight, Rooney thought.

As pretty coming in as she did going out. She had that glow he'd noticed about her for a while now.

Gathering her coat against the wind, Erica Wheaton bent her head into the fur collar.

"Thanks, Mr. Rooney," she said, shaking her great head of hair.

Another thing Rooney liked was her calling him "mister," like everyone used to. "Not "Rooney," like they mostly did now.

"Winter drawers on," Rooney said, laughing at the same joke he swore he'd never use after cringing when his father said it for all those years.

Erica Wheaton also laughed, waiting for the big man she was with to catch up with her. It only took him a few strides.

"Good evening," he said crisply, happily.

"Evening, sir," Rooney answered, charm oozing. He'd seen him with Mrs. Wheaton quite a few times now. Tall and well-dressed, he was good-looking even without a lot of hair. Seemed like a true gent, too, and not because of his English accent. By rights, an Irishman like Rooney should hate a Tory like him. But they looked nice together. If he was the cause of Mrs. Wheaton's glow, Rooney approved.